MISSING IN THE KEYS

A GREENE WOLFE THRILLER - BOOK 1

NICHOLAS HARVEY
DOUGLAS PRATT

HarveyBooks

1

Prizren, Kosovo: 1999

The turbines of the WG 13 Lynx swirled dust and trash through the air as it dipped toward the clump of scrub brush. With nothing taller than three feet, there was no way to conceal the chopper's approach. The pilot dropped the helicopter to a level glide over the dirt and bushes.

"Prepare to disembark," a voice announced through their earpieces.

Gray Fox glanced toward Windsor, giving him a single, jerky nod of her chin. She was ready. The tall Englishman stared back at her with glacial blue eyes. He pulled open the sliding side door. A rush of dusty air flushed into the cabin. Most of Gray Fox was covered in Desert Night Camouflage. Protective glasses shielded her eyes, and a hood disguised the rest of her features. The only thing exposed to the onslaught of Kosovar dust was her lips, and she tasted the grimy landscape.

The landing skids of the WG 13 Lynx brushed against the earth with a single thud. Windsor gestured toward the door as if to tell her, "Ladies first."

Damned genteel British. She rolled her eyes at him in vain.

She stepped off the chopper. Despite landing on the firm ground, her feet continued to vibrate as though she was still on board the Lynx. Windsor's hand pressed against the small of her back as he exited the copter. Before she could turn back toward the man, the pilot pulled back on the stick, twisted the cyclic, lifting the chopper's skids off the ground.

Thirty seconds later, the only sound from the aircraft was a rhythmic thumping as it raced west. Gray Fox wiped the back of her sleeve across her exposed lips, hoping to clean away some of the stinging sand.

"We need to move," she urged Windsor. She guided her finger up the hills toward the edge of the city.

"The Slavs might have spotted the chopper," Windsor advised.

Fox nodded, suggesting, "Let's put some distance between us and the LZ."

Gray Fox took the point, keeping her stature crouched as she jogged toward the ridge. They'd dropped three clicks from the city limits. Reports indicated the city was firmly held by the Slavs, and Aleksandar Lazović's men cordoned off every path. At least every road, she thought to herself.

Windsor stayed on her six, shuffling his feet as they traversed the narrow path climbing down the hill. The sun was already dipping below the horizon, and the two were descending the eastern slope leaving them in an ever-darkening shadow. From their angle, they could see the city of Prizren which spread out over several hundred square miles. Lights began to flicker on as night climbed across the landscape.

Despite the glow of the city lights, the stars glittered bright enough that she could make out the path ahead of her. A familiar thumping echoed over the hill. Windsor let out a shrill whistle, signaling her to take cover. By the time his whistle stopped, she was nowhere to be seen.

Like an angel appearing above them, a glow of white crested the hill followed by the beating rotors of an Apache helicopter patrolling the territory. Dissecting the landscape, the beam of light cut through the brush.

Fox peered up from beneath a shrub of European privet. Branches, leaves, and dirt whipped all around her from the thrashing blades. She lowered her head as the spotlight illuminated the brush where she crouched. Motionless, she held her breath and waited, praying the privet and camo blended harmoniously.

The chopper banked away, and the hillside sank back into darkness. She blinked a few times as she attempted to readjust her eyes to the night.

"Close one," Windsor whispered in her ear.

"Let's move," she urged, bounding to her feet.

At the bottom of the hill, they slid gently along a sandy slope into a ravine. All four of their feet splashed into six inches of stagnant water. The last rain was three days ago, and the stream hadn't dried up. When the next storm passed through, in a day or so, this ditch would flow almost to its brim as the rain washed the grime from the streets of Prizren out to the White Drin, a river winding its way east through Kosovo.

Windsor pushed at her back as she trudged steadily along the gully. She slowed as she came to a pile of trash blocked by a grate that operated as a catchall for the city's garbage in the mouth of a large pipe. Fox inhaled a lungful of fresh air before she climbed up the heap and pressed through the wet accumulation of cardboard, paper, and assorted decaying masses she'd rather not identify.

The pile of refuse was almost a foot and a half deep, and by the time she slipped through the bars of the grate, emerging on the other side, she was dripping wet. The camouflage fabric did nothing to protect her from the moisture. The lingering odor of rot clung to the inside of her nose.

The drainage pipe was six feet in diameter, and Fox straightened up in the opening. A metallic thump signaled Windsor's attempt to follow suit, only to bang his scalp against the top of the pipe.

"Damn," he whistled under his breath.

Fox motioned for him to stay close as she moved down the dark passageway. The decision to continue in the dark was decided prior to the mission. There wasn't a perfect map of the tunnel, and with no way to ensure that the pipe wasn't accessible through open drains or grates, it was decided to maneuver in pitch dark.

The water lapped over their boots, and Fox's face contorted as the first bit of moisture oozed between the tightly bound leather and her skin. Based on the smell of the rank water, she couldn't bear to think about what might be soaking into her socks.

She ran her gloved fingers over the ridged wall of the pipe just to assure herself there was something still there in the dark. Otherwise, she listened to the sloshing of water and the annoying sibilant sound Windsor made as he breathed behind her. Annoying but somehow consoling in the blackness.

When the first remnants of light appeared in the distance, she almost ignored it, thinking it was nothing more than a trick her eyes were playing on her. The glow wasn't really a glow. More like a blurred gray appearing in a sea of black. Each step allowed the blur to spread until the contours of the pipe became more evident.

"Ahead," Windsor announced, somewhat pointlessly since she was in the lead and could already make out the exit.

Gray Fox decided there was no reason to comment. He wasn't going to change.

The drainage pipe opened under an old cistern built at least fifty years earlier. Initially, the reservoir was designed to collect the water for the building's occupants, however as the local water began to be sourced from the White Drin, the cistern became nothing more than an ornate water feature.

Gray Fox pressed her shoulder against the grate under the cistern until the rusty bars creaked. Windsor's arms extended over her head as his fingers laced between the bars. A grunt emanated from him as he pushed upward.

Fox stopped him. "On three," she whispered.

Windsor nodded, and Fox's head bobbed—once, twice, a third time.

On the third nod, they both shoved up against the grate. The metal cracked loudly, echoing in the underground chamber. Fox paused, halfway expecting the noise to alert someone overhead. It wasn't that loud, she assured herself.

The round metal closure slid over to the side, leaving a two-foot opening. Windsor laced this fingers together to create a step for Fox. She put the sole of her boot in his palms, and he hoisted her through the hole.

As she climbed out into the cistern, she realized that everything she'd traipsed through in the pipe was now all over Windsor after using him as a ladder. She found herself lying in a puddle of rainwater that remained at the bottom of the trough. Rolling over, she dropped her right hand down to give Windsor a lift. In the darkness below, his hand gripped her wrist squeezing tightly.

He pulled himself up as she lay prostrate on the bottom. Once he got his free arm through the opening, she released her grip and moved back out of his way. The Englishman emerged from the drain, crawling through the water. At least this water was cleaner, she thought as she splashed the water over her boots.

Windsor rose up on his knees and gave her a nod, indicating he was ready. According to the city diagrams, Lazović was located on the seventh floor of the next building. His troops would be guarding the entrances, leaving the best ingress from above.

The two moved through the shadows to a side wall. Old ceramic pipes snaked down the face from the roof, ten stories above. When the cistern was first designed, these pipes caught the rain and funneled it down to the cistern. Several turns and screens had been added to catch debris and trash before it reached the bottom.

Fox put both hands on either side of the pipe and began to ascend the side of the building. Years of training made this free-hand climb easy. The brick wall provided enough traction and footholds to speed her ascent.

When she crested the top, she stretched her legs as she waited for Windsor to follow her up. From the peak of the building, she had line of sight into the one next door. Constructed only an alley width apart, Gray Fox and Windsor had to traverse across a line to the next roof before dropping down three stories to find their target.

Windsor appeared behind her. He pulled a foldable grappling hook from his pack. "You ready for this?" he asked as he threaded the rope through the eye and secured it tightly.

"I'm ready for the extraction, and maybe a nice glass of Chardonnay."

The man shook his head with a wry grin. "Half an hour," he relayed. "Then we'll head to the coast."

The hook soared from his hand across the divide. The flash of silver vanished into the dark, but the clang of metal against brick rang out. Windsor pulled the slack out of the line until the hook caught on the edge of the building. Once the line was taut, he tied it off, creating a tightrope between the buildings.

Gray Fox doubled checked her SIG Sauer P228 pistol with its suppressor extending the barrel of the semi-automatic. Securing it back in the custom holster strapped to her waist, she gave Windsor a nod before grabbing the line with both hands and swinging out over the abyss. Her feet wrapped around the rope and crossed at her ankles. Two clips on both of her boots slipped deftly around the rope securing her feet. She didn't want to trust the thin pieces of metal to defy gravity completely, but they were designed to prevent her feet from dropping off the line and throwing her climb off-balance.

With a final glance at Windsor, she offered a hint of a smile, filled with confidence. He winked at her and tapped his watch. *Time to move.*

She slowly shimmied along the line, reassuring herself that the rope would hold. During training, she'd made similar climbs a hundred times, but the real world tended to interfere with the most intricate of plans.

Despite any attempt by Murphy to subvert her, she reached the other building. Lifting her feet off the line, she twisted her body around until she could hook her knees over the edge. The tricky part of this whole maneuver was disembarking. The grappling hook's hold was always the uncertainty. Pull the rope the wrong way, and the hook might dislodge. Sure, the other end wasn't going anywhere, but it would be an impressive feat to cling to the rope as it swung into the other building.

When her feet touched the roof, she breathed a sigh of relief and released her grip on the rope. She glanced back at Windsor who offered her a congratulatory signal. From here, she was on her own. Windsor would make his way down to cover her escape if she found herself running hot.

A metal door howled on corroded hinges as it opened across the roof. Gray Fox dropped, pulling her gun free of the holster. As she raised her head, she spotted a single sentry walking the roof. As they'd suspected, the top of the building wasn't guarded as well as the main entrances. Lazović wasn't worried about trouble from above. He controlled the entire block.

Fox crept along behind a row of exhaust fans and slowly raised the SIG.

The barrel snapped once with no more than a *pfft*. The guard lifelessly dropped, and Fox moved to the corpse. He had a radio and an MP-40 machine pistol with a thirty-two-round magazine hanging impotently off his shoulder.

Hard to defend yourself when you aren't prepared, Fox thought wryly.

She picked up the radio. The MP-40 wasn't much better than her pistol except for the number of rounds. In this case, she needed stealth more than firepower. At least, that was the plan.

At the door the patrol came through, Fox found a staircase leading down. She couldn't see any more guards. The singleton was likely the only one making rounds to the roof. If the rest of

Lazović's patrols were as effective, then she had nothing to worry about.

On the eighth floor, she paused, hearing voices below. At first glance, the stairwell was still clear. The voices were coming from the other side of the door on the seventh level. Lazović's floor. Fox stepped behind the door so that when it swung open, she'd be hidden. With the P228 at the ready, she pressed the transmit button on the radio she'd pilfered and tossed it down the steps. The radio bounced and clattered as it tumbled loudly down the stairs. She hoped the men on the other side could hear the racket, either on their radio or through the door.

As if on cue, the door opened. A male voice announced something in Russian, but Fox held her breath, waiting. Two men stepped onto the landing and the door swung closed behind them. Both men moved toward the stairs and peered down. Fox raised the gun. *Pfft. Pfft.*

The men collapsed on the steps. These two appeared somewhat more vigilant. One carried another MP-40 while the second held a Soviet-made PPS-41 submachine gun. Fox removed the radio from the one with the PPS-41. If her presence became known, the radio might warn her.

Aleksandar Lazović's flat was on the northeastern corner of the building. According to MI6's intelligence, his top aides were in the city of Pristina, leaving Lazović alone except for his security detail.

Fox moved along the corridor. It was hard to imagine this building was holding a war criminal. It could have been an apartment building in any city in the US. The gold wallpaper and floral carpet didn't strike Fox as the décor of a despot.

She found the door to the flat. Before she took the time to pick the deadbolt lock, her fingers fell upon the gold-plated handle. The knob turned, and the latch clicked open.

How does a monster who slaughtered hundreds of citizens in cold blood not lock his door? Fox wondered. He thought he was invulnerable, she assumed. Or that his security was infallible.

The door swung open revealing a lavish, at least for Kosovo, apartment. White tile led through a foyer, past a large mirror on one wall and a poorly painted portrait of a naked woman. Fox cautiously moved forward, holding the pistol up at the ready. Movement in another room caught her attention, and she stalked toward the sound. She turned the door handle, and pushed it open.

A rotund man in the nude turned toward her. His pale body was covered in thick curly hair that formed in patches with no discernable pattern all over his body. Aleksandar Lazović's eyes widened as he saw her standing in the doorway. She raised the barrel. *Pfft.*

The despot tumbled backward as the bullet pierced his skull. She took a step forward. *Pfft. Pfft.* Two rounds into the chest.

Then Gray Fox noticed the young woman on the bed.

The girl was in her teens, Fox guessed. She was tied to the bedpost with a thick rope. Fox leveled the barrel at the female who cowered, sobbing into a pillow.

Fox keyed her own radio. "Windsor come in," she called.

"This is Windsor, report. Why are you breaking protocol?"

"I have a problem," Fox admitted. "There's a girl here. Lazović has her trussed up like a pig."

"No witnesses," Windsor advised.

"I'm not shooting a teenage girl who's been brutalized by this asshole."

"You have to do something," Windsor advised. "There is a unit coming in the door. I imagine they will be checking in on the colonel at some point."

Fox cursed. She lifted her hand to signal that she meant the girl no harm. Pulling down her face covering and holstering her weapon, she pulled a three-inch knife from her boot. The blade sliced through the rope, and the girl scrambled away from the assassin.

"Run," Fox told the child who obviously didn't understand English. She motioned for her to go, and the girl seemed to comprehend. She bounded off the bed and ran out of the room.

Fox wasted no time. She flung open the sliding glass doors that led out to a small balcony. She pulled a small contraption out of her pack. The device could have been a retractable dog leash, but it was three times the size. A stainless-steel carabiner hung from the end, and Fox snapped the hook around the railing of the balcony.

Her other hand retracted four feet of line from the block. With a quick snap, she connected the line to the harness around her waist. She climbed up onto the railing and dropped down on the other side, hanging seven stories above the street.

Fox glanced through the doors at the naked corpse and wondered if the girl would make it out alive. Then she stepped back off the railing, the line feeding out as she fell back.

2

London, England: Present Day

Charlie looked at her watch. Again. It was six thirty in the morning. Miami was five hours behind London, which meant it was twelve thirty there. *No, wait,* she thought. *Shit. One thirty.* Apart from nodding off a few times on the sofa, she hadn't slept properly in days. The empty bottle of Chardonnay on the coffee table had also contributed to her befuddled state. Or more precisely, the wine which the bottle had formerly contained.

Her Bengal cat, Stanley, opened one eye and stared at her disapprovingly from the overstuffed chair he'd claimed as his own since he'd been a kitten.

"Bugger off, Stanley," Charlie mumbled. "Don't judge me, you judgmental... judging... fur ball."

The cat closed his eye and went back to sleep. She loved Stanley with a passion. He on the other hand was little comfort in her times of need, occasionally granting her permission to make a big fuss of him. The big cat usually slept on her bed with her which probably explained his disgruntled mood. Maybe he cared after all as he hadn't ventured into her bedroom since Charlie had sequestered herself in the living room, with occasional trips to the kitchen and bathroom.

Her hair was a mess. A quick sniff told her she was responsible for the stale aroma hanging over the sofa, and her T-shirt and jogging shorts were long overdue for the laundry hamper. Charlie had been in a funk for weeks, but now, alone in her father's flat, she'd slipped further into a melancholic despair. He'd left on a business trip to the US four days ago, and she hadn't heard a word since.

Keith Greene worked for a company who made security systems for *things*. What *things*, she'd never been sure, nor interested enough to ask her father. He in turn, preferred to leave his work in the office and enjoy his free time. Although he always seemed to be on his cell phone dealing with more work-like things she didn't pay attention to.

It had been an arduous step, moving back in with her dad after having her independence for the prior eight years. She'd left home for university at age eighteen, riddled with guilt for leaving him alone, despite his encouragement and offers to help financially. After university, she'd entered the National Detective Programme in Warwick, south of Birmingham. It was the cheapest place to live she'd been able to find near a training center. Working evenings in a restaurant, and living in a rented room, Charlie passed the exams and applied with constabularies in London and the surrounding suburbs. Unbelievably, she was accepted by New Scotland Yard.

Sharing a tiny flat with a friend, she struggled to make ends meet on her meager police salary, so when the shit hit the fan and her world crumbled, she had no choice but to move back home. The plan had been to stay with her dad for a week or two while Charlie figured out what would come next. That was two months ago. *Next* had been a stubborn problem for someone who ever since she could remember wanted to be a police detective. She'd never considered any other line of work.

She groaned and wriggled out of the pillowy sofa, forced from her sanctuary by the requirements of nature. Her bare feet fell heavily on the reclaimed wood floor as her petite but toned five-foot, six-inch frame plodded across the room, past the closed door to her father's office, and on to the guest bathroom. Sitting on the toilet looking back down the hallway, her focus stayed on the office door. *Why did he keep it locked?* He'd always told her it was because his work required him to keep customers' security data which by contract had to be under lock and key. Now that she thought about it, the reason seemed thin. If someone made it past the two locks on the hefty front door, the office didn't seem like much of a challenge.

Charlie flushed the toilet and pulled up her shorts, hurriedly washed her hands, and walked down the hallway, halting in front of the tall, white, solid-wood door. It was possible her dad had been crazy busy and missed a suitable time to call, text, email, or message her. But that would be a first. Even when she was away at university, he would text her to say he'd landed in whatever country he was heading for, and text again when he was home. Four days of silence was beyond unusual. His cell phone was going straight to voicemail and his hotel room in Miami just rang and rang.

In the movies and television shows, police personnel all knew how to pick locks, but they hadn't taught her that in the detective training program. Thoughts of her former career sent little blades into her heart once more, and she clenched her fists. Charlie rested her back against the opposite wall and kicked the crap out of the office door. Fine carpentry splintered from the jamb as the wood gave way and the large door swung inward. They *had* taught her self-defense and she'd taken five years of Taekwondo as a teenager.

Over the years, Charlie had stood in the room too many times to remember, but now she realized, this was the first time in over twenty years she'd been in his office alone. Memories rushed over her, triggered by the slightly musty smell of old books. One wall was lined from floor to high ceiling with shelves, packed with novels, non-fiction, and a special section down low for the books she'd cherished as a young girl.

She knelt and ran a finger across the well-worn novels by Enid Blyton, and the Harry Potter and Hunger Games series. After a while, she stood and looked at the broad oak desk, conjuring an image of her father in his antique leather chair. Her mind blended the years and she saw him as a handsome young man not much older than her today, before he morphed into the fifty-six-year-old she'd last seen less than a week ago. Distinguished, with gray streaks invading his full head of hair. Those sparkling blue eyes which never failed to comfort her.

Where has father gone? Surely, if he'd been in an accident she would have been contacted by now, she thought, trying to reassure herself. Her number was his emergency contact on every device and form. A stream of crazy ideas raced through her tired mind, from a wild fling with an American woman he'd met, to a mundane work issue consuming all his attention. If it was one of the two, she hoped for the fling. The man deserved a little slap and tickle occasionally.

Charlie had never seen her father date a woman. Whenever she'd brought up the subject, he'd always said her mother, Dee, was the only partner he'd ever needed. As Charlie had no memories of her mother, she could only miss the idea rather than the person. She suspected that wasn't the case for her father, but in his usual unselfish way, he never burdened Charlie with his pain.

With hands on hips, she looked around the room. Her trained eyes began processing, the way she'd been taught to evaluate every scene, every situation. The desktop was clear of any paperwork and his laptop computer was undoubtedly with him. Three small, framed pictures sat alone on the smooth wooden surface. She sat in his chair and tried each desk drawer, one by one. The upper few held basic office supplies, empty spiral-bound notepads, and blocks of unused sticky notes. The lower drawers on each side were locked.

Searching through the supplies, Charlie hunted for a key without success. The idea of breaking into the piece of antique oak furniture sent chills through her body. She pictured herself bumbling through an explanation of why his prized desk was royally buggered thanks to her paranoia. Her state of mind lately would not help her defense.

She didn't even know what it was she hoped to find in the office. He'd gone on a business trip like he often did and left her his hotel details and flight information. What more could she learn that might explain his lack of contact? Charlie couldn't come up with an answer to her own question, but sitting on the sofa watching Stanley sleep and waiting for the phone to ring had been driving her crazy. She had to do something.

Turning to the sideboard against the back wall, she opened the long drawers and fingered through a sea of hanging files. Charlie knew her father was a meticulous man, but it appeared he kept every sheet of paper which had ever touched their lives. Utility bills from ten years ago, a file full of her school reports, but nothing related to his business of supplying security for things she'd been too self-absorbed to pay attention to.

Charlie glanced up at the framed photographs on the desktop. All three were of her and her dad. When she'd been five or six years old, she'd asked to see a picture of her mother. He'd explained that all their possessions had been lost in a fire, including their family albums. At the time she'd wondered if it would be comforting to see her mother's face, or make the void seem even larger.

To her left was the bay window where the early light streamed through the panes, illuminating the fine dust particles hanging in the air. Charlie's gaze moved to the wall across from the desk. In the center was the door and the splinters of broken wood scattered across the floor. On either side of the opening were two large oil paintings. One depicted the Battle of Trafalgar, and the other, an English knight on a rearing white horse.

Cursing herself, Charlie leapt from the chair and rushed to the ornately framed painting of the knight. She peered behind the frame, pressing her face to the wall. It appeared to be firmly fixed in place as though the whole back of the frame were glued to the wall instead of dangling from a hanger. Moving across the room she yelped as she trod on the sharp pieces of wood with her bare feet. Looking behind the other painting, she could see it was fixed in the same manner.

Reaching up, Charlie firmly tugged on the left side of the frame. It didn't budge. She tried the right side, but it truly appeared to be screwed to the framing of the house. Carefully avoiding the broken wood, she returned to the knight. Frustration was creeping in, and she wrenched at the left side of the picture, almost falling over when it swung away from the wall.

"Bugger me!" she blurted, staring at the modern safe, flush mounted into the wall of the Victorian era flat.

Her father had never mentioned a safe, and Charlie had never seen it before. A gut instinct had driven her to search, partly from knowing her dad and how security conscious he was, and partly from somewhere deep inside where she processed situations with machine-like efficiency. That was how the Chief Inspector had described her during her last review. The one a few months before she'd been sent home, endured a series of painful interviews and an official review, then dismissed.

Growling under her breath to push the distraction away, Charlie looked at the keypad before her. Her keen nose had found the safe, but now she had no idea how to open it. Trotting back to the living room, she hunted for her cell phone. Stanley raised himself up and took a stretch, filling the width of the chair. He gave her a cursory glance, then dropped to the floor and sauntered toward the kitchen in search of food. Charlie stepped over him as she made for the end table where her cell phone was plugged into a charger.

Returning to the office, she searched online for the brand of safe, discovering their codes were six digits. That was a million possible combinations. Charlie stepped back and leaned against the desk. Her father was too cagey to use simple birth dates or family names. She went back to the keypad and tried "Greene" converted into numbers just to prove herself right. The small LED screen flashed "incorrect code." She returned to leaning on the desk.

She tried to think of something less obvious that was important to her dad. He was a car enthusiast. A Jaguar F-Pace SUV sat in the garage, mostly unused. He took a taxi everywhere in London as parking was a nightmare. She tried "Jaguar," using the corresponding numbers for the letters which appeared in tiny type below the numeric digits. "Incorrect code." Charlie began circling the room impatiently, racking her fatigued brain for other ideas. As she passed by the desk chair, the three framed photos on the desktop caught her eye. One was of the two of them seated in an old 1960s sports car. She grabbed the frame.

"That old car!" she blurted.

She then stood there for over a minute trying to remember what kind of car it was. Her father still owned it as best she knew. It was safely tucked away in the countryside somewhere. *Bollocks*, she thought, berating herself. What the hell was it called? Putting the frame down on the desk she moved to the bookshelves and began scanning the hundreds of spines lined up in neat rows.

Typical of her father, the books were arranged by category. Charlie found a section near her children's books, filled with automotive and car racing editions. A whole row was dedicated to a tall annual called "Autocourse." Her tired eyes flitted from cover to cover on the next shelf up until she yelped in glee. "Austin-Healey bloody Sprite!"

With three different six-letter options, she franticly rushed back to the keypad and typed them in one at a time. When "Sprite" returned the same negative result as the first two, Charlie swung the picture frame closed with a bang.

"Bugger me, Dad! I don't need this shit right now!"

She ran her fingers through her light-brown hair and glared at the rearing horse and its gallant rider. She swung the frame open once more and typed in the numerical equivalent of "knight." "Correct code."

More surprised than excited, Charlie turned the handle and opened the safe door. Inside were several small boxes and a stack of files. A strange feeling tightened her stomach. She was prying into her father's private safe. The idea she'd find something not meant for her eyes made her hesitate. What would her dad have that was so secret his daughter couldn't know? He was the most loving, honest, and straightforward man she'd ever known. Shoving her doubts aside, Charlie reached inside the safe and pulled out the stack of files.

Spreading them across the desk, she studied the carefully labeled tabs, recognizing her father's neat handwriting. Most were property deeds, insurance, car paperwork, and other papers found in most families' fireproof safes. But one of the files was marked "Edwards." Charlie couldn't think of anyone she knew named Edwards. Flipping open the folder revealed a large manila envelope. She dumped the contents onto the desk and stared in astonishment.

A State of Florida marriage certificate showed Daniel Edwards had married Diana Turner on December 3, 1995. Baffled, she slid the paper aside and found two eight-by-ten color photographs. The first was of a couple standing outside a courthouse. The woman looked beautiful in a simple yet elegant white wedding dress. The man was tall and handsome in a suit and tie, his face full of joy with a broad smile and twinkling blue eyes. Unmistakably her father.

Charlie fought for breath and returned her attention to the woman. It felt like she was looking into a mirror, their likeness was astounding. All logical processing from her life as a detective went out the window. Her world had just been turned upside down.

Could Diana be Dee? The name her father had always used.

She reached out and picked up the photograph. Beneath it was the second picture. She dropped the first and grabbed the next one. The same couple sat on a sofa, with the same beaming smiles as their wedding day. Cradled in the woman's arms was a baby.

"Mum?" Charlie whispered as tears formed in her eyes.

3

The heat and humidity hit her like a heavy blanket as Charlie walked to the curb outside international arrivals. Overhead, the departure level shaded her under a concrete roof providing shelter from the blazing hot early afternoon sun, but trapping the exhaust fumes and heat from the mass of vehicles passing by. Strange, larger cars and SUVs than she was used to in England.

Slipping off her leather jacket, she cradled the garment between the handles of her duffle bag and followed signs toward the ride-share pick-up area. She'd heard about these companies that were cheaper than taxis, which had now appeared in London, but she'd never used one as she usually took the tube. According to the app she'd downloaded during the flight, Alfonso in a blue Ford was three minutes away.

Charlie joined a huddle of people all staring at their cell phones and dropped her duffle to the pavement. In the whirlwind past twenty-four hours, she'd maxed her credit card out on a flight to Miami, shoved possibly a poor selection of clothes into a small carry-on bag, and deposited a complaining Stanley with a cat-friendly neighbor. Finally feeling like she had a purpose, she'd mercifully managed to get the most sleep she'd had in a week on the flight. Refreshed might not be the perfect description, but almost human felt better than the zombie-like state she'd been immersed in back in London.

Alfonso arrived in a dark blue SUV which appeared to have endured its fair share of scrapes with city traffic. She climbed in the back, and he turned and spoke to her in Spanish.

"*En inglés, por favor*," she responded, using up most of her Spanish vocabulary in one sentence.

"Little," Alfonso said in heavily accented English, holding up two fingers close together to reiterate how little. "Cubano," he added, pointing at the national flag of the foreign country hanging from the rearview mirror.

"*Bueno*," Charlie said, exhausting the last of her Spanish.

Alfonso turned around and blended into traffic by making it clear he was changing lanes regardless of what the other drivers chose to do. She figured he had the destination in the app so he knew where he was supposed to be taking her, and relaxed back in the seat. Steamy air flowed liberally through the open front windows as apparently it wasn't hot enough for the Cuban driver to bother with air-conditioning. Charlie disagreed and wished she hadn't worn jeans which now clung to the perspiration covering her body.

The four-mile drive took fifteen minutes on a broad street with three lanes in each direction. They passed by businesses and restaurants with big signs displaying names Charlie didn't recognize. The traffic was heavy, but she was used to that from the hustle and bustle of London. Alfonso made a left turn, to where the new street was lined with snazzier buildings. He pulled under a covered entrance on the right-hand side and came to a stop. The Hyatt Regency Coral Gables was a grand looking structure with a high, arched doorway into the lobby.

"Welcome to Miami," Alfonso said in broken English with a big, tip-inducing smile.

Undoubtedly, he assumed Charlie was staying at the expensive hotel and was hoping for a generous addition to the fare. Little did he know that she not only wasn't registered at the Hyatt Regency, but she didn't have a hotel booked anywhere. She tried to reserve the cheapest place she could find online, but her card had been declined. She held her breath for the fare to clear through the app and when it did, she handed Alfonso a pound coin with her thanks. She left him with a baffled look on his face as he turned the coin over in his hand.

The hotel was beautiful inside. Polished marble tiles, high-backed upholstered chairs, and an elegant chandelier decorating the entranceway, with a bar lounge to the right, and a carpeted sitting room to the left. Charlie felt out of place in her jeans and tank top with the duffle thrown over her shoulder. Goose bumps raised on her arms from the chilly air conditioning, and her nervous expectation of finding her father in his room.

Making her way to the front desk, a Hispanic woman greeted her in accented English, welcoming her to the hotel with a well-practiced smile.

"Hello," Charlie said, summoning a bright smile. "I'm here to see my father, Keith Greene. He's staying with you."

"Certainly, miss. Would you like me to call his room?"

Charlie nodded. "That would be lovely, cheers."

The woman tapped away at her keyboard for a few moments before looking up. "His last name is Green, miss?"

"Yes. With an 'E' on the end."

"Ah, one moment. Let me try that." After more keystrokes, the receptionist smiled. "Here we are, Mr. Keith Greene." She picked up a phone, hidden from Charlie's view, and dialed the room extension.

Both women stood in silence, Charlie with a lump in her throat. Her father was clearly still registered in the hotel, but he hadn't answered the phone in the room for four days and still didn't appear to be picking up.

The receptionist hung up the receiver. "No answer, I'm afraid, miss. Our restaurant is currently closed, but the bar will open soon, and we have a sitting area where you're welcome to wait."

"I'll just take a room key, please," Charlie replied. "I'm knack-ered after the flight. I'd love a shower."

She watched the woman's face tense and knew what was coming next.

"I'm afraid we can only provide keys to registered guests, miss. Perhaps you could try your father's cell phone?"

Charlie pulled her passport from the side pocket of her duffle. "Here," she said, sliding the passport across the counter. "You can see I'm Charlotte Greene, his daughter."

The woman slid the passport straight back. "I'm so sorry, miss. It is the hotel's unwavering policy not to issue keys to unregistered guests."

Charlie contemplated pulling the ridiculously polite woman across the counter by the silk scarf-like thing she wore around her neck, but quickly reminded herself that rash decisions and unorthodox persuasion were the reason she was currently unemployed.

"I'll wait for him," she muttered and gathered up her things, stomping toward the sitting area, her Doc Martens boots clunking loudly on the tile floor.

She dropped into a pillowy overstuffed chair, letting her duffle fall to the floor. Charlie had been constantly vacillating between logical detective mode and stunned daughter mindset ever since opening the envelope from the safe. As lost as she'd felt before that moment, it seemed like a stable place from where she stood now. She questioned everything about her life, her father, and why he'd lied to her about not having pictures of her mother. Unless that wasn't her mother. In which case it was another child, by another woman, in a secret life her dad had omitted to mention. Ever.

What about the names on the marriage certificate? It was all too much to process. She groaned and forced her thoughts back to her immediate problem. It was now midafternoon, she was in a foreign country with nowhere to stay, very little money, and still no clue where her father was. She needed to get into his room. Looking around, Charlie spotted a hotel pamphlet on the glass coffee table, listing the amenities, local restaurants nearby, and the hotel extension numbers. She made note of the room service number and looked around for a house phone.

"Hello, this is Mr. Greene's personal assistant. He'd like lunch delivered to his room please," she said as the call was answered.

"Certainly, what can we get for Mr. Greene?"

Charlie realized the snacks and miniature packages of crap the airline called food had long since left her hungry.

"He'd like a burger please, and a beer."

"How would he like the burger cooked?"

"Medium well."

"Certainly, and what side?"

"Chips please."

"We have sweet potato fries, truffle fries, French fries, fried yucca, salad, or fresh fruit, ma'am."

Charlie was about to point out that she'd already asked for chips, when she remembered that chips were crisps in America. "French fries, please," she replied, unsure what all the other variations were apart from the salad… and she was too hungry and emotionally unbalanced for salad.

"Domestic or imported?"

"Heineken, please," she ordered, figuring that was imported in both countries she'd been in that day.

"Anything else we can get for you?"

"I think that's everything, thank you."

"And Mr. Greene's room number?"

Charlie half covered the phone with her hand. "Oh, okay. I'll be right there. I'm just ordering his food." Removing her hand she spoke into the receiver, "I'm sorry, I'm being called away. It's Mr. Keith Greene's room. I'm afraid I forget which one that is, we have so many rooms booked with you. Thanks a lot, and please make sure there's tomato ketchup with it. Ta-ta for now."

She rolled her eyes at her own bumbling and groaned to herself as she unzipped her duffle and rummaged through her clothes. Pulling out a hooded sweatshirt, she slipped it over her head and dug deeper for a pair of tennis shoes. She loved her Docs, but they were more suited to kicking in doors than stealthily sneaking through them. Tying her hair up in a low bun and putting a dark brown newsboy cap on her head completed what she hoped would be enough of a transformation for the receptionist to ignore her.

Standing near the edge of the sitting room, she waited for a couple to approach the front desk before striding confidently down the hallway, past the reception toward the elevators. She pretended to be engrossed in her cell phone as she went, while actually scanning the hall for signs giving her a hint of where to go. Beyond the elevator, a door on the right was marked 'staff only' and she opened it boldly, prepared with a gushing apology.

It opened into a short hallway which met a wider corridor running behind the elevator toward the offices to the right, and the kitchens to the left. Voices emanated from both directions, but no one was in sight. She noticed one of the elevators had a rear door for service access. In about ten minutes, a waiter with a tray would come out of the kitchen and get in that elevator—or so she hoped. Charlie's challenge was staying out of the way until then and timing her coincidental appearance into the same elevator from the guest side.

Leaving the staff area, she stayed close to the wall by the first elevator where the woman at the front desk would have to lean over her counter to see her. One of the elevators opened and a couple came out, too engrossed in their own conversation to pay attention to Charlie. She checked her watch; it had been seven minutes since she'd placed the call.

Charlie felt more nervous than the times she'd been part of a police raid. Then, it had been adrenaline, anticipation, and usually armed officers in full tactical gear who entered first. Far more seemed to be at stake here. All it had taken was a few pieces of paper in an envelope for everything she knew about her life to be thrown into question.

A vibration through the wall and a low groan told her the service door was opening. Charlie lunged for the button and prayed she wasn't too late. A door opened, but it was the middle elevator which the couple had exited from. She looked from open door to closed door and realized only one would open at a time.

"Bugger!" she growled and stepped into the open elevator.

Hitting the button for the top floor, she pressed her ear against the side of the elevator. She heard a faint mechanical whirring and knew a burger and chips were on their way up to a floor she didn't know. She hit the close door button six times with no effect. Finally, the polished metal doors began to slowly close until a hand reached in and stopped them.

"Bloody hell," Charlie moaned and pressed her ear against the wall of the elevator again.

The neighboring elevator was still going up. Her own doors were now open again and a young boy around twelve years old stood there staring at her with his mouth agape.

"You're either in, or you're out, mate. What'll it be?" she ordered.

The kid stared at her in complete confusion. Nothing in his twelve years on the planet had prepared him to face a good-looking woman barking at him while pressing her ear to the side of an elevator.

"Well?"

The boy's eyes grew wider, but he stepped into the elevator. Charlie leaned over and hammered the close door button once more, rewarded with silence and a stationary elevator.

"Bugger!"

The sound of the other elevator was drowned out by her own doors finally closing and the elevator smoothly accelerating upward. Charlie tried to distinguish between the matching tones from the two elevators but couldn't tell them apart. The boy reached over to the array of buttons to select his floor.

"Don't you dare!" Charlie said, and the boy retracted his arm as though it would be severed if left extended.

The elevator tone changed slightly, and she guessed the neighboring one had stopped. She began counting in her head, trying to match the time delay between the two elevators. The little screen above the door continued checking off floor numbers. Charlie reached out and pressed the button for the next floor. The elevator jerked to a stop and the doors slowly opened. She poked her head out and looked down the hallway to her right. Nobody, and an employees' door beyond the elevators was closed. Her heart sank, but she swung around and checked the other direction and saw a maid's cart outside a room, and beyond that, a man pushing another cart.

"Thanks," she said to the boy, hoping she hadn't traumatized him for life.

"Cool," he stuttered and peeked out into the hallway to watch her swiftly walk away.

Humming came from the room the maid was cleaning, and dangling from her cart was a key card. Charlie wrenched at the card as she passed by, snapping it from its tether, without missing a step. The waiter was knocking on a door farther down the hall.

"Sorry," Charlie called out. "I'd just popped downstairs for a…" She couldn't come up with a good reason to leave the room after ordering food, so she resorted to a flirty smile. "…I'm bloody starving, thanks for bringing the grub so fast."

The young man smiled in return and couldn't help his eyes wandering across her figure. She wished she'd ditched the sweatshirt to give him a better view, but he appeared to be suitably distracted so she quickly held the key card to the electronic reader on the door and breezed inside.

Holding the door open, she looked around the luxurious room, which at first appeared vacant. For a moment she stopped breathing as she considered the idea that she'd followed the wrong service cart. Frantically, she scanned the room, looking for signs of an occupant, who she prayed was her father. The waiter pushed the cart inside and Charlie fumbled for another pound coin, wishing she'd exchanged her dwindling cash at the airport.

"Thanks," she repeated and continued holding the door as she handed him the coin.

"You're welcome, ma'am," he responded, then made a hasty exit once he realized her flirtatious smile had vanished.

Charlie stood in the room and looked around. Not a suitcase, piece of clothing, or personal item was visible. She slid back the mirrored wardrobe door, and there, hanging neatly were several shirts and pairs of trousers. Someone was still occupying the room at least, which explained why the hotel hadn't closed out the bill. She quickly moved across the room and opened the bedside cabinet drawer. Inside, lay a Rolex watch and a wedding ring. Her father's watch, and the ring he only took off at night. The gold ring he continued to wear despite losing his wife—Charlie's mother—over twenty years ago.

4

Charlie sat on the side of the bed and stared at the watch and ring. Her father always took them off while in the house and wore them whenever he left. It had been habitual for so long, he'd tell Charlie it felt like he was naked if he stepped outside without them, and as though he was wearing a raincoat in the house if he didn't take them off when inside. *Why would he leave without them now?* He wasn't a paranoid man, but he'd never leave them in a hotel room while he was gone for any extended period of time.

Next to the watch was a car key fob and the slip with a spare key card to the room. The plastic key fob tag had the rental car company's name and details on one side, and the vehicle information on the other. Taking all four items, she placed them on the bed and continued searching the hotel room. In the bathroom was a familiar distressed leather toiletry bag she'd seen her dad pack a hundred times. Meticulously opening every drawer and cabinet throughout the room, she found nothing more of interest. She even searched the pockets of his trousers and the sport coat hanging with the other garments in the wardrobe.

After flying all this way and sneaking herself into the room, Charlie felt no further along than before she'd left London. She sat in the chair by the small desk and ate the burger and fries. The Heineken tasted refreshing, and with a full stomach, she soon felt sleepy. The bed looked tempting, but an afternoon nap wouldn't bring her any closer to finding her father.

Putting her police cap back on, she wondered about approaching the local authorities and reporting him missing. With no signs of foul play, they'd be reticent and hard-pressed to do more than fill out a missing person report which would do little unless he popped up in the system leaving the country. Charlie couldn't imagine him leaving without his watch and beloved wedding ring.

Wiping the ketchup from the corner of her mouth, she swigged the last of the beer, and quickly changed into a fresh tank top and a pair of capri leggings. Gathering up the things from the bed, she placed her own cheap watch in the bedside table along with a quickly scribbled note saying she was in Miami, and to call. She didn't want to miss him if he came by the room while she was looking for his rental car.

Leaving the room, Charlie tucked the key card with the maid's in her pocket, the watch on her wrist, and the ring over her thumb as it was too big for her ring finger. She said hello to the maid who was franticly searching all over her cart for something and paused. Deftly retrieving the stolen key card from her pocket, she reached down and pretended to find it on the floor.

"Looking for this?" she asked, handing it to the woman.

"Gracias," the maid enthused, clearly relieved, and adding a bunch more words of gratitude Charlie didn't understand as she hastily made her way to the elevators.

Below the reception level, there were two buttons for parking levels and Charlie pressed the bottom one, figuring she'd work her way up. The elevator door opened to a sea of concrete and vehicles. She began walking the rows, repeatedly pressing the unlock button on the key fob and listening for a beep. It was stiflingly hot below the hotel where not a stitch of air was moving. Sweat began weeping from her pores, and she was glad she'd ditched her jeans.

With no success on the lower level, Charlie continued up the long ramp which also served as more parking spots. Tired of clicking the unlock button, she hit the red one instead and a car horn began loudly honking, the sound echoing around the concrete walls.

"Bollocks," she muttered.

For someone who was trying to move covertly around, a horn blasting was less than ideal, but nobody else paid attention to the racket beyond a few annoyed glances. Her father's rental car was a big, black GMC Yukon. Clicking the unlock and silencing the horn blasts, Charlie opened the driver's door and found the steering wheel and pedals were missing.

"Damn it," she groaned, having forgotten she was in a country which drove on the right-hand side.

She moved around to the left and climbed into the driver's seat. The vehicle was roasting hot inside which promoted the odor of chemicals which many referred to as the "new car smell." Charlie wrinkled her nose as she began searching the SUV. The ice chest-sized center armrest held no clues, the numerous cup holders were empty, and the glove box contained nothing more than the rental paperwork. At the top of the windshield behind the rearview mirror was an odd plastic box marked "SunPass." Charlie had no idea what it was, but it appeared to be attached as though it came with the vehicle. A parking ticket was wedged into the edge of an air vent, and she checked the date. The SUV had been parked four days earlier.

She searched for the slot to put the key into the ignition, but realized there wasn't a fold-out key, and no place to put one. Finding the "start" button on the dash she pressed it, but it worked as well as the "close door" button in the elevators. It was an automatic transmission, which Charlie wasn't used to, but after several minutes of poking, prodding, and swearing, the engine finally fired up when she had her foot on the brake as she pressed the button. She wondered if the elevator had a brake pedal that she'd missed.

In less than a minute, cold air belted from the vents, and she put her face near the closest one, taking off her cap and letting the air-conditioning cool her scalp. A television-sized screen lit up in the dash area between the seats offering more menu options than her local Indian restaurant. Playing with the touch screen, Charlie found her way to the GPS which showed a map of the United States of America.

"I know that much," she said to the screen, looking for an option to locate her current position.

She looked outside at the low-ceilinged concrete tomb she was in. No way the satellite signal was reaching the vehicle down here. Feeling like she was about to maneuver the QE2, Charlie dropped the Yukon in drive and eased out of the cramped parking spot and came to an abrupt halt. She could hardly see over the wheel, and her bum was slipping off the front of the seat when she pushed the brake. It took several minutes to find, fiddle with, and correctly adjust the seat, lower the steering column, and turn off the heated seat she'd accidentally bumped on.

Driving slowly to remain unnoticed—but more because she was worried about hitting something or somebody—Charlie made her way to the exit where a barrier awaited. She slipped the parking ticket into the machine which in return showed a fee of thirty dollars a day times four days. Before she had time to panic, the barrier went up and she quickly exited to the street, relieved it was billed to the room.

Pulling out onto the street, she searched for a place to pull over and park, but the street appeared void of any such thing. Caught in two lanes of busy late afternoon traffic, she went with the flow to the end of the road where it met another street and a traffic light. Glancing down at the GPS screen, Charlie noticed it had now found her location. Thankful the light was red, she pressed around the options until she found the GPS history, expecting to find the route from the airport to the hotel. That did come up, but it wasn't the most recent map, there were two after it. Pressing the last directions programmed it showed a highlighted line leading from a place in the Florida Keys back to the hotel. When she pushed the back button, the previous map showed a route her father must have taken south to the Keys.

A car honked its horn behind her, and she realized the light was green and the traffic ahead had already made the turn. Pulling forward, she quickly selected the directions. By the time she'd made the corner and accelerated up to speed, a synthetic voice began guiding her toward Key Largo.

Miami traffic at 4:00 p.m. on a Saturday turned out to be nearly as hectic as negotiating the city streets of London at just about any time of day. Charlie just wasn't used to doing it in a Challenger tank-scale vehicle, or from sitting in what she perceived as the passenger seat, but at least the mass of cars made it clear which side of the road she should be on.

Once she reached a freeway, things rolled a little better and she quickly discovered two things. In Florida, it seemed people either drove incredibly slowly, or like complete lunatics. Motorcycles flew past at over a hundred miles per hour, dodging around gardener's trucks overloaded with cuttings going fifty in the middle lane. Passing, it seemed, was permitted wherever space for a car existed, rather than the outside lane only. Her second realization was at the first toll road signs, where the word "SunPass" appeared, and she finally understood the little plastic box was part of an automatic billing system for the toll.

When what she knew as a motorway, but was locally called a turnpike, finally ended, she was in a town called Florida City. Looking around, Charlie decided the place didn't really deserve to be named after the whole state, but maybe she wasn't seeing the good part. Businesses, gas stations, and fast-food restaurants gave way to thick shrubs and low trees lining a road called Highway One, which soon became one lane each way of busy traffic stretching as far as she could see. Occasionally, the looneys on bikes zipped by on the hard shoulder, and when she came to a passing lane, everyone sped up and nobody actually passed anybody else.

Swampy lagoons began appearing on both sides, then larger bodies of water which could have been lakes, or the ocean, Charlie wasn't sure. Finally, the traffic crawled over a long, tall bridge high above the water with boats and a resort-looking place below, and to her right. On the far side of the long bridge, the road curved right and became two lanes again as she reached Key Largo. Charlie knew the name from an old black and white movie she'd watched with her dad.

Key Largo seemed to go on forever with small shopping centers lining each side of the highway. The traffic had slowed to somewhere in sight of the forty-five-mile-per-hour speed limit and passing a few police cars along the way told Charlie why. Everything about the place was tropical. Palm trees, brightly colored business signs, boat dealers, and restaurants all claiming to serve the freshest fish.

When the GPS voice told her she'd arrived at the address on the right-hand side, Charlie slowed the SUV, but wasn't sure what to do. A car park was full of vehicles in front of an elegant red brick building signed "Adaline & Bennett Funeral Home." When cars began honking their horns behind her, Charlie turned into the parking lot and her GPS informed her she'd arrived at her destination.

5

It was too cold for Grant. He wondered if there was some fear by Adaline and Bennett that if they turned up the temperature, the corpses would start rotting on-site.

Lilacs and lilies flooded the room with floral scents, which mixed with the faint smell of formaldehyde that every funeral home attempted to mask. Grant's nose endured the assault, which was worsened by wafting fragrances of Chanel No. 5 and Estée Lauder, neither of which Grant could place if he wanted to.

The sanctuary of the handicapped stall in the men's room offered him an oasis for a few moments. He leaned forward, pressing his shaking hands against the metal door. The onslaught of condolences and unwanted hugs grated against him, leaving him raw.

Grant hated people. As a whole species, they sucked. Most of the women—and they all seemed to be women at the visitation— circled the room like buzzards. He never considered his mother old. And in Key Largo, where the average age was somewhere between sixty-one and sixty-eight, she barely squeezed into that bracket. Still, some of her clientele at the hair salon pushed into their nineties. They loved Fiona Wolfe. Whenever they climbed into her chair, she dished gossip with each of them. In fact, Grant often joked that his mother knew more about each of the island's denizens than they did themselves.

Deep breath, he told himself. He lowered the lid on the toilet and sat back on it. A nerve in his leg quivered and made his muscle twitch. Grant winced.

His hand slipped inside the pocket of the dark blue sport jacket he was wearing. He only had one black suit, and his mother would have rolled over in her coffin if she thought he wore it to the wake and the service. If she had her way, he'd change before heading to the cemetery for the graveside service.

"Grant?" a feminine voice called from outside the men's room.

"I'll be right out, Angie," he called.

When the door to the men's room clicked closed, he pulled out the small amber bottle. After twisting the top off, he tossed his head back and flicked the bottle to his mouth. Two light blue oxycodone tablets flew into the back of his throat. He didn't bother to make sure he'd only taken two—in fact, the instructions only stated to take two a day. Since his doctor cut the prescription in half, Grant used his own discretion to measure out his dosage.

The instant relief almost made him laugh. The opioids hadn't had time to get into his bloodstream, much less give him the relief he told himself he needed.

He stood up and exited the stall. The restroom was empty. That was a relief, as if someone in the room might have witnessed him popping those Percocets.

After sitting, his sport coat bunched up around his torso. With a quick snap on the bottom of each lapel, the jacket slipped into a more presentable appearance. He didn't want his mother to disapprove.

Outside the bathroom, Angie Wilkerson stood holding the silver chain that kept the brown mutt from running off. Wrench would have, too. The damned dog wanted to greet everyone.

"Thanks, Angie," he told the woman before leaning in and kissing her cheek.

"I'm going to run in a bit," she told him in a warning tone.

Wrench pulled at the leash despite being seated on his haunches. His lips pulled back in a snarl that Grant recognized for the dog's sunny smile.

"Okay," he replied to Angie. The two of them had been in an on-again, off-again romance since the seventh grade. Currently, they were off again, which meant little except they might date a few other people.

"I have to get to work," she explained, even though Grant never asked.

"Will you be by tomorrow?" he asked.

She nodded and waited for him. He stared blankly at her.

Suddenly, she leaned forward and patted down the sides of his jacket. He flinched but didn't pull back. When the pills in the inside pocket rattled, her eyes narrowed.

"Grant Wolfe," she said with exasperation. "How many did you take?"

"I'm fine," he assured her.

"You are far from fine," she retorted. "You don't get to eat them like candy."

"I know," he said. "I'm trying not to."

"But how many did you take?"

"Two," he admitted. He thought his head drooped and he pulled it back, resisting the urge.

"Dammit," she cursed. "Do I need to worry about you?"

"No, Ange, I'm fine," he assured her again.

She rolled her eyes.

"Are you working?" she asked.

"A divorce case right now. Husband thinks his wife is running around."

Angie lifted an eyebrow. "You hate divorce cases," she pointed out.

"They pay the bills."

Angie stared at him. Grant didn't move.

"Take the damned dog," she finally told him.

"Oh, sorry," he apologized, grabbing the leash from her hand. Wrench shook excitedly.

Angie wrapped her arms around him and pulled in against his chest. Grant inhaled her herbal shampoo. Her comforting arms tightened around him.

The last time they broke up was all his fault. He'd been relying on the pills more and more to steady himself. Grant convinced himself the old wound in his leg was hurting more. He took the meds he needed to function. Angie had warned him if he didn't get it under control that she couldn't be with him. He didn't.

Nothing new. The sheriff's department wouldn't let him come back either. Grant raged about that for a while. He'd taken the bullet while on the job. The round embedded in his femur, and the resulting surgery to remove it created an embolism that damaged the nerves along his thigh. After all that, the department benched him because he couldn't piss clean. If it hadn't been for his mom and Angie, the bitterness would have overwhelmed him.

"I know today is a lot," Angie whispered, still gripping him. "Don't let it get to you."

He said nothing, but his head pressed into her shoulder as he nodded.

"I'll be by in the morning," she promised. "I'll bring you guys some breakfast."

"Thanks, Ange," he replied as she let the hug go.

Angie bent over and massaged Wrench's face. The pit-lab mix huffed through his nostrils with excitement.

"Take care of him, boy," she told the dog. Looking back at Grant, she advised, "You better get back in there. I think you have some family that showed up."

Grant's brow furrowed. "What family?" he asked.

"I don't know," Angie admitted. "She kinda looks like your mother. I assumed she's a cousin or something."

Grant's face twisted.

"See you tomorrow," she told him again before turning to walk out of the funeral home.

Grant watched her leave. He missed having her around. This was just another hiatus. Since he met Angie in junior high school, the two had gone on eight breaks over fifteen years. His mind came back to her comment. *Family*? He didn't have any family. Just his mother. And her damned dog, which he assumed was now his dog.

Otherwise, there was no one. His mother's parents were long dead before Grant was born. Fiona Wolfe had no siblings and therefore no extended family.

In that instance, it hit him. He had no family. There were never a lot of stories about his father. Grant knew he had died before his mother found out she was pregnant. Over the years, she'd tell him a little bit, but only when he asked. Even that was like pumping water from a well. If he didn't continue to ask her questions, she'd dry up.

Something wet touched his hand, and as Wrench licked his fingers, Grant came back into the present.

"Come on," he urged Wrench, who bounded to his feet and followed Grant.

Fiona Wolfe found the mutt on her way back from Miami. Someone dumped several puppies off the highway. She guessed it was some twisted kid trying to feed an alligator, but Wrench was the only one she found still alive. Fiona brought him home swaddled in her blouse. Grant remembered seeing his mother come through the door wearing only her bra and pants. The wet dog's muzzle stuck out of the silk blouse.

That was two years ago. Wrench, whose name came from the first thing Fiona saw when entering the house that day, became her constant companion. He'd plop in a chair and wait while she teased hair in the salon, then follow her home behind her bicycle. If Fiona went somewhere, Wrench was right there with her.

Except that last day. She'd left him at home to run to the store. When the sheriff called Grant to tell him a hit-and-run driver struck Fiona while she was on her bike, he expected to find the dog nearby. It wasn't until he went back to her house that he found Wrench whining and pawing at the door.

The dog seemed to realize Fiona wasn't around, and he'd latched onto Grant. The two always got along—Wrench loved to go running with Grant when the latter's leg had allowed him to run. Most of the time, it was a steady walk.

Wrench obediently remained just to Grant's right as they moved back into the chapel. If the floral aroma seemed pungent in the halls, it overwhelmed Grant in the main room. His mother hadn't received that many flowers. He'd bought a large wreath with calla lilies, since those were her favorite. Her boss at the salon sent a smaller wreath of roses, something Grant wondered about. Roses never seemed like a funeral flower, but his knowledge of such things was limited to what his mother or Angie told him was proper.

"Oh Grant, you have Wrench with you," Mrs. Tellison announced as if Grant might not know he had a dog attached to a leash.

The older woman worked at the coffee shop currently, however, for a few years she'd worked the chair next to Fiona's in the salon. Mrs. Tellison's husband died long ago, and for almost as long as Grant could remember, the woman reveled in widowhood. While she was at least ten years older than his mother, the two women were close friends. Mrs. Tellison often watched Grant when he was still too young to be left alone.

"Yes, ma'am," he responded to her. "We're about to go back inside."

"I'm sure going to miss Fiona," the woman assured him.

He nodded—a gesture he'd grown accustomed to doing. Usually "Thank you" followed it.

"Is that a cousin I didn't know about?" she asked curiously.

"Who?" Grant wondered aloud.

"The young lady I just passed near the…uh…casket," Mrs. Tellison explained.

"I don't think so," Grant replied. "I don't have any family."

"Really?" Mrs. Tellison questioned. "She's the spitting image of Fiona."

Grant shrugged, curious who this person, both Angie and Mrs. Tellison, confused for his family. Most likely, he guessed it was another one of her customers. As a cop, he'd learned most people are terrible witnesses. Their brains adjust what they see to something familiar. It's why the ladies at the shop often referred to the postman that delivered the mail as the "Jerry Seinfeld Mailman." He had the same facial features as the comedian, but his eyes were the wrong color. Not to mention, the mailman was a good four to five inches shorter than the television star.

Wrench tugged at the leash.

"Wait, boy," Grant urged the dog before turning back to Mrs. Tellison, saying, "I'll keep an eye out for this woman."

"Maybe she's a long-lost family member," the woman mused.

Wrench vibrated as if every muscle in his body was about to explode. Grant turned to follow the dog's gaze until he saw a woman heading out the door of the funeral home. Her head was down, but he caught a brief look at her face when she glanced over her shoulder. Her expression suggested confusion or anger, Grant couldn't distinguish which. He recognized what Angie and Mrs. Tellison had said. She did favor his mother. Of course, now watching her from behind again, she could have been any brown-haired woman with a good figure.

"Excuse me," he told his mother's friend. "I think Wrench needs to go out for just a minute."

Mrs. Tellison agreed, squeezed his free hand, and stepped away.

Grant and Wrench stalked down the hallway to the exit door. He opened it to find the glare of the Florida sun blinding. While the funeral home was ice cold, the outside was baking at nearly ninety-eight degrees.

The woman was stomping across the yard toward a black GMC Yukon.

"Excuse me," Grant called out, pulling back on Wrench's leash.

The dog obviously mistook the woman for his mother, and after several days without his companion, he was ready to launch after her. The woman crossed a stretch of cemetery and clicked a key fob to unlock her vehicle's doors.

Tires squealed across the lot, and Grant watched as a black Suburban raced toward the stranger. She deftly leapt out of the way, but the SUV screeched to a halt. Two men bounded out of the Suburban. From where he stood, he saw the first man pull out a Makarov pistol.

Before Grant could react, Wrench took off. The full weight of the dog hit the end of the leash at a full run, and Grant had no chance of holding the handle. He chased after the dog, who had already covered half the ground.

Then the gunshot echoed through the tombstones.

6

With every nerve tingling after the weird looks she'd received inside the funeral home, Charlie ignored the stranger calling her. She couldn't wait to get in the rental car and leave. Already primed like a coiled spring, the SUV screeching to a stop a few feet away was the last straw. As she wheeled around, a dog began furiously barking, as a man stepped from the black vehicle and aimed a gun across the parking lot.

Everything became a blur, as instinct and training kicked in. Charlie took a step toward the assailant and swung at his arm. The gunshot rang in her ears as she wound up to punch the man in the throat, but she was too late, he was gone. A brown missile flew past Charlie at chest height, latching onto the man's arm, and crashing them both into the side of the Suburban.

The man, who had the stern look and buzzed hair of a soldier, somehow stayed on his feet with the dog writhing and snarling still locked on his forearm. The man screamed in pain and swore in what sounded like an Eastern European language as blood splattered from the dog's jaws and the gun dropped to the ground.

Charlie suddenly remembered the second man and turned, but

he'd already ducked back into the passenger side of the vehicle, fumbling inside the glove box. She lunged for the dropped gun.

"Gun!" came the voice of the man who'd been calling to her from outside the funeral home.

"No shit," Charlie muttered as she tried to recall everything she'd learned in her brief firearms training too many years ago.

She took two steps away, and the dog suddenly released the first assailant and bounded around the front of the car. Charlie aimed at the second man who was getting out, now brandishing a weapon.

"Drop the gun and stay where you are!" she yelled, but no one seemed to pay attention.

The second gunman lunged back into the car and slammed the door a moment before the dog reached him, leaving the mutt leaping at his door with claws grinding down the glossy black paintwork. His bloodied cohort dived into the driver's seat and yanked the car into drive, spinning the tires in a plume of smoke and squealing rubber.

Charlie leapt back as the car lurched past her, landing in some-one's arms. She shook them off as she watched the dog chase the car to the road. Instinctively, she wrestled her cell phone from her pocket, unlocked it with her thumb, and clicked a photograph of the car as it took off down Overseas Highway.

"Wrench!" the man next to her yelled. "Here, boy!"

Charlie turned to see a guy around her age in a dark blue blazer. If she hadn't been ready to spit nails, she would have paused to look longer. He was a good-looking man, albeit a little too clean-cut, square-jawed, Mister America for her taste. He was tucking his own cell phone back in his pocket, having snapped a similar shot.

"What the bloody hell was that all about?" she groaned, watching the dog trotting back toward them with his tongue hanging out and his leash trailing along the ground.

"Beats the fuck out of me," the guy replied. "Are you okay?"

Charlie looked at the gun still in her hand. "Everything I heard about Florida is bloody true. First day here and I've already been shot at." She looked up at the man, realizing she had no idea whether he could be trusted. "Who the hell are you, and why are those wankers shooting at you?"

"How the fuck should I know?" he said, running a hand through his neatly groomed hair.

"You don't know who you are?" Charlie quickly rebutted.

" I'm Grant," the man said impatiently. "I don't know who *those guys* are. And technically, they weren't shooting at me. I figured they were after you."

Charlie felt a wet nose rub her hand as the dog lean against her leg. His big eyes looked up at her and he wagged his tail. He had a small piece of bloody fabric hanging from his jaw.

She frowned at the mutt. "You seem nice when you're not ripping someone's arm off, but you should know I'm not a dog person."

"Wrench likes you," Grant said in a calmer voice.

"Wrench?" Charlie repeated. "What kind of a name is Wrench? No wonder he's aggressive. You gave the poor bugger a stupid name."

"I didn't name him," Grant replied defensively. "My mother did."

"Well, she gave him a…" Charlie trailed off, recalling the picture of a woman on a stand inside the funeral home. A woman who was a stranger to Charlie, yet somehow familiar. She hadn't seen Grant inside, but now wondered if he was related to the deceased. He was attending her funeral, so he must know her at least.

"Is everyone okay?" came a voice from across the parking lot and they both turned.

A crowd had gathered outside the funeral home and an older man in a black suit was calling to them. Charlie had seen him inside and the man had appeared in charge of the service.

"We've called the police," the man said. "Are you both all right?"

"Shit," Grant groaned. "We're fine, sir. Thank you," he added in a louder voice. "No one's hurt and the men have gone."

The man in the suit didn't come any closer. "Was that the gun we heard go off?" he said, pointing at Charlie.

"Oh. No," she replied, holding the gun out in front of her as though it were burning her fingers.

"Actually, it was," Grant corrected her in a whisper.

"Bugger," Charlie moaned. "Well, yes, sir. It was this gun, but I didn't fire it. I hate guns."

The funeral director furrowed his brow. "No firearms are allowed inside, I must insist we adhere to that rule, young lady."

Charlie wasn't sure what to say to that, or what to do with the gun in her hand. It all felt like she'd landed in the middle of a modern-day wild west show. A siren wailed in the distance, and she breathed a sigh of relief. Help was on the way.

The funeral director looked at his watch, then at Grant. "I'm sorry, Mr. Wolfe, but we must proceed with the service. We have one more this evening so we must conclude on time and we're already behind schedule."

The siren was getting closer, and Grant shook his head. "Do whatever you need to do," he replied. "I guess I'll miss my own mother's funeral."

"I am sorry," the director replied, but quickly began herding the crowd back inside.

"Fucking leech," Grant muttered. "Do you know what a racket this is?" he continued, looking at Charlie. "They charge a fortune and bang out these services like a fast-food joint."

"I'm sorry about your mum," Charlie said, still bewildered and becoming more and more uncomfortable holding the gun.

Grant took a deep breath and his shoulders dropped. "Thanks." He looked down at the dog who took a step toward him, keeping his butt against Charlie but getting close enough for Grant to reach down and stroke his head. "We miss her, don't we, Wrench?" Grant said and looked back up at Charlie. "Hit and run. Full of life. One minute we're having breakfast, next minute I get a knock on the door, and they tell me she's dead."

"I'm sorry," Charlie said again as she had no idea what else to say.

"Thanks for saving Wrench," Grant said. "The guy was shooting at him."

Charlie replayed the chaos in her mind. She knew the memories would become distorted and her brain would begin filling in the gaps and uncertainty with anything which helped the situation make more sense. She needed to anchor the details she knew as truth. Grant was right, the man had tried to shoot the dog as he was the immediate threat. If they'd wanted to shoot either her or Grant, they could have done it without ever getting out of the car.

Blue and red lights flashed all around them and the ridiculously loud siren made her head spin.

"Place the gun on the ground!" a policeman ordered.

Charlie looked up, annoyed they were screwing up her processing of what had taken place. The cop was behind his open car door with a gun leveled at her. His partner was in a similar position on the opposite side of the car. The lights practically blinded her.

"Drop the gun, now!" he barked. "Get on the ground, face down. Both of you!"

Charlie was scared the gun might go off if she tossed onto the asphalt, so she leaned down and placed it on the ground.

"Don't be a dick, Hernandez," Grant said, and stepped between Charlie and the police car. "She took the gun off the guy who was doing the shooting."

Charlie stood stock-still. The day continued to deliver new and bizarre situations. She was now caught up in an episode of some American police drama.

"Stay right there, Wolfe!" the cop shouted. "You're a damn civilian now and we'll treat you as such."

Grant shook his head. "Put your fucking guns away and bag this one," he said. "The longer you fuck about, the farther away they're getting, and I'm missing my mother's funeral."

The two policemen looked at each other, then reluctantly holstered their weapons, stepping from behind the doors.

"And turn off the berries and cherries before someone has a seizure," Grant added. "Black Suburban with Florida plates, heading north. Two male perps. Caucasian. One has a dog bite injury to his right forearm. He's Eastern European. Clean shaven. Short, dark hair. Both looked to be former military—just not our military. Other guy was heavier. Both in dark slacks and polo shirts."

Charlie was impressed and tried to recall anything she could add. "Second bloke had a beard," she said. "And the driver's side will have claw scratches down the door. Wait…" she thought a moment, remembering the vehicle was left-hand drive. "Passenger side. Forgot you drive on the wrong side. I have a picture of the reg plate."

All three men stared at her.

"And who are you?" Hernandez demanded, while his partner retrieved the gun from the ground.

"Charlotte Greene," she replied, shielding her eyes from the flashing lights they were yet to turn off.

"Australian?" Hernandez asked in a smoother tone, puffing out his chest a little more and eyeing her up and down.

"English," she replied curtly, baffled how anyone could confuse the two accents.

"You knew these two guys in the Chevy?" Hernandez asked sharply, sensing he wasn't impressing her.

"No. How should I know them? I only flew in this morning."

"How do you know Wolfe?"

"I don't."

"But you were attending the funeral?"

"No."

"Then why were you here, Miss Greene?"

Charlie opened her mouth to reply but had no idea what to say. The lights were making her squint and as the adrenaline wore off, she was feeling desperately tired. *Why was she here?* The truth would sound like the ramblings of a lunatic. Her head spun from the madness the day had dealt her from beginning until now.

She stared into the distance, looking past the police car, and through the strobing red and blue, she caught a glimpse of a man getting into a parked car.

"Miss Greene? Why were you attending the funeral?" Hernandez asked again, moving closer and blocking her view.

"I was lost, and happened to pull into this car park," she lied, taking a deep breath to clear her mind and pull herself together.

She stepped to the side, trying to see the distant car again, but between the refrigerator sized policeman and the stupid lights, she couldn't focus or see properly.

"We can do this here, or at the station if you'd prefer," Hernandez insisted. "Either way you need to answer our questions and make a statement."

Charlie closed her eyes for a moment. "I'll give you a bloody statement, all right? Just give me a minute. I know you lot shoot at each other every day, but it's rather new to me." She opened her eyes and glared at the policeman, taking another step to the side.

The car was a beat-up looking Toyota or Honda with faded silver paint. She couldn't see the driver clearly as he pulled out onto Overseas Highway and turned the same way that the Suburban had gone.

But Charlie couldn't shake the notion she'd just seen her father.

7

"Grant, I'm so sorry about Fiona," Tracy told him as she placed a cold pint of Sharkey's Hammerhead Red Ale on the bar in front of him. She added, "I wanted to make it to the service, but I was here all day."

"Thanks, Tracy," Grant acknowledged. "If it makes you feel any better, I missed the service, too."

"What?" She gasped. "Why?"

Grant twisted his head to peer at the woman next to him. "I'm not sure yet," he replied.

Tracy reached over and squeezed his forearm as she offered a slight smile. "I'll get Wrench some water," she told him.

Grant nodded.

"I'm sorry you missed your mother's funeral," Charlotte remarked. "I feel horrible about the whole affair."

The woman's British accent continued to surprise him. He had trouble taking his eyes off her. The resemblance to his mother was uncanny. Add thirty years onto this lady and the result would be Fiona Wolfe. Even Wrench struggled with the likeness. If he'd only seen her from afar, Grant might have sworn it was his mother's spirit.

I suppose it's lucky she opened her mouth, he considered.

Tracy appeared at Grant's side with a silver bowl filled with water and two chicken tenders.

"The chicken is from Jeff in the back," Tracy told Grant.

"What?" he joked. "I don't garner free chicken."

"Jeff says he likes Wrench better than you," Tracy remarked as she walked back around the bar.

Wrench's head bobbed as he picked up the first piece of chicken and tossed it to the back of his mouth before chewing it three times and swallowing. He repeated the method with the second piece before sniffing around the floor for bits of breading he'd dropped.

"We need to start at the beginning, I guess," Grant commented, turning his attention back to the woman. "Who are you?"

"I already explained that to you," Charlotte snapped.

"Yeah, yeah," Grant moaned. "Charlotte Greene. You got lost and turned around. I don't expect Hernandez bought that line of crap either."

"The officer?" she questioned. "He was a bloody prick, wasn't he?"

"That's the polite way of saying it," Grant retorted. "I'd use douchebag, but that's an insult to douchebags everywhere."

He thought he saw the corners of her mouth twitch.

"Why don't you start over with me, Charlotte?" he suggested. "Let's start with what you were doing at the funeral home, and maybe we can discuss why you are the spitting image of my mother."

Charlotte picked up the Chardonnay she'd been served and took a drink. She seemed to study the decor of Sharkey's as she considered her response. Her eyes shifted to the Marine Corps flag draped across the ceiling.

"She might have been my mother," she finally said.

Grant nodded. It wasn't a big shocker, at least not at this point. In fact, once the adrenaline subsided after the gunmen fled the cemetery, he relaxed enough to piece together that possibility. Of course, it didn't dull the stabbing pain he felt in his chest.

Grant and his mother had been close. Even in his teen years, she'd given him a wide enough berth to make his mistakes without pushing him away. But she never told him he had a sister.

Stories about his father were few and far between. From what she told him, he died before his mother even realized she was pregnant. It seemed to be a brief affair, but it was one thing she didn't like to talk about.

"Who is your father?" Grant asked.

"Keith Greene," she answered, studying Grant for a reaction. "Did your mother ever talk about him?"

He shook his head. "Never heard of him."

The woman beside him let out a sigh before shrugging her shoulders. "He told me my mother was dead," Charlotte explained. "Cancer. I was a baby."

Grant sipped the red ale and considered the situation. "As far as I was aware, my father died before I was born. If I remember, it was some kind of accident, but Mom never talked about him much. I always guessed it was too much for her."

"What if they didn't die?" she asked.

"Why would they lie about that?" Grant questioned.

Charlotte reached into her bag and pulled out a picture. Grant took the photo and studied it. The woman in the picture was his mother and an exact clone of Charlotte Greene. The couple sat on a sofa, beaming over a baby in the woman's arms.

"I'm pretty sure that's me," she told Grant.

"He's wearing a ring," Grant pointed out. "I can't make one out on her hand." He struggled to force his brain to identify the woman in the picture as Fiona Wolfe.

"If that is me, we still don't know how you fit in," Charlotte commented.

"But if they were together, then we may share the same mother." Grant mused. "And they must have divorced. Maybe she's trying to hide from him?"

"This is hardly solid proof," Charlotte pointed out. "And my dad's the nicest guy in the world, so why would she hide from him?"

"Have you asked him?" Grant asked. "That seems like the easiest thing to do. Go straight to the source."

Charlotte shook her head. "I can't find him. He came to the States and vanished."

A dull pain grew in his leg. Grant fumbled in his pocket and pulled out a blue pill. He popped it in his mouth and washed it down his throat with the ale.

"Have you called the cops?" Grant asked.

Charlotte slowly turned the wine glass clockwise. In his head, Grant heard the click-click-click as if each rotation triggered an imaginary sound.

"My father wouldn't want the authorities involved," she explained. "He's the head of an international security company. The publicity might be damaging."

"Not any more damaging than being dead," Grant advised as he waved at Tracy for another beer.

"I don't think he's dead," she retorted. "I just don't know where he is."

"What about the men at the cemetery?" Grant asked. "They were coming after you."

"I've never seen them before," she responded.

"What kind of work do you do?" Grant asked. "You fought them off like a champ. Do you do security work, too?"

She shook her head. "No," she answered. After a second, she finished, saying, "I was with New Scotland Yard."

"Scotland Yard?" he asked. His tone grew looser. "Like a cop?"

She nodded.

"Scotland Yard sounds a little pretentious," he remarked. "You know, Sherlock Holmes and what have you."

"At least I didn't name my dog after a spanner," she quipped.

"A what?"

She rolled her eyes with deliberation. "Never mind. You used to be police, too?"

He nodded. "The keywords are 'used to be.'"

"That wanker—what was his name? Hernando?"

"Hernandez," Grant offered.

"Yes, he worked with you?" she asked.

"Yeah, I was a deputy with the Monroe County Sheriff's Department."

"Deputy sounds just as pretentious as constable," Charlotte noted.

Grant shrugged a surrender.

"I need to find my father," she said. The tone wasn't pleading, but Grant heard the request.

He sighed. "What made you assume he was at the funeral?"

"The car I'm driving was his rental," she explained. "I found it at his hotel. The last destination in its history was the address which turned out to be the funeral home. I had no idea he was coming there."

Grant crossed his arms. His eyes caught Tracy, and he signaled for another beer. "Another wine?" he asked.

Charlotte glanced at the empty glass and nodded.

Grant pieced together a few of the puzzle pieces he imagined in his head.

"Your father knew the funeral was happening," he said aloud. Talking out loud about the problem often helped him visualize it. Plus, he tended to talk more once the pill took effect.

"I would think so," she replied.

"They must have still been in contact," Grant surmised.

Charlotte Greene's brow furrowed. "Why would they hide it from us?"

In Grant's experience, everyone had secrets. Usually, they were a form of protection from something. Since becoming a private investigator, he'd seen more couples scrambling to hide things than any criminal he'd encountered.

His first thought had been his mother had been hiding from Charlotte's father. *Who could possibly be his father.* It felt strange to consider that. He'd never had a father. In fact, he couldn't remember ever missing that fact. Sure, in school, there were always friends whose fathers would take them out fishing or boating, but he never missed it. It was never a reality he'd experienced.

If they were in contact, though, that meant Fiona Wolfe wasn't hiding from this man. Then why not tell Grant about it?

Grant was never one to leave things alone. He pulled at every illogical string until he came up with a truth that fit into his brain. Now he was staring at a mess of strands that made no sense.

But what did it matter? His mother was dead, and if he had a father out there, the man never gave two shits about Grant. His life was a mess right now. The last thing he needed was this woman around, who seemed to be irritated by every word that came out of his mouth. He didn't need that.

He still had the Robertson case. The husband had hired him to catch his wife cheating, and with his mother's death, he'd slid the whole thing to the back burner. James Robertson had offered to pay a hefty bonus if Grant could get the evidence. After all, it would mean she'd violated their prenuptial agreement, and Robertson wouldn't have to split his thirty-million-dollar estate with his bride.

All he had to do was catch the wife.

Everyone had secrets.

"Only one thing makes sense to me," Charlotte continued, breaking Grant out of his thoughts. "I don't know about your mother, but my father has never had another relationship. I think he still pined for her."

Grant shook his head, saying, "Mom dated a few guys, but it never went past a few weeks."

"What if they split up to hide from something?" she asked. "Or someone?"

"My mother was a hairdresser," Grant pointed out. "Who wants to go after a hairdresser? It's just as possible that they split up right after getting married. Perhaps they realized it was too much or not right."

"Those men at the cemetery were after something," she argued. "What if they expected my father to be there?"

"They didn't go after your father," Grant corrected. "They came after you."

She slumped down, disappointed. Grant studied her expression, recognizing it from the disappointed look his mom often gave.

"Unless…" he mused.

"Unless what?"

"Your father didn't show, but you did," he suggested.

"Why would they be after me?"

Grant tapped his finger on the old photograph. His fingertip patted the image of his mother. "You look just like her."

"Bollocks," she uttered. "Well, okay. A bit, I suppose."

Tracy interrupted them with two fresh drinks. Charlotte grabbed hers and took a gulp. Grant sipped his with more contemplation.

"They knew who my mother was," he thought aloud. The idea of men with guns storming his mother's funeral disturbed him. He'd seen those types of eyes on men before, too. They were on a mission, and somehow his mother was involved. "Okay," he relented. "I am curious who these guys with the guns are."

She nodded. "I got a picture of the registration. Can we track them down?"

"It's not all that easy," he admitted. "I don't have a lot of friends left in the department."

Charlotte stared at him, but he didn't elaborate.

"I'll see what I can come up with," he added. "I can make a call tomorrow."

She drained the rest of her glass. She reached for her wallet when he waved her off. "I got it," he promised.

"Thank you. I need to find a hotel, I guess. Where do you recommend? Someplace cheap. And when I say cheap, I mean *really* bloody cheap."

"There's a Hampton over on the highway, but I doubt it's cheap."

"I'll find something," she stated as she stood up. "Can I call you tomorrow?"

Grant nodded, and scribbled his cell phone number on a napkin, handing it to her. Charlotte took it and started walking past the pool table for the exit. Wrench whined and pulled against the leash attached to the barstool. Grant realized the dog was pining after the woman who looked so much like his owner had.

He sighed.

"Charlotte," he called to the woman he was trying to imagine being his sister.

She paused and turned back.

"Look, I live at my mom's place, and there's plenty of room if you want to stay. It's not Buckingham Palace or anything, but it has a marvelous view."

Charlie smiled. "Thank you."

Wrench's tail thumped against the stool as she came back to the bar.

"Also, call me Charlie," she said, and he nodded to the woman who could be his sister.

8

Lost in the dreamy, half sleep of morning, Charlie felt the warm breath of a lover close by. It had been a while since she'd dated anyone, and her body quivered in anticipation of the man's touch. She'd sewn her wild oats in her late teens and found the empty feeling accompanying her hangover the following morning wasn't worth the clumsy and mediocre pleasure of a fleeting encounter. It had taken making the same mistake a few times, but finally she'd learned. In theory.

If she'd been awake enough to think it through, she'd have contradicted that statement, but as it was, she simply moaned and felt for the man lying beside her. Her fantasy slowly eased into the reality of waking, and she stared into the dark eyes of... Wrench. His big head rested on her arm and his slobbery tongue hung partly out his panting mouth.

"Bloody dog!" she yelled, bolting upright and yanking her arm away.

Wrench leapt to his feet, his mass bouncing the bed and his thick tail thrashing the air in excitement.

"What the hell is going—" Grant shouted, running from an

adjacent room before coming to an abrupt halt in the doorway. "Oh shit! I just saw… I mean…"

Grant hid his eyes as Charlie snatched up the bed sheet, quickly covering her naked breasts. Wrench was beside himself. He hopped from one front foot to the other, looking back and forth between the mortified man in the doorway and his new best friend in the bed.

"Your bloody dog is…" Charlie squealed, unable to form a complete understanding of exactly what crime Wrench had committed. Her face flushed with embarrassment at her own sleepy desires.

Grant peeked through his fingers then took his hand from his face once he was sure the woman he was potentially related to had covered herself.

"He likes to sleep on a bed," he said defensively. "He misses Mom and he's taken a real shine to you."

Charlie shoved Wrench's shoulder, but the dog just licked her arm as though she'd barely flicked his solid muscle. "Argh," she groaned and waved a hand at Grant, switching her grip on the sheet. "Turn around before you get another eyeful."

Grant spun around and faced the hallway and Charlie couldn't help but notice his lean, toned shoulders and strong arms. "Bugger me," she hissed, getting a bad case of the willies. That was probably her brother she was ogling. It was bad enough he'd just seen her boobs. Her face pulsed in a red glow.

She patted around the sheets until she found the tank top she'd worn to bed. At some point she must have tossed it aside, which reminded her how hot it was despite the whirling ceiling fan above her.

"How the hell do you sleep in this heat?" she complained, slipping the tank-top over her head and stepping from the bed, making sure the shirt hung low enough to cover her butt.

Grant laughed. "This ain't hot, girl. I have the AC on."

Wrench leapt across the bed, nuzzling her arm with his cold, wet snout.

"What is up with this bloody dog?" she said, striding across the room. "Excuse me," she demanded, and Grant quickly stepped out of her way.

Charlie marched by with Wrench on her heels. "I think your AC's broken, mate. It's like the Sahara in here."

"Oh, well the temp is set to eighty, but without the AC it would be ninety and dripping with humidity. The main thing is it dries the air out."

"It's gotta be broken," Charlie repeated, opening the linen closet door in search of the bathroom.

"On the left," Grant said.

She wheeled around and stomped past him down the hall.

"It's not broken, but it costs a fortune to run the AC all the time," he added.

"I'll chip in a tenner if you'll turn it down from Sahara to pleasant summer day," Charlie responded, closing the bathroom door behind her before Wrench could bulldoze his way in with her.

"Once you go outside and come back in it'll feel great in here," Grant assured her.

Charlie plonked herself down on the toilet and let out a long breath. The chaos of the past few days came flooding back to her and she buried her head in her hands. Nothing made any sense. Her pee hitting the water in the bowl sounded like rainwater pouring from a broken roof gutter, and she felt self-conscious and embarrassed all over again.

"Are you both standing out there staring at the bathroom door?" she asked, frowning as she picked her head up and looked at her side of the door, realizing she hadn't locked it.

Grant laughed again, this time a little nervously. "Wrench is. I'm about to make coffee. You drink coffee?"

Charlie finished her business and flushed the toilet. "Yeah."

"Wait, did you just flush the head?" Grant asked from the hallway.

Charlie paused, about to wash her hands. "Of course."

"Yeah, water's expensive here too. Can you save a flush for when you've knocked out a number two?"

Charlie stared at herself in the mirror, her jaw hanging open. She had to be asleep and dreaming all this madness.

Grant laughed, his voice fading as he walked away. "Just kidding. Flush till your little limey ass is content."

Charlie's shoulders dropped and she sighed again. If this wasn't a dream, then she must have stepped through someone's whacked-out looking glass. She dried her hands and opened the bathroom door. Wrench's face lit up and his tail swept the tiled floor like a severed high-pressure air hose, his backside wiggling back and forth in reaction.

"Listen, lover boy, we need to come to an understanding," she said, and his tail slowed. He tilted his head as though trying to understand her accent. "I'm barely a cat person and certainly not a dog person, so I need some space, okay?"

Wrench's mouth opened and closed as though he'd spoken a silent word. Charlie returned to the bedroom to get dressed and the dog followed, jumping onto the bed, and collapsing with his bulbous face resting on his outstretched front paws. Charlie shook her head, but extended a hand and stroked the dog's short, coarse hair, scratching behind his ears.

Wrench looked up at her with half-closed eyes as though his life was now complete. Charlie couldn't help but smile, which became a giggle when the dog began groaning softly in euphoria.

They'd arrived late at the house the night before and Charlie had been too tired and disorientated from the madness of the day to pay attention to much. In the morning light, she realized the little house was on a straight waterway lined by other properties. Some were similar little square or rectangular cottages, but others were far bigger, extravagant newer homes.

Her face glowed with perspiration although it was only eight in the morning. Grant had been right, the inside of the home was warmer than she was used to, but nowhere near the tropical oven outside. A breeze brushed her skin, and the relief was instantaneous.

"Notice how much cooler it is here than in Miami?" Grant said, handing her a coffee mug.

"No," she replied honestly, although beyond the underground parking at the hotel, she realized she hadn't spent any time outside beyond rushing out of the airport to catch the Uber. It all felt like her flesh would begin dripping from her bones at any moment. She looked at the steaming mug in her hand and decided she had a caffeine addiction issue as the hot liquid didn't repulse her despite standing in a sauna called Florida.

"We get a constant breeze through here which really knocks the edge off the heat," Grant persisted. "Up there, all the traffic and concrete produces even more heat which gets trapped in amongst the city buildings. It's usually five degrees cooler here."

"I'm not sure I can notice five degrees in the middle of an inferno," she grumbled, not bothering to ask whether he was talking centigrade or Fahrenheit.

"Down the end," Grant said, stepping to the railing at the rear of the deck and pointing right, "our canal meets the main one leading to the ocean. We're only a three-minute idle from the open water."

A back yard extended between the house and the waterway, which was more of a concrete patio with beds of pebbles where Charlie expected grass should be, and beyond sat a shiny white boat on a lift. She made out the words "Grady White" on the side.

"Is that your boat?" she asked.

"Yeah, well it's my mother's..." he said before his voice trailed off. Grant cleared his throat. "It *was* my mother's. I suppose it's mine now," he finished despondently.

Charlie sipped her coffee. Knowing what to say in difficult moments had never been her strength, which was strange, considering her father always seemed to have the right words for any situation. The vision of the man across the funeral home parking lot shot through her mind, and she instantly recognized her memory had already adjusted. The figure was no longer a vague image she'd barely glimpsed, but clearly her father.

"So, what do we do now?" she said, turning and heading inside.

Wrench's nose made a wet smudge along the pane of glass as she pulled the slider open to step inside. Grant followed and slid the door closed behind him.

"Track that plate, I guess," he replied. "It's about the only lead we have."

Charlie picked up her cell phone from the dining table next to the open plan kitchen. No calls or texts. She hit speed dial number one, calling her father's cell phone again. She hung up when it went to voicemail.

"He must have ditched his phone so he can't be tracked," she said.

Her police training along with every thriller on Netflix told her this was a sensible move while on the run. The question, however, remained as to why he was running, and from whom.

"Let's assume my dad was here for your mother's funeral," she mused aloud. "If he was, why didn't he show up sooner?"

"And why did he run?" Grant added.

"Maybe the two yobbos were there for him," Charlie suggested, and Grant looked at her in puzzlement.

"Yobbos?"

"Yeah," she said, wondering what confused him. "You know, thugs, or whatever slang you have for them over here."

"Thugs works," he replied with a grin. "But you had me with yobbos."

"Bloody hell, whatever, yeah? The two geezers with guns. Maybe they were there for Dad, and we just got in the way."

Grant shook his head. "I don't think so. I'm not sure the gobos..."

"Yobbos," she corrected.

"Yobbos," he repeated. "I'm not sure the yobbos ever saw your old man. Shit, I didn't see anyone, and from what you've told me, you barely saw him."

"Hmm," she grunted. He had a point. "So, they were after one of us."

"If by one of us, you mean you, then yeah, I think you're right."

Wrench nuzzled against Charlie's leg, and she looked down.

"I know, I know. You saved my arse, didn't you, snot face?"

Wrench leaned against her leg until she reached down and scratched his ear.

"So, Mr. Former Copper, what's the plan for tracking the plate?" she asked, looking up again.

"Well, Miss Former Cop, I'll make a call to the station."

"You still have friends there?"

Grant let out a long breath. "Let's go with, 'I have a few people who don't hate me as much as others.'"

"That's good," Charlie replied. "'Cause that wanker yesterday definitely seemed to hate you."

9

"They'll shitcan me, Grant," Macabee moaned over the phone.

"C'mon, Tony," Grant said. "It's like ten keystrokes."

"The captain will have something to say," he remarked.

Grant rolled his eyes, pulling the phone away from his ear as if Macabee might catch the facial expression over the line.

"I know as well as you do that Captain Rich has no idea how to even check who you pulled the tags for," Grant pleaded. "I'll throw in a fishing trip."

"Psh," the deputy on the other end scoffed. "You were going to do that whether I pull this tag or not."

"Look, Tony, this woman showed up at Mom's funeral yesterday…"

"Oh, yeah, Grant, I'm sorry about your mother. Several of us sent some flowers," Macabee offered.

"I ended up missing the service," Grant whined.

"Was that where the shooting was?" Macabee asked. "Hernandez's dumb-ass probably wrote it up as fireworks."

Grant laughed. "That's assuming Hernandez could spell 'fireworks.' The people with the guns were after this British chick."

"Oh, you got a British babe?"

"No asshole. This woman is the spitting image of my mother."

"No shit!" Macabee exclaimed. "Is she related or something?"

"I think she's my sister, or half-sister, or something," Grant explained. "I need to know what the hell is going on."

Macabee sighed into the phone. Through the speaker, the tapping of a keyboard was audible. Grant had no doubt Macabee would give in. He just had to make a show about not doing it so he could justify doing it.

"It's the registration for a Black Suburban, owned by T&R Luxury Leases out of Marathon."

"Any chance you can see who the lessee is?" Grant asked.

"You know better than that," Macabee scolded. "I can't do all the work."

"Thanks, Tony," Grant acknowledged.

"Next weekend," Macabee said. "I want to wet a hook."

Grant agreed and hung up.

"What did your friend tell you?" Charlie asked.

"It's a rental," Grant answered. "Or rather, a lease."

He started typing on the keypad, searching for T&R Luxury Leases. When he found the number, he clicked the link that automatically dialed the number.

"Luxury Leases," a woman answered. "How can I help you?"

"Yes, ma'am," Grant began. "This is Detective Hernandez with the Monroe County Sheriff's Department."

"Yes, sir," the female on the other end responded.

"I didn't get your name," Grant pointed out.

"Oh, I'm so sorry," she replied. "It's Jazmine—with a z."

With a z, Grant thought ruefully.

"Jazmine, I'm following up on one of your SUVs that was involved in a shooting yesterday. We requested the information late yesterday, and we still haven't received it. This is an urgent matter."

"Oh, I'm so sorry," she repeated. "I must have already left. My chemistry test was last night, and I needed to study beforehand."

Charlie sat on the sofa. Her left leg crossed over her right, and her foot was bouncing with nervous energy. Grant studied her as he talked to Jazmine. Wrench stared at the woman from about three feet away. The poor dog sat motionless with his eyes locked on Charlie.

"Going to night school, eh?" he asked politely. "I hope you passed your test."

"I got an A," she boasted.

"Good," Grant cooed. "But about the SUV."

"What did you need, Detective?"

Grant read off the license plate to the girl. "I need the name of whoever leased that vehicle."

"Um, I'm not sure I'm supposed to give out that information."

"Jazmine, we already requested it with the owner... What's his name?" Grant shuffled through some papers.

"Dammit," Grant blurted out before halfway placing his hand over the microphone and saying, "Tony, what's the name of the owner over there?"

"Mr. Rolton?" Jazmine asked, nervously.

"Yeah, that's right, Rolton," he answered, covering the phone again to say, "We got it, Tony."

Charlie smiled as she watched the way Grant performed. Wrench's tail thumped against the floor when he saw her grin. Her eyes cut to the dog before she rolled them.

"Okay," Jazmine said. "It's currently leased to XF Finance. The company's address is in Moscow."

"Russia?" he asked.

"Uh, yeah. But there's a Florida address, too."

She read it off to Grant, who scribbled it down. It was in Miami.

"Thank you, Jazmine," Grant said into the phone. "Can you tell me how they are paying for the vehicles?"

"I'm not sure I can do that," Jazmine stated.

"Jazmine, these guys shot up a funeral yesterday. We need to track them down before they hurt anyone else."

"Well," she replied, somewhat wishy-washy, "it was a credit card."

"Look, I'll send a detective down there if it makes you feel better," Grant offered. "But I'll have to comb through all your records."

"Oh," she said in a worried tone. "It's a Visa." She rattled off the numbers, and Grant hastily jotted them down.

"Thank you, Jazmine," he repeated. "If I have any more questions, I'll reach back out."

"Yes, sir," she stammered.

When he hung up, Charlie smiled. "You are a devious bugger."

"You don't know the half of it," he responded. "I was counting on the fact that the poor girl was scared of both the cops and her boss."

"What made you think that?" Charlie questioned.

"The tone when she gave up her boss's name. She was too willing to share the information I wanted rather than face him," Grant explained. "It seemed she wouldn't want to tell him the police were coming to go through his records."

"Aren't you a sneaky one."

He opened his laptop, typing into the search engine the address in Miami. Charlie moved over to stand behind him, reading over his shoulder.

"Post office box," Grant noted when the results pulled up a Mailbox Emporium. "It's a trick some use to make it appear they have a legitimate business. It looks like an actual place, and hell, people can send them mail. So, to some extent, it is."

"We could watch the mailbox?" she asked.

"We could," Grant acknowledged. "But I doubt it would get us anything. Most of the time, they forward everything to another address. I've seen a chain of forwarding that goes on forever. If we had the right resources, we could track it all down."

"Damn," she cursed. "What do we do?"

Grant offered her a cajoling grin, and she appeared to notice the small dimple on his left cheek, which showed when he gave a half smile. He clicked an icon on his computer's desktop, and when the program opened, he typed in the string of numbers the girl at the leasing company gave him.

"I helped a guy out who ran into a little bit of trouble with a pimp and a couple of call girls. Brayden Barnes. Goes by BeeBee. He didn't want to pay me traditionally, but he works for a credit bureau. He can run the number and give me the charges for as far back as we want."

"That has to be bloody illegal," Charlie said with a knowing grin.

Grant nodded. "It *is* bloody illegal," he agreed. "And bloody effective."

He hit a red button at the bottom of the screen.

"How long will it take?" Charlie asked.

"The guy's usually quick," Grant told her. "We could go grab us a bite while we wait."

She huffed.

"Look, he's fast, but not instantaneous," Grant scolded. "I need something in my stomach, and I'm sure Wrench does, too."

"He's coming?" Charlie questioned, sneering at the pup.

Grant cocked his head sideways. "You could be a little more courteous, given you took the boy's bed."

She rolled her eyes as she turned and walked away from the man and his dog. "I'm going to the loo first," she announced.

When she vanished, Grant glanced at Wrench, mimicking her in a high-pitched badly imitated British accent, "I'm going to the loo."

Wrench folded his front paws and let his hindquarters sink to the ground. He stared at Grant disapprovingly.

"Screw you," Grant told the dog. "You switched allegiances a little too quickly, buddy."

The computer dinged, and Grant clicked the notification.

"Must be a slow day," he said to Wrench. "He's already back with me."

The toilet flushed. Grant chuckled, recalling the joke about not flushing.

"We're in luck," he announced when she returned to the living room. "I got the results."

Charlie folded her arms, waiting.

Grant's boyish grin appeared again as he said, "You aren't the father."

The woman's left eyebrow shot up with a questioning stare.

"You don't get Maury over there?" he asked.

"What's a morry?" she asked with a frown.

Grant shook his head in disbelief. "I have the charges. Looks like there are at least four car leases... and here we go. Cheeca Lodge and Spa. There's a hefty charge there."

"Where's Cheeca Lodge?" Charlie inquired.

"A little south in Islamorada," Grant explained. "Swanky place. Certainly not the Key Largo Motor Lodge."

"Motor lodge?" she questioned.

"It's a motel—usually an older one. It has something to do with pulling off the road and right to your room."

She stared at him curiously.

"With your motor vehicle," he said slowly, enunciating each syllable.

"Don't be a fucking wanker," she snapped. "I understood that."

"Want to take a drive south? We'll take my car. These guys might recognize your rental."

When Grant stood up, Wrench bounded to his feet. Charlie paused, watching the animal who seemed to wait for her to take the lead.

"What's he doing?" she asked.

"He's a good Southern dog," Grant told her. "It's ladies first."

Charlie rolled her eyes and followed Grant down the exterior steps to the carport under the stilted home.

"What the hell is this?" she muttered when he climbed into the somewhat worn-down, faded red Honda Del Sol.

"It's my car," he stated, as she looked to the street where the shiny rental Tahoe was parked.

"It looks like a roller skate," she quipped, turning back to the Honda.

Grant lifted an eyebrow as he opened the door. Wrench raced behind the vehicle and leaped behind the driver's seat. Ignoring Charlie, Grant slid behind the wheel and cranked the engine.

Once Charlie was in the passenger's seat, she stared at the interior of the car.

"How old is this pile of rubbish?"

"Wow, you have the manners of a toad," Grant pointed out. "It's a 1996 model."

"It's the size of a model," she remarked. "Why didn't you get the full-sized version? I thought everything was bigger in America?"

"What do you mean? This baby has been with me since high school," Grant replied, passing on the obvious comeback. The whole sister thing was starting to mess with his head.

Charlie's mouth curled up in a droll expression. "I'm guessing you were a virgin until uni."

Grant rolled the driver's window down as he backed out of the car port. Wrench's head popped up between the two front seats, and he licked Charlie's cheek.

"Bugger," she hollered. "Get back there." Her hand pushed the dog away from her.

A second later, his muzzle reappeared. Grant wrapped his arm under the dog's chin to scratch his ears.

"It's so bloody hot," Charlie moaned. "Don't you Americans have air-conditioning in your cars?"

"There's air," Grant assured her, adjusting the dials. "Kinda."

The compressor under the hood started blowing cool air through the interior of the Del Sol. Charlie relaxed, leaning against the headrest as Grant drove out of the neighborhood. When he turned left onto Highway One, he rolled his window down halfway. As he sped up, the air suddenly stopped.

It took about a minute before Charlie opened her eyes. She reached for the controls to find the fan blower set to high speed.

"You might want to crack your window," Grant advised. "The AC gets persnickity at about forty-five miles per hour."

"Seriously?" she groaned as she pressed the button on her door.

"Just crack it," he warned as she let the glass disappear into the door.

He shook his head.

"What?" she asked.

"It sticks if it goes all the way down."

Charlie huffed. "This car is a piece of shite."

10

The air-conditioning continued to come on and off based on their speed and to Charlie's relief, the busy traffic moved slowly. Wrench panted, slobbered, and was convinced she needed a lick if she turned even slightly his way. Grant indicated left, pulled to the center turn lane, and nipped across between a pair of lifted pickup trucks with ridiculously large-diameter wheels and super low-profile tires.

"Bugger me," Charlie muttered. "What on earth do they do with those things?"

"Nothing useful," Grant replied as they drove down a palm tree-lined lane. "But they spend a fortune to make them look that stupid."

Ahead, beyond a sign for the Cheeca Lodge, a guard shack split the lanes and a man in a uniform stepped from the shade to greet them. His eyes roamed across the Del Sol before settling on Grant as he came to a stop.

"Can I help you, sir?" he asked in a heavy accent, his expression one of concern.

"With the band," Grant said confidently.

The guard studied a clipboard in his hand. "I'm not seeing any band listed."

"Last minute gig," Grant countered. "The van is a few minutes behind us. We're playing the Tika Bar in…" he slid his sunglasses down his nose and looked at his watch. "Shit. In ten minutes, man. We gotta get set up, she has to change into the outfit. These last-minute deals are always a shit show, you know what I mean, man?"

The guard scratched his head then tapped his clipboard. "Not on the list I'm afraid, sir. I'll have to call the office."

Charlie leaned over, shoving Wrench back so he didn't intercept her with his tongue. "Seriously, love, they told us they'd have it all squared away by the time we got here. Someone's made a bollocks of it, yeah?" Charlie said, laying on a thick London accent. "Be a dear. I swear this outfit they have me in is a skimpy bugger, but takes forever to get into it. Has this little stringy thing that about cuts me bum in half."

The guard stared at Charlie with his mouth slightly open. "You sound like that one who was big, and now she's small, and she wins all the awards…"

"Blimey, love. If you say Adele out loud, you'll have a line of paparazzi at your cute little hut in minutes," Charlie said, giving the man a big wink.

The guard reached into his hut and grabbed a hang tag, handing it to Grant while staring at Charlie. "It was nice meeting you, miss," he said. "I'm a big fan."

Grant shot forward before the guard came to his senses and began laughing once they were clear. "I'm devious?" he cackled. "That was Oscar worthy."

"I can't believe it worked," she replied, truly surprised. "Now what? This place is huge," she added as they wound around the entrance road with buildings, tennis courts, and swimming pools seemingly everywhere.

"Where would you go if you were staying at an oceanfront resort in the tropics?" Grant asked.

"Pool bar," Charlie quickly replied.

"I would too, but who knows what Russian thugs do in their spare time."

"It's a long shot they're even here, yeah?" Charlie said, looking around as Grant slowed in a large parking area behind a long row of two-story rooms. "Hey, look!" she shouted, pointing to a black Suburban.

"That was dumb luck," he said, and found a parking spot several rows away. "Doesn't give us a room number, though, so we either sit here and watch the Suburban, or try the bar."

"I hate surveillance jobs."

"Me too," Grant agreed. "Bar it is."

"What about Sir Slobber-Chops?" Charlie asked as she got out after trying in vain to wind the window back up.

"Come on Wrench," Grant called, and the dog didn't wait to be asked twice, leaping from the back of the car.

Grant clicked a leash to his collar, and after Wrench swiftly cocked his leg on a neighboring car tire, the three set off for the Tiki Bar near the water.

Two curving pools sat adjacent to each other with a thatched roof palapa housing the Tiki Bar between them. Beyond the second pool were the beach and the ocean, where a mixture of bronzed and burning bodies lay on deck chairs in the bright sun. The first pool was well shaded by tall palms, and Grant and Charlie scanned the loungers for the two men from the funeral home. If they were still wearing their dark trousers and shirts, they'd stand out like sore thumbs.

No one looked familiar and Charlie realized they were the two who were overdressed, as everyone one else wore a bathing suit of some description. She was beginning to think leaving her carry-on bag at her dad's hotel had been a mistake. Not that she had a lot of options packed, but the singular outfit in her possession was going to get a bit whiffy in this heat. She sat next to Grant who'd found two empty barstools under the palapa, and the bartender moved their way.

"What'll it be, guys?"

"Corona," Grant replied without hesitation.

"We're sort of on the job here," Charlie whispered, then in a louder voice. "Just a water, please."

The bartender looked at her as though he didn't understand the meaning of water.

"Water," she repeated slowly, raising one eyebrow.

"Water and a bowl for the dog. Got it. What would you like?"

"I want the bloody water, mate," she said irritably.

The bartender shook his head and turned away to get the drinks.

"Nice going," Grant hissed. "Bartenders are the best source of info and you just pissed ours off right out of the gate."

"Getting pissed isn't going to help anything," Charlie snapped back.

"That's what I'm saying," Grant reiterated.

"Then why are you ordering booze at ten past something in the bloody morning?" she said, looking at her dad's watch as she realized she had no idea what the time was.

"Because I don't want the bartender pissed at me," Grant replied, rolling his eyes.

Charlie scoffed. "This one of those American things where you lot buggered up a perfectly good language, isn't it?"

Grant looked at her like she had two heads.

"Pissed means drunk in England," she explained. "Pissed off means you're mad about something. But not the mad about something meaning you really like it. The cheesed off type."

The bartender set a Corona bottle and a stainless-steel bowl full of water in front of Grant, and a child's size glass of water by Charlie.

"Just let me handle this one," Grant said quietly, shaking his head at Charlie and placing the bowl on the ground before turning to the bartender. "Hey buddy, have you seen a couple of Eastern European guys kicking around? Buzz cuts, pissed-off looking," he said, emphasizing the words and throwing a glance at Charlie.

"Drinking vodka straight like some people drink *water*?" the bartender replied sarcastically, giving Charlie a sideways look.

"Been by today?" Grant asked.

The bartender looked back and forth between the two of them. "You cops?"

Grant shook his head. "Private."

"I don't need any trouble in the bar, bro," the bartender said, leaning closer to Grant. "Reflects badly on us, according to management."

Grant slid a twenty-dollar bill across the bar which quickly disappeared under the bartender's hand.

"Haven't seen them this morning, but they've been by a few times during the day earlier this week. Word has it they're here till the bar closes at night though. Shitty tippers, loud, pissing everyone else off."

The bartender straightened up, wiped the already clean bar top with a cloth, and moved on to another customer.

Wrench slurped at the water in the bowl, splashing more of it over the floor and the bar than he consumed.

"Eww," Charlie complained as her feet got wet.

"We might have to come back tonight." Grant said, swiveling on his stool to face the pool.

"I've been thinking," Charlie said, turning the same way. "We've tracked the plate, found where the yobbos are staying, and now we're doing what, exactly?"

Grant looked at her blankly. "What do you mean?"

"Well, the last time we ran across these wankers, they tried to kill one of us, so why are we sitting here like shooting range targets? Wouldn't it make more sense to call the copper who hates you and tell him we found the shooters? Let him come here and nick 'em."

Grant looked slightly away while she was talking, popped something into the corner of his mouth, then swallowed it with a swig of beer.

"First of all, Hernandez has probably shoved this case to the bottom of his stack, simply because I'm involved. I doubt he'd come. And secondly, there's no way these guys will say a word if they're arrested. They'll lawyer up and we'll never know why they were coming after you."

"Or why my dad's involved..." Charlie added, gently nodding. "Fair enough. So, what do we do when we see them?"

"Play it chill. Follow them."

"To their room?" she quizzed unenthusiastically.

Grant shrugged his shoulders. "I guess."

"You're making this up as you go, aren't you?" Charlie groaned, frowning at him.

Grant shook his head. "Well, it's not exactly routine territory for me," he growled in annoyance. "I just buried my mom yesterday, had a pair of Russians, or whatever they are, shoot up the funeral, and some chick who looks the spitting image of her show up in the middle of it all. Fucking right I'm making it up as I go!"

She wriggled from her barstool. Everything felt out of control. From the doubts about getting on a plane in the first place, to the questions over her dad, and the madness ever since she'd arrived in Florida, Charlie was about at her limit. "Don't be a tosser about it! I didn't ask for your bloody help. You can go back to popping pills and drinking before noon for all I care. I bet Hernandez won't mind helping *me*."

Grant slapped his beer on the counter. "Fuck you," he muttered. "I gotta take a piss."

As he strode off, Charlie looked down at Wrench who stared back up at her.

"You're supposed to go with him," she said, realizing she couldn't stomp off, leaving the dog alone.

"Hey, good-looking, he giving you trouble?" a voice came from behind her, and Charlie whipped around to face a tall, muscular, shirtless man who reeked of sunscreen. "I'd be happy to put him in line for you."

The man rested a hand on her shoulder and gave her his best

knee-wobbling smile that probably sent some girls immediately horizontal.

"Mind your own bloody business," Charlie snapped, and brushed his hand away.

"Whoa, don't get all femmed up, baby," he said, throwing his hands up. "I was just offering some help. Seemed like you needed it."

"What, because I'm a woman? You think I can't look after myself?" she said, stepping closer toward him with her hands on her hips. She had to crane her neck to give him the stink eye.

He reached down and lightly pushed her shoulder. "How about you get back on your barstool. Clearly, it was my mistake. I didn't realize you were fucking crazy."

That was the straw… Grabbing the guy's hand, Charlie twisted his wrist. The man would have had more than enough strength to resist her move if he'd been ready, but she was too fast. He sunk to the ground and let out a loud yelp, until her right hand punched him in the throat.

"What the fuck?" another man shouted, stepping forward to assist his friend.

His mistake was looking down to check on his cohort, whose face was contorted in pain with his twisted arm still held in Charlie's vise-like grip. She met the new guy with an open palm punch to his nose, feeling the bone and cartilage give under the blow. He grabbed his face with both hands while Charlie followed up with a kick to the groin. The man crumbled to the floor, landing awkwardly on top of his friend where the two moaned and groaned, Wrench hovering over them, snarling.

"Who's next?" Charlie gasped, looking around her like a wild, cornered animal.

She heard the bartender's voice and whipped his way. "Security, get to the Tiki Bar, now!"

Charlie glared his way, ready to pull the guy across the bamboo bar.

"Some English chick is beating up half the bar!" he continued into the radio, holding his free hand up. "What did I say about no trouble?!" he shouted, looking at Charlie.

"English chick?" A voice she recognized from the security shack said over the radio. "You mean Adele?"

"Charlie!" came Grant's voice behind her, and she took a few breaths.

"This twat put his hands on me," she said, slowly calming and realizing every face was turned her way.

She let go of the man's wrist. People around the pool were standing, watching, and the whole place had fallen silent except for the calypso music playing from the speakers.

"Remember the *play it chill* part?" Grant said, picking up Wrench's leash. "This is not *chill*."

Charlie stepped over the legs of her victims and the crowd parted, clearing a path to the first pool where they'd entered from. On the far side of the water stood two men, staring at her along with everyone else. One was shorter, bearded, overweight, and wearing a Speedo. His friend was taller, toned, with tattoos on both arms and across his chest. His right wrapped in a bandage.

"Oh, shit," Charlie muttered.

Wrench growled and pulled to the end of his leash.

11

The Russian in the Speedo pointed at Grant and Charlie, signaling his tattooed companion to go after them.

"We need to leave," Grant urged.

"But we fucking found them," Charlie squawked, storming toward the pool.

"Charlie!" Grant snapped, pulling against the leash as Wrench strained to follow the cantankerous woman.

"They had guns," Grant murmured to himself, realizing Charlie didn't seem to have an off switch.

The tattooed Russian now broke into a run on a direct path with the charging Charlie. Grant saw the man reach behind his back for what he guessed was a gun.

"Dammit!" he cursed, releasing the tether.

"Get 'em Wrench," Grant commanded.

With a pop, the leash cracked in midair as the dog went from a ready stance to a full speed bolt. The brown mutt shot like a bullet past Charlie as the tattooed man's Glock 17 appeared from behind him.

Wrench launched himself into the air and slammed against the Russian's chest. The tattooed figure flailed back as fifty pounds of canine muscle plowed into him. The Glock flew out of the Russian's hand.

"Sodding dog!" Charlie wailed as she slid to a stop.

Grant's attention shifted as the Speedo-clad thug rushed at Charlie. The man screamed something in Russian.

"Charlie!" Grant shouted in warning, but she didn't hear him.

Charlie was frozen in place, eyes locked on Wrench, who'd wrapped his teeth around the tattooed man's throat. His fangs applied just enough pressure to immobilize the man without tearing his throat out.

Speedo grabbed Charlie, who threw an elbow into the man's face. Grant sprinted toward the pair. Charlie and Speedo twisted around, both falling to the side. The entwined duo splashed into the pool. Grant stopped at the side of the water, preparing to dive in after them, when Speedo surfaced with a howl.

"Fucking arsehole!" Charlie screamed as she came out of the water.

Grant froze, trying to understand what he was seeing. When he realized Charlie had a claw-like grasp on the front of the man's crotch, he winced uncomfortably.

"Don't you fucking move, you twat!" Charlie commanded.

Grant retrieved the Glock, which had landed on the edge of the pool.

"Wrench, come!" he ordered, and the dog released his victim's throat.

The tattooed man, now freed and enraged, with blood trickling in streaks down his chest, turned to attack the retreating canine.

"Don't do it, asshole," Grant warned, leveling the pistol at the man's head.

The Russian recoiled, pulling his hand up to his throat to feel the punctures around his neck.

"Charlie!" Grant yelled again.

"Where the bloody hell have you been?" she bellowed.

"Let go of him," Grant suggested.

"I have some questions for this yobbo," she countered.

"Stop!" Speedo begged.

Charlie released the man's groin, but she caught him by the back of the head with her other hand. In a swift motion, she slammed the man's face into the sidewalk around the pool.

She pulled his bloodied countenance away from the edge, and Grant saw a single tooth on the concrete. He winced again.

"What were you doing at the cemetery?" Charlie demanded. Her fingers wrapped in the man's hair, threatening to bash his head a second time.

The man said something in Russian. Blood bubbled from his lips as he spoke.

In the distance, there was more shouting. The security guard who'd let them through the gate came running from the tiki bar. Two more men arrived from the other side of the pool. Those two carried handguns and a distinct foreign appearance.

"Shit, Charlie," Grant snapped. "We gotta go."

She allowed Speedo's head to drop and glanced over her shoulder. Grant grabbed her hand to heave her out of the pool.

"C'mon," he urged, running through the rows of chaises filled with guests. Eyes and a few cell phones trained on the trio as they bounded over the last row.

"Sorry," Grant apologized as Wrench leaped over a woman who jerked up from her stomach so startled she forgot to grab her bikini top.

As he turned to glance behind him, he saw the two new men, whom he could only assume were more Russians, in pursuit. They seemed to ignore their injured comrades.

Charlie was right on his heels. Her dripping clothes hung to her body, and rage filled her face.

"Keep up!" he demanded, afraid she might turn on the two armed men chasing them.

"Run faster!" she panted.

Grant focused on the path in front of him. He saw his Del Sol sitting where he'd parked it. He fumbled in his pocket for the keys as his feet pounded the asphalt. Wrench's paws made a scratching sound as his claws scraped across the parking lot surface.

"Why the hell would you lock this piece of shit?" Charlie shouted as Grant slipped the key into the door. "Nobody in their right mind would nick it."

Ignoring her, he jerked the door open, letting Wrench jump into the back seat. Charlie slid into the passenger's side as he started the Honda while simultaneously shifting into reverse. The rear bumper slammed into one of the men, knocking him off his feet. The other man fired a shot at the trunk of the red Del Sol.

"Everyone has a bloody gun!" Charlie screamed.

The tires of the little sportster jumped a curb, a loud scrape emanating from the underside of the car.

"Dammit," Grant moaned. "I think that broke something."

The Del Sol vibrated violently for about six seconds before it smoothed out.

"I can't believe your shitty car just got shittier," Charlie snapped.

"Not now," Grant blurted out as he gunned the four-cylinder engine, sending the needle on the tachometer toward the redline at 5000. Flying past the security gate, the motor whined as Grant turned right and raced north on Old Highway One, a two-lane remnant of the original road connecting the Keys together.

"They're right behind us!" Charlie howled.

Grant glanced in the rearview mirror to see a black Suburban squeal out of the Cheeca Lodge's cobblestone drive.

"Dammit," he moaned under his breath.

"Go faster," Charlie urged.

"My foot is on the floor," he retorted back to her. "They have a bigger engine."

"What the hell kind of sports car is this?" Charlie asked with a huff.

"The kind with a sunroof," he said. "This is the Keys. No one needs to drive fast here. There's too much traffic."

A pop sounded behind them, followed by another.

"The bastards are shooting at us again," Charlie groaned.

"Yup, I'm aware," Grant groaned as he touched the brakes, approaching the stop sign at the intersection with Overseas Highway.

"Here, shoot back," he declared, tossing the nine-millimeter to her.

Charlie fumbled with the gun, dropping it behind Grant's seat.

"Don't drop it!" he shouted as he cut the wheel to the right, giving a cursory glance at the oncoming traffic. A string of cars heading north on the road bore down on the intersection, and Grant stomped the accelerator again.

The little car jerked with the front tires squealing in protest, throwing Wrench off-balance and into the left side of the back seat. The dog let out a short whimper.

"Sorry, buddy," Grant told the mutt.

The driver of a red Chrysler Sebring laid on the horn as they braked hard to avoid hitting the back end of the Honda. Grant straightened the wheels and shot north on the highway.

"You're going to kill us," Charlie blurted out.

Nine cars filled the initial line of vehicles that Grant barely avoided hitting. There was a momentary gap, followed by another six vehicles.

The reprieve was small, but Grant took advantage of it. The red Del Sol charged up behind a Jeep Grand Cherokee with two bright orange kayaks strapped to the roof and a pair of bicycles hanging off the rear door.

His teeth ground together as he warned, "Hang on!"

Grant tried to pass the Jeep, but a motorhome barreling south at sixty-five miles per hour dissuaded him. He jerked the wheel to the right, and the Del Sol's passenger side tires dropped off the highway as he passed the Jeep on the edge of the road.

"What the hell?" Charlie shouted. "Are you insane?"

When Grant bounced the little Honda back onto the road, he let out a sigh.

"Beats getting shot," he pointed out as he sped ahead.

Charlie craned her neck to see if the Russians were behind them. The black SUV attempted to follow Grant around the Jeep on the shoulder. The width of the vehicle was too much, and the Suburban clipped a telephone pole, veering the big SUV left, slamming into the Jeep.

"Shit!" Charlie gasped.

"That ought to slow them down," Grant announced, continuing north.

"How many are back there?" Charlie wondered aloud.

"Too many," Grant mused.

"We needed to grab one of them and question him," Charlie pointed out.

Grant turned to stare at the woman. "You're kidding, right?" he asked.

"They know something about my father," she stated.

"They have a hard-on for you, too."

Charlie gaped at him. "A hard-on?"

"Yeah," Grant acknowledged. "They want you, too."

"I understood what you meant," Charlie barked. "It was how you said it."

Grant shook his head. "Look, these guys tried to grab you at the cemetery. Just now, they came after you. Neither of those two Russians at the pool were expecting us, but they sure as hell knew they wanted you when they saw you."

"That doesn't make any sense. Why would they want me?"

Grant shrugged, slowing to turn off the highway. "We need to get out of sight for a minute," he suggested. "They probably have another vehicle coming behind them. I bet your buddy in the Speedo wants to have a one-on-one chat with you now."

Charlie curled her lip in disgust.

"That was a pretty gruesome move," Grant admitted. "I've seen some crazy shit, but you take the cake."

"They won't stay at the Lodge," Charlie pointed out, flinching a little at his crazy comment.

Grant shook his head. "No, and I doubt they'll let *us* come back ever again."

"How are we going to find them now?" Charlie asked. Her eyes lit up. "We could go back for the guys in the Suburban. We know where to find them."

"Along with their guns," Grant added. "I would be surprised if they stick around until the cops show up, anyway."

"I should just let them grab me," Charlie remarked.

Grant's head swiveled around again. "You bitch about my driving, but you're willing to be kidnapped."

"Of course, I'd expect you to protect me."

Shaking his head in disbelief, Grant commented, "Something doesn't make sense to me. Why were they looking for you at the cemetery?"

Charlie shrugged. "They were there for my father?" she suggested, questioningly.

Grant pulled into the parking lot of a Sandal Emporium. When the Del Sol came to a stop, he sat still, staring out the front window.

"Why would they wait for your father there?" he asked, looking at her.

Wrench leaned forward and sniffed at the back of her head.

"Your damned mutt," Charlie scoffed.

"He was my mother's," Grant stated.

Charlie blinked. "Yeah, sorry."

"He thinks you look just like her," Grant suggested.

Charlie said nothing.

"There seems to be an obvious reason why your father was at my mother's funeral."

Her eyes shifted to the rearview mirror.

"I didn't—"

Grant continued, almost talking to himself. "On top of that, why were the Russians expecting your father to show up at the funeral?"

Charlie straightened up. "They must have known your mom and my dad were—well, you know."

"If they knew that," Grant said in an increasingly louder tone, "they knew he wouldn't miss her service."

Charlie sucked in a breath. "You don't think they—"

"Killed my mother?" Grant interrupted. "I think it's time to dig a little deeper into her accident."

12

Charlie reached behind the seat, pushing Wrench's muzzle aside, and retrieved the gun. She held it between her thumb and index finger, letting it dangle like a dead fish.

"We could hand this in and see if your police mate can pull prints," Charlie suggested, attempting to find a way forward rather than let them both dwell on what may have happened to Grant's mother.

He took the Glock from her, leaned over, opened the glove box, and dropped the gun on top of the car's tatty-looking handbook. Charlie noticed a few fast-food wrappers, a flashlight, and an oily cloth also residing in the small compartment. Grant didn't seem like the organized and tidy type.

She felt exhausted again. The adrenaline had dissipated, replaced by a bruise or two, a sore hand, and the realization she'd lost control of herself at the resort. A mixture of embarrassment and annoyance brewed inside her, as she pictured her old boss shaking his head.

"I have a guy," Grant said, as he closed the glove box, bringing her back to the moment.

"A guy for what?" she questioned.

"For prints," he said, putting the car in gear.

"Why not the police?"

"That takes too long," he replied, pulling up to Overseas High-way. "Besides, I need to restrict my favors with the department, or the well will dry up."

"I would think they'd be keen to get their hands on a gun used in attempted murder," Charlie scoffed.

Grant shrugged his shoulders. "Hernandez gets wind of the gun being handed in and he's more likely to slow-boat the prints instead of fast-track them."

"What a wanker," Charlie muttered.

"You don't know the half of it," Grant said, driving south.

"Your pathetic little clapped-out piece of shite stands out a bit much," Charlie pointed out. "And you're now driving back toward the place we just ran away from."

"I know, I know," Grant replied impatiently. "We'll switch later, but it's not far to this guy's place."

"I hope we do run into those tossers," she mumbled. "If you hadn't made me let him go, Ivan in the Speedo would have sung like a canary. Ten minutes with one of them and we'll get some answers."

Grant looked at her, his brow knitted. "What exactly got you kicked off the force?"

Charlie's cheeks flushed. "The chief had it in for me, that's what."

Grant nodded. "I get that, believe me. I'm sure department bull-shit runs deep everywhere, no matter the country." He paused a moment, considering his words before continuing. "But what did he use to get you booted?"

Charlie shifted in her seat and felt Wrench's hot breath panting from behind her. She knew why Grant was asking, and would love to avoid the subject, but it was bound to keep resurfacing, so she decided to get over with.

"According to him, I was a bit heavy-handed with a suspect," she said, downplaying the story as best she could, choosing not to use the actual words the man had raged at her while thumping his desk with his fist.

"Uh-huh," Grant responded, as though he expected her to carry on.

"The guy was a prick," she said defensively.

"Your chief, or the suspect?"

"Both."

Charlie struggled to conjure the right words to both satisfy Grant's curiosity and make the incident sound less damning than it really was.

"I had no way of knowing the suspect had a disc problem in his back," she said, her anger rising once more. "I leaned on him a bit hard when I arrested him. He was a bloody low-life drug dealer, and we were after his supplier, you know. His twat of a lawyer gets him transferred to the hospital, where they operated and put plates and screws in the wanker's back. Hot-shot lawyer sued, and the department settled with me as the sacrificial lamb."

They rode in silence for a few moments and Charlie decided she preferred the questions to the judgmental cloud now lingering over the Honda.

"You broke the dude's back?" Grant finally asked.

"No!" Charlie barked, as Grant took a side street off the highway. "He already had a buggered up back. I just… tweaked it a bit. He'd been on NHS's stupid-long waiting list for a surgery, then I put a knee in his back when he resisted arrest, and Bob's your uncle, the lawyer makes it out like I tortured the bastard and gets him moved to the front of the queue."

Grant frowned. "Who's Bob?"

Charlie rolled her eyes. "You know, Bob's your uncle, Fanny's your aunt?"

Grant looked at her in confusion.

"Means quick as you like. Easy to do," she replied, shaking her head.

"Oh," Grant said, pulling into the gravel front yard of a small block of apartments. "I just ask, because you kinda went postal back there at the resort."

"Postal?" she questioned, but she had a pretty good idea what he meant.

"Yeah. Nuts would be another way of putting it," Grant said. "You really lost it there for a moment."

Charlie gritted her teeth, biting back the reaction she knew would only confirm his suspicions. She took a few long breaths.

"Sometimes..." she began cautiously, "I get overly focused and... perhaps a teeny bit aggressive."

"You think?" Grant replied.

"Sod off," she snapped, but he was already getting out of the car. "Better than popping pills like bloody Smarties!"

He leaned back in. "Bring the gun with you," he said, and closed the driver's side door.

Charlie yanked the glove box door open and stared at the Glock. Their plan was to dust it for prints, yet they'd both handled it already, making the task a step harder. She pictured a stereotypical detective from old TV shows holding the gun with a pen through the trigger guard.

"Bugger it," she mumbled and picked it up with her index finger.

She got out of the Honda and followed Grant up the steps to the front door to one of the apartments. He knocked slowly three times. Charlie noticed the door had a second peephole, which she presumed was a camera, and another small camera was aimed at the landing from the window to their left. White blinds blocked their view inside the apartment.

"I'm busy," came a voice from a speaker above them.

Charlie looked up. A small, round speaker grille was mounted in the soffit.

"C'mon, Rat, don't be a dick. My money spends as good as anyone's," Grant said, staring at the peephole.

"This guy's called Rat?" Charlie whispered.

"Yeah," Grant replied, turning his head away from the camera. "You got any cash?"

Charlie scoffed. "You know I'm skint."

The door opened and a skinny young man with the pimples and wispy facial hair of an adolescent peered outside. Except Charlie guessed the man was at least thirty years old by the thinning hair-line. His skin was far paler than her own English sun-deprived tone, he wore a T-shirt which hadn't seen a washing machine in too long, and grubby-looking black jeans. The scent of body odor and stale food reached her nose, and she stifled the urge to turn away.

"That's more like it, buddy," Grant said, either oblivious to the smell, or hiding his reaction well.

He could have warned me, she thought, holding up the gun.

Rat looked at it dangling from her finger. "Ballistics or prints?"

"Prints," Grant replied. "Yesterday."

Rat glared at him. "Costs extra."

Grant nodded. "I know."

"Cash up front," Rat said, and held out a skinny hand.

"Gun is collateral," Grant replied. "Call me as soon as you have something. I'll drop the cash by later."

Rat looked at the gun again. "A hot gun? No way, man. Cash."

"You'll get your cash. Later. We have to go back to the house; we've been running around all morning."

Rat laughed, which came out more like the cackle of an evil elf. "That was you then?" he said, eyeing Charlie one more time.

"Get us the bloody prints, Rat-man," she snapped, and he took a step backward and pulled the door half-closed.

She held out the gun and he tentatively took it from her, eyeing her in the way an animal surveys a new creature, unsure whether it's prey or threat.

"Get on with it!" Charlie barked and Rat's hand quickly with-drew, and the door closed with a bang.

"Smile for the camera," Grant said to Charlie with a grin. "I think he likes you. He'll be having a date with *little rat* once we're gone."

Charlie smacked Grant's arm. "That's bloody disgusting," she moaned and swiftly made for the steps.

"I heard that," Rat's voice came over the speaker. "The price just went up."

Charlie turned and held up two fingers to the camera. "Get the prints done or I'll be back to wring your scrawny little neck."

Grant steered her down the steps. "Damn it, Charlie. You go from idle to wide open like a top-fuel dragster."

She shrugged his hand away. "Your mate's a bloody perv."

"He's not my *mate*," Grant retorted. "But he's damn good with forensic evidence, and anything computer related. And yes, he's a creepy perv."

She opened the car door and paused. "But a different guy from the one who owes you for letting him off the creepy shit with the tarts? The bloke who got you the credit card info?"

"Correct," Grant said, somewhat tentatively as he got in the driver's seat.

"So what did you let Rat off the hook for?"

"Nothing," Grant laughed. "The opposite, in fact. That's why he was reluctant to help us. Rat worked for our forensics lab, and they suspected he was spying on the ladies' locker room. They used me to lure him into sharing pictures of an officer I told him I had the hots for. He got kicked out and blames me."

"Did you?" Charlie asked.

"Did I what?"

"Did you have the hots for the officer?"

Grant laughed. "At one time."

"So, you didn't mind seeing his pervy pics then," she said as he backed out onto the street.

Grant shrugged his shoulders. "Nothing I hadn't already seen."

Charlie smacked his arm again. "Pig," she muttered.

Grant drove down the street to Overseas Highway and made a right, heading south. "Hungry?" he asked.

Charlie hadn't thought about food, but now he mentioned it she realized she was. "Famished, actually."

He looked over at her. "I take it that means, yes?"

"Yeah. Famished, you know? Starving."

"Oh," he said, and pulled to the right in front of a small, single-story older building with a sign for Mrs. Mac's Kitchen.

There were three other cars parked out front, leaving room for one more, but Grant drove down the side of the restaurant and parked behind it near a dumpster. The Honda looked at home between the trash and two beaten-up cars Charlie presumed belonged to the employees.

Twenty minutes later, Charlie sat back from her empty plate and let out a sigh. Her belly felt stuffed to the gills with Caribbean Style Crab Cakes. Grant washed down his Blackened Fish Sub with a swig of Corona, the lime wedging into the neck as he drained the last of the beer. His pocket buzzed, and he switched the bottle for the phone, receiving the call and putting it on speakerphone.

"What the hell are you into?" Rat asked instead of offering a greeting.

"Not your concern, man," Grant replied, turning the volume down so others couldn't hear. "What did you find?"

Rat grunted his displeasure. "Nothing from police records, or immigration."

"But..." Grant led him.

"Got a hit from Interpol. Your man is Russian."

"Rat, for fuck's sake, tell us something we don't know," Grant said impatiently.

"Okay, okay. Your British girlfriend still with you?"

"She's not my girlfriend," Grant instantly retorted. "She's my... Damn it, Rat. Just tell me what you found!"

Charlie heard another grunt. "Maksim Prutsev. That's the name that came up. Wanted for questioning about a murder in Prague."

"Not wanted in connection with?" Charlie asked. "Just questioning?"

"Oh, hi," Rat stammered. "There you are. Yeah. That's what it said."

"Same thing isn't it?" Grant questioned, looking at Charlie.

She shook her head. "Usually, it means local law enforcement doesn't have enough evidence to hold them, or it could be a ruse to lure the suspect in. We know this guy is someone's thug, so I don't think they'd waste time trying to trick him into dropping by the station. He's never going to fall for that."

"You owe me money," Rat said, reminding Charlie he was still on the line.

"Text me the correct spelling of that name. I'll be by this afternoon," Grant said, and hung up, cutting off whatever response Rat was attempting.

"What now?" Charlie asked.

Grant thought for a moment. "That name doesn't do much for us, does it?"

"Not really," she agreed. "He must be traveling under false ID or immigration would have flagged him entering the US."

"Fuck," Grant muttered, reaching into his pocket until he caught Charlie watching him. He brought his hand back out and drummed his fingers on the table instead. "I guess we're still shit outta luck."

Charlie was glad he'd not shoved another pill in his mouth, but she knew he would as soon as she wasn't looking. Putting her concerns aside, she thought through what they knew. Still way too little, was her summation, which didn't take long to conclude.

"I don't know what security systems your dad sells," Grant said, and her eyes met his. "But he's mixed up with some bad people, or it's a cover story. These Russians must be connected to him in some way."

Charlie's first instinct was a defensive one, but she swallowed her words and sucked in a deep breath. Grant was right.

"They have to move from the Cheeca Lodge, right?" she said. "Assuming they didn't get arrested."

"True," he replied, nodding.

"So, reach out to your credit card guy again," she said, her voice sounding more optimistic than she really felt. "Let's see where they went."

Grant picked up his phone and opened the mobile app for the same software he'd used to reach his contact on his desktop. He typed a message, and they waited.

13

As Grant pulled onto Atlantic Boulevard, Wrench straightened in the back seat. His tail swished rapidly.

"Stop breathing on me, dog," Charlie moaned.

"You could call him by his name," Grant suggested.

"His name is stupid."

Grant cut his eyes over to her. "I'm guessing you didn't have a lot of friends to play with when you were a kid."

"Sod off," she growled. "Who's at your house?"

Parked in front of Grant's home was a red Volkswagen Jetta convertible. The top was down.

"That's Angie's car."

Charlie glanced at Grant. "Is that your girlfriend?"

"At the moment, no."

She lifted her eyebrows as Grant pulled into the driveway.

"What's she doing here?" Charlie asked.

"Well, I don't know, Charlie. I haven't talked to her yet."

"She still has a key?"

"Yes," Grant grunted as he got out of the car. "C'mon, Wrench."

The dog jumped past Charlie, bounding out of the driver's door.

"There isn't time to wait around," Charlie snapped as she exited the Del Sol.

"Right now, all we can do is wait," Grant pointed out. "When we get a hit on the credit card, we can move."

"Ugh!" Charlie groaned.

When Grant opened the front door at the top of the steps, Wrench squeezed through the opening and scampered across the tile floor. Grant followed the dog to the kitchen where Angie stood over the sink, washing dishes.

Wrench skidded to a stop beside her, dropped on his haunches, and teetered with excitement.

"Hey, boy," Angie bellowed at him in a high-pitched voice. "Give me a smile."

The dog's lips curled in what looked like a snarl, but his tail flapped back and forth vigorously. The woman brushed her brown hair over her right shoulder as she knelt down. Wrench threw his front paws up, and Angie caught them with one hand while the other scratched at his chest.

The dog vibrated with excitement as she rubbed under his neck and head. Finally, she made some slight gesture, and Wrench dropped back down with all four paws on the ground.

"That's my boy," Angie praised him. "I'm happy to see you, too."

"And me?" Grant asked.

She straightened up and looked at the man. "Of course," she told him as she moved forward, wrapping her arms around him. "I wanted to check on you after yesterday."

"It's been a strange and crazy day," Grant acknowledged. "Or two, I suppose."

Angie's head lifted as a figure appeared behind Grant.

"Uh, hello," Angie greeted Charlie.

Grant stepped back as Charlie offered a curt nod.

"Angie, this is Charlie. Charlie Greene."

As she stared at her, Angie said, "Wait, I saw you at the service."

"She's looking for her father," Grant explained.

Her eyes fixated on Charlie's features. "Are you two related?" Angie asked finally.

Grant glanced at Charlie. "Um…" he muttered.

Charlie's head shook with resignation. "Not really. We suspect my father might have known Grant's mother."

The brunette stared back in disbelief. Then a smile creased up on her lips. "Might have known?" she questioned wryly. "You are the spitting image of Fiona Wolfe."

"My mother is dead," Charlie refuted.

The smirk vanished off Angie's face. "I'm sorry."

Charlie replied, "Oh, she died when I was a baby. I never knew her."

Angie turned to Grant. Her eyes begging for some answers. Stoically, he stared back without responding.

"You are kidding, right?" Angie finally snapped. "You don't remember your mom, but you are a near doppelganger for Fiona."

"Why would my father lie to me about this?" she asked.

Grant cleared his throat. "Why would someone kill my mom?" he wondered aloud. "Right now, we have too many questions about everything."

"Wait, Grant," Angie interjected. "What do you mean? Fiona was murdered?"

Slowly, he nodded. "These guys were at the funeral waiting, we think, for Charlie's dad. When she showed up, they tried to grab her."

"They recognized her?" Angie asked, trying to wrap her head around it.

Grant looked back at Charlie. "Like you said, she's the spitting image of Mom."

"Holy shit!" Angie muttered, sliding into a chair at the table. "She's your sister."

"Now, wait a bloody minute!" Charlie blurted out. "We don't know that."

Her voice trailed off and Grant caught her eye. He was recalling the picture she'd shown him and guessed Charlie was as well. The one she'd found in her father's study. The woman holding the baby girl. The woman who looked just like Charlie.

"Why would your parents hide it from you?" Angie asked. "This sounds like some Parent Trap shit here."

"Parent Trap?" Charlie asked.

"Yeah, from the Disney movie. This couple splits up when their girls are babies. Each one takes a sister, and they move to opposite sides of the world—never to talk to each other again."

Charlie's head furrowed. "Why would anyone do that?"

Angie stated, "Don't worry. The girls eventually run into each other at a camp or something. They figure it out and switch places so they can meet their other parent. After that, they just try to get their parents back together."

"How would that work? How did they even know they were related?"

Grant grinned. "Oh, I forgot. The girls are identical twins."

"That's a stupid movie idea." Charlie scoffed.

"They made two of them," Angie offered in a hushed tone.

"People will watch anything Hollywood spews out," Charlie muttered.

"I'm still confused," Angie said. "Who is after your father? And why?"

"Russians," Grant explained. "That's really all the information we have."

"Russians? Is your dad like James Bond or something?"

Charlie snorted with some distaste. "Not at all. He runs a security company."

"Did he do business here in Florida?" Angie asked. "Or, Grant, maybe your mom was in... I'm guessing, England."

"I don't think she ever left Florida," Grant said. "At least she never told me about it."

Charlie gave a cough. The other two faced her.

"I found something in my father's safe," she explained. "It was a picture of Dad with a woman who... Who looks just like Grant's mum, and she was holding a baby."

"You showed me yesterday," Grant pointed out.

"Can I see it?" Angie asked.

Charlie gave Grant a concerned look.

"You can trust Angie," he said.

"It's not that," Charlie responded.

"Then what's the problem?" Grant asked.

"I also found this in my father's safe with the photo," Charlie said, handing over an embossed certificate.

Grant studied the paper, reading the bold lettering at the top declaring the State of Florida recognized this marriage certificate. He scanned down the page. The groom's name, written in embellished script, read Daniel Edwards. On the line for the bride's name in the same calligraphy—Diana Turner. Date of nuptials read December 3, 1995. Below were signatures of the clergy as well as a witness, but the second signature was illegible.

Charlie passed him another photograph. The same couple from the photo she'd already shared were on the steps of a courthouse. The white neoclassical building stood atop nearly a dozen marble steps. Two columns held up the entablature and bordered the entrance. Palm trees lined the plaza in front of the steps.

Grant glanced back at the marriage certificate. The paper showed they filed the certificate in Lee County. Fort Myers. His investigative mind unfurled the bits of information he had, trying to fit the pieces together.

For several seconds, the kitchen fell deathly quiet. Grant and Charlie held each other's gaze as this new information needed time to settle into reality. The awkward calm suddenly ended as Wrench began lapping up water from his bowl. The chain collar hung loose around his neck and banged against the metal dish with a steady rhythm.

"Why didn't you show me these before?" Grant asked.

"I didn't know how much I could trust you," Charlie replied.

They continued staring at each other until Grant finally turned his attention back to the documents.

"You think that's your parents?" Angie asked.

"I've never heard either of those names," Grant replied.

"But you never met your mom's folks, did you?" Angie asked him.

His head shook slowly from side to side.

Angie turned to Charlie. "What about you? Did you know your grandparents?"

"No, they died before I was born."

"Hmm," Angie mused.

"Fuck me," Grant swore. "We need to figure out who these two people were."

"It's pretty bloody obvious to me," Charlie retorted. "They are our parents. They've been keeping secrets from us for our entire lives. I could strangle my dad right now, if I could find him. And after I hug him. The lying bugger." She grew more animated as she stomped around the kitchen. Wrench moved around behind her in quick lines as he tried to keep up with her motions.

"Dammit, Wrench," she cursed at him.

"Hey, you used his name," Grant noted with a slight grin.

"Why aren't you… what did you call it? Pissed about it?"

He shrugged. "The fact that our parents lied, or that you hid this stuff from me?"

Charlie frowned at him. "Both, I suppose."

"It's been a long week. I don't think it's in me to be pissed at my dead mother for something she may or may not have done."

"Ugh!" she groaned, pacing some more. "It infuriates me."

Grant sighed.

"Why don't you track down Diana Turner and Daniel Edwards?" Angie suggested. "If it's them, the state would require them to give some information when they got their marriage license."

"Can you do it at the courthouse?" Grant asked Angie.

"I am heading there next to pull some paperwork, anyway."

"Wait, you're a solicitor?"

Angie laughed.

"A solicitor?" Grant questioned.

"She means lawyer," Angie explained. "No, I'm a paralegal, studying for my law degree."

Charlie nodded.

"I still can't understand why anyone would kill Fiona," Angie mused.

"If they were both in hiding, it makes sense," Grant pointed out. "What if they found Mom first? Killing her and making it look like an accident was just bait to get your dad to show up."

"What made them think he'd come?" Charlie asked. "Or even about your mother's death? It seems safe to assume they haven't talked in years. Decades, probably."

"Unless they did," Angie offered.

Both Grant and Charlie stared at her.

"Think about it," Angie explained. "They must have loved each other. If this Daniel and Diana are them, they had a family together. It's not like a regular divorce. I know your mom, Grant. There is no way she'd refuse to ever see her daughter again unless she had to."

"The best way to hide was to split up," Charlie said, following the same train of thought.

"Yeah, but if they still loved each other—and it sounds as if neither of them moved on from the marriage—they might find a way to stay in touch."

"Okay," Grant conceded. "Let's say they did that. We still don't have a clue who or what they were hiding from."

"I need to get going," Angie told them. "I'll see what I can get from their marriage license. It should, at least, list a next of kin."

She leaned in and kissed Grant on the cheek. "It was nice to meet you, Charlie," she told the other woman.

"You too," Charlie agreed.

Wrench jumped to his feet when he realized Angie was leaving. She knelt down and scratched him on the back of his head. The dog reciprocated with several tongue laps across her face.

"Call me," Grant told her.

She nodded as she left.

When the front door closed, Charlie said, "She likes you."

"We've known each other our whole lives," he explained.

"Let me guess," Charlie interjected. "You buggered it up with those pills."

Grant's eyes narrowed. "Those pills are under control," he assured her.

"If I were you, I would do whatever I could to fix it," Charlie suggested. "Otherwise, someone is going to come along without the myriad of issues you have."

Grunting, Grant marched to the refrigerator, pulling out a bottle of Corona.

"I think we need to figure out who our parents really were," he commented. "Do you have anyone at Scotland Yard that can run Daniel Edwards's name through the system?"

"I might," she admitted.

"Good. I'll see if my friend Macabee can run Diana Turner through his. I should ask him this one in person. Hell, we might as well see if either of our guys can pull both. Obviously, they were together in Florida at some point to get married. Perhaps they left a trail over in England too."

"I think this is going to sound stupid," Charlie remarked.

"What is?" Grant asked.

"I guess it's two things. The first is trying to wrap my head around the fact I have a brother."

"And the second thing?" Grant asked.

"I'm just wondering if what Angie asked was true," she answered. "What if my dad is like a James Bond? Maybe our parents were spies?"

14

Charlie opened the front door, looked toward the road, and froze.

"We've got a problem," she said, and quickly closed the door again.

"What's wrong?" Grant asked, gathering up his phone and keys.

"We're idiots, that's the first problem."

"Are the Russians out there?" Grant asked.

"Just pulled up," Charlie confirmed. "We should have known they'd know where you live. Hopefully they didn't see your future ex-wife."

Grant ran to the back of the house and peeked through the blinds in his room, seeing two men getting out of a large black four-door Cadillac.

"Where do these guys find these cars in Florida?" he muttered, ignoring Charlie's jab. "No one has a black car in Florida."

"Apparently T&R Luxury Leases in Marathon do," Charlie replied.

Grant raised an eyebrow. Charlie was right. "We could easily have been grabbed last night. That was sloppy not to think of it," he muttered, berating himself.

"Gives me the willies thinking someone could have been watching the house while I was having a kip," Charlie responded, twitching her nose.

"I don't think they were, or they would have invited themselves in," Grant replied. "We don't know what they're after or why they may have killed Mom, but I'm starting to think you being here surprised them as much as me. Maybe last night they were trying to figure out their next move."

"How do they even know who I am?" Charlie replied.

"Because you look just like my mom," Grant said. "Your mom... I guess."

Charlie went to say something more, but the thoughts were too jumbled in her mind. Frustration brewed again, and she felt her anger rising.

"We need to get out of here," Grant said, gently releasing the slats of the blind.

"Let's go ask them who the hell they are," Charlie fumed, stomping out of the bedroom. "I'm tired of running from these wankers."

"Are you crazy?" Grant groaned, rushing after her.

"What are they going to do, shoot up the whole town?" Charlie rebutted, heading for the front door. "This isn't a bloody Tarantino movie."

Grant caught her arm before she could turn the door handle. "Charlie! What have you seen about these guys so far that tells you they *won't* shoot up the town?"

She glared at his hand, but relaxed a little when she looked up at his face. He was genuinely concerned.

"Besides, I'm not sure they want to kill us. Or you, at least. I think they want to *take* you," Grant said. "Running out there, you'll be serving yourself up."

Charlie considered her brother's words and found herself speechless over the fact she was now thinking of Grant as a sibling. Something they couldn't be certain of, yet it felt accurate. *Half-brother perhaps?*

"I have a better plan," Grant continued, steering her back into the house. "We'll take the boat."

Wrench had trotted behind them both as they'd run back and forth through the house, but now he stayed at the front door with his head tilted and ear cocked, listening. Charlie slid to a stop.

"The only way out is down the steps," she pointed out. "Which means going out the front door."

Grant shook his head. "There's another way. We'll drop from the deck."

Charlie frowned. "To the bloody ground? That has to be at least three meters."

Grant moved to the sliding door leading to the deck and pulled it open. "I've no idea how many meters it is, but if that translates to nine or ten feet, that's about right."

"Yeah..." she muttered. "I think I'd rather face the Russians with guns. We'll break our bloody legs. Besides, what about his nibs?" she added, pointing to the dog. "He'll splat like one of them Mexican thingies full of sweets that the kids wallop with a stick."

"A *piñata*?" Grant guessed.

"That's the thingy."

Grant seemed too stunned to speak for a few moments, then recovered. "We can discuss children's party favors later when Russian gunmen aren't about to burst through the door, Charlie. You'll drop Wrench over and I'll catch him."

Charlie looked at the fifty-pound dog. "I'm not sure I can lift him up. He's like The Rock of mutts."

"It'll work, trust me. I've dropped from this deck a hundred times," Grant urged, omitting the part that he'd been a youth most of those times.

He called Wrench, who threw a last glance at the door, accompanied by a low growl, as a creak resonated from the steps outside.

"Sod it," Charlie grumbled, grabbed her car keys, and jogged over to the sliding door.

"I'll be right back," Grant said, suddenly turning and running across the living room toward the bedrooms.

"Grant!" Charlie hissed.

Confronting the thugs on the street in front of potential witnesses was one thing, but being cornered by them in the house was another situation entirely. She tried to remember if he'd brought his gun in from the car, but they'd been griping at each other, and she hadn't noticed. He's getting another one, she decided, based on her growing theory that Americans kept guns like the rest of the world kept loose change... you could find one just about everywhere.

She heard the door lightly rattle as one of the Russians tried the handle. She was relieved it was one of those locks which was secured from the outside whenever the door was closed. Charlie softly walked across the deck and peered over the railing. From straight above it looked even farther than she'd imagined, and the landing was concrete.

"Couldn't be grass down there, could it?" she groaned to Wrench, who looked generally confused by what was going on. "In the movies there's always a handy rubbish bin below."

Charlie looked over her shoulder as Grant ran back across the living room and squeezed through the sliding door, closing it behind him. They both started when a thump sounded. The Russians were trying to break the front door open. Grant went to the corner of the deck and swung his leg over the railing. Easing himself down, he clutched two railings and let his legs dangle from the deck. Charlie looked over and it still appeared to be a long way from Grant's feet to the ground. He released his grip and dropped, bending his knees, and rolling to the side as he hit the concrete.

He quickly bounced to his feet and held up his hands. "Drop Wrench to me."

A crashing sound came from inside the house, and Charlie spun around to see a brawny man she hadn't seen before standing in the open doorway with splintered wood scattered at his feet. Their eyes met. The man raised his arm and pointed a gun her way. Charlie raised her hands in the air and carefully moved to the sliding door.

The gunman beckoned her to come inside, so she reached down and pulled the glass door aside.

"Get 'em, boy!" she shouted, and Wrench was through the gap and racing toward the man before he could figure out what was happening.

His moment of hesitation was all it took for the dog to cover the distance in two strides, leap into the air, and barrel into the man with his teeth wrapped around the Russian's forearm. Charlie turned and bolted to the corner of the deck, swinging over the railing, and precariously planting her feet on the edge while clutching the corner post. She grabbed low down on two railings before slipping her feet from the deck and feeling herself drop. Her body weight, as slender as it was, combined with her momentum, yanked her grip free of the railings, and she fell for what seemed like forever.

Charlie wailed. She was rotating backward and was about to crash into the concrete below with her arms frantically windmilling in the air. She hit with a thud that didn't feel as solid as she'd anticipated and realized something had broken her fall. Grant's moan and sudden gasp of air from his lungs explained the cushioned landing as they both sprawled to the ground in a heap.

"Wrench?" Grant managed to splutter.

"He's busy," Charlie replied, rolling off her brother and helping him to his feet. "We should leave." Miraculously, she still held the SUV keys in her hand.

"Damn it," Grant muttered, but stumbled toward the dock at the end of the yard. "Get the bow line," he ordered.

Charlie didn't know a lot about boats, but she was pretty sure the stern was the blunt end, and the bow was the pointy bit. The rope was wrapped around a cleat screwed to the concrete and she frantically unwound it and threw the line onto the boat. The sound of a gunshot echoed from inside the house, and she froze. There was only one thing still in Grant's house to shoot at, and Charlie realized with a lump in her throat that she'd be devastated if the

Russians killed Wrench. For a second, she considered running back inside, but Grant's voice grabbed her attention.

"Get the stern line but don't release it yet," he ordered.

Charlie ran to the other end of the dock and fumbled with the line, awkwardly keeping hold of the car keys as the boat's twin outboard engines rumbled to life.

"Why did you bring those damn keys?" Grant yelled. "Throw them to me."

As she stood, holding the line hooked around one end of the cleat, she tossed the keys in Grant's direction, just as he looked away. Charlie watched them sail past him into the canal.

"You idiot!" Charlie bellowed, catching Grant's attention. The man's face looked desperate. He put two fingers in his mouth and let out a shrill whistle.

"Wrench! Here, boy!" he yelled.

They both looked up at the deck and then the top of the steps by the front door. For a moment there was no movement at all, but then the second Russian appeared on the landing and began trotting down the wooden steps beside the house. Halfway down, he raised his gun and fired, the sound of the bullet hitting metal reaching Charlie a split second before the report of the gun.

"Come on!" Grant yelled, and Charlie unhooked the line and tossed it aboard before leaping over the gunwale herself.

With the wheel turned to port, Grant pushed the throttles forward and the Grady White leapt away from the dock toward the center of the channel. They both instinctively ducked at the sound of another gunshot, although the bullet would have already hit whatever fell in its path before the sound ever reached them. Charlie looked over her shoulder.

"Wrench!" she screamed, and Grant swung around to see the dog bounding across the backyard.

The Russian was just taking careful aim when he was hit from behind, the gun going off, firing harmlessly into the ground. Wrench took a bite out of the man's ear as he careened over the Russian's crumpled body and continued toward the dock.

"Come on, boy!" Grant called out, pointing along the concrete seawall and docks running down the edge of the canal behind every home.

Each property was divided from the next by a small fence or wall, which the dog bounded over without breaking stride. Grant aimed the center console at a house three doors down who didn't own a boat, and eased back on the throttles.

"Jump, Wrench!" Charlie screamed, and the dog obeyed, launching at an angle off the dock in the direction of the boat.

"Oh, bugger!" Charlie yelped as fifty pounds of canine came flying over the gunwale, bowling her over.

Grant sped the boat away as Charlie looked up at the sky, dazed and hoping she hadn't broken anything. Wrench scrambled to his feet, panting and slobbering. Before she could bring her hands up to stop him, the dog slurped at her face with droplets of blood and spit flying everywhere.

"Stop it, you stupid hound!" she squealed, wrapping her arms around him and pulling him close so he couldn't lick her face, her eyes closed. "You're leaking Russian all over me."

Grant swung the Grady White around the corner into the main channel before easing back on the throttles, letting the boat drop back into the water after badly waking out his neighbors.

"You two are really starting to bond," Grant said, looking down with a grin.

Charlie opened one eye. "No chance," she replied, then gave Wrench a big kiss on the top of his massive head.

15

The Grady White skimmed across the water. Grant stood at the helm as Wrench paced to the open bow and back to the stern three times before he suddenly seemed comfortable. The dog climbed up on the starboard bow seat, facing forward. The wind whipped his ears back.

"He likes it?" Charlie asked.

"He loves it," Grant acknowledged. "He'll end up sitting there until we stop. I'm positive the only reason he paces is to make sure he doesn't get settled, only for me to stop the boat."

"That mutt's insane," Charlie commented. A smile crept onto her lips.

Grant relaxed now that they were away from the dock. He leaned back against the captain's seat.

"Shit, this fell out of your pocket," Charlie announced, bending over to retrieve the item.

When she straightened up, she held an amber-colored prescription bottle between her right index finger and thumb. Her face twisted.

"Oxycodone?" she demanded. "Is this what you went back for?"

"No," he lied.

"Bullshit. It was," she howled over the twin Yamaha 350 horse-power motors. "I assumed you were getting a gun—or something important. But it was bloody pills."

"It's not like that."

"Your damned dog almost died!" Charlie shouted. "I almost died! Just so you could get your next high."

In a fit of anger, she rotated around on her left foot and hurled the container off the back of the boat.

"No!" Grant called, letting go of the wheel for a split second as the container soared into the wake.

Twisted 180 degrees, he stared out behind the boat at the spot where the plastic bottle hit the water.

"You have a problem," Charlie snapped. "I can't believe it."

"It's not that," Grant said, turning around finally to stare forward.

"Whatever," she declared. "Why don't you drop me off some-where? I've had just about enough of your help here."

"Charlie, these guys are after you," he reminded her.

"Yeah, and I don't need some pill-popping stoner watching my back. That seems like the best way to get shot."

Frustrated and annoyed, Grant sighed. "Fine, I'll drop you at the marina up here."

The next fifteen minutes passed without a word between them. Wrench sat on watch until they passed the No Wake buoys around the marina. When Grant pulled the throttle back, idling the dual outboards, Wrench bounced off the seat in the front and ran to the back, where Charlie sat with her arms crossing her chest.

The dog laid his muzzle on her leg, and she stared down at him. Without realizing it, she rubbed the area on the back of his head. Her fingers kneaded his thin, floppy ears. Wrench strained his neck so she would continue.

As Grant edged the Grady White toward the pier, Charlie stood up. Wrench took a step back, wondering why his ear rubs had ended.

"If you need me, you can call me," Grant told her.

Charlie didn't say a word as she stepped on the gunwale with her right foot and climbed onto the wooden dock.

"Charlie," Grant called, but she continued walking away.

Wrench ran to the bow, jumping up onto the bowsprit. He let out a high-pitched bark, calling for the woman to come back. She didn't stop to look back. Grant watched her until she reached the shore, wondering what the hell her plan was.

Once she was out of sight, he pushed off the dock, slipping the engines into reverse. With precision, he swung the bow around to the open sea.

A few minutes later, he passed the No Wake markers and pressed the throttles forward.

Grant was angry. Right now, his blood boiled. How dare the Russians barge into his house? His mother's house. Even worse, how dare Charlie abandon him? Unfortunately, she wasn't wrong. He'd realized he had no more oxy. All this running around gave his leg an aching throb. He knew he was struggling with it, but what the hell did she know? How can this woman pop into his life suddenly and think she can do better? He'd seen how she reacted to everything—ready to fight anyone. Charlie was an angry, broken mess.

The more he considered it, the angrier he got. How was it his fault that her mom had bailed on her?

His mom.

She was mad because she'd never met her mother all the while Grant grew up with her.

Well, that was bullshit. He'd never had a father, and Charlie got that. Hell, it sounded like good old Dad actually had a lot of money. It must have been nice living in London with their rich father.

Now, he was furious with this unknown parent. And his mother, too. How dare they do this to them?

Grant pulled the throttle back to neutral. The hull slowed, plowing the bow into the waves. Wrench, who'd resumed his watch at the front, turned to stare at Grant. He'd taken the boat a mile offshore. There were a few boats buzzing to and from the coastline. But, mostly, he was alone right now. Grant wanted a minute of quiet. As pissed as he was, he might not have even slowed the boat for several miles, he wasn't sure.

The Florida sun beat down on him. His face burned, and Grant almost couldn't stand it. He stood up and walked to the back of the boat. He stripped his shirt and shorts off before diving into the blue waters. When he surfaced, his tongue ran over his lips, tasting the sea. He savored the salinity of the water. The current and the waves had already grabbed the boat, pulling it away from him.

His arms dug into the water as he kicked toward the vessel. Out here, it only took seconds to get separated from the boat. Most of the time, he carried a line in the water to tether him to it, but in his irritation, he'd forgotten. Now, the speed of the current drove him to swim faster. It took nearly forty seconds to catch the back of the boat.

Grant's left foot pushed up on the anti-cavitation plate just over the propeller on the starboard engine. He hoisted himself over the stern, rolling onto the floor of the fishing boat.

Wrench stared at him from his perch.

The dip in the ocean cooled his temper. With some clearer thoughts, he stretched out on the deck of the boat.

His mother worked her entire life to take care of Grant. Angie was right, too. Fiona Wolfe would never abandon her daughter unless she had to. Something forced Daniel Edwards and Diana Turner apart. Everything pointed to the Russians being involved in her death. Now, he was certain they were after Charlie, too.

All of this had to lead back to their parents. The phrase he remembered from his training with the Sheriff's Department was "inciting incident." There had to be one that caused all of this. Right now, it seemed the only person who might have those answers was Charlie's father.

Who could also be his father.

After lying in the sun for half an hour, Grant suddenly sat up. Pulling on his shorts then grabbing his shirt. He needed to get back to shore. Charlie was on her own, which might be for the best as at least the Russians had less chance of finding her, however, Grant didn't sit idle very well.

Angie shouldn't take too long getting the marriage certificate, which was public information, but he still had to reach out to Macabee. Maybe his buddy could dig into his parents' real identities. Going there in person was off the table, but he could still call him.

He started the motors, and Wrench's tail thumped the vinyl seating with rhythmic excitement. Grant couldn't help smiling at what it took to make the dog happy. Just the prospect of the boat moving thrilled the canine.

Pushing the throttles forward, he headed south. A fishing buddy, Clayton, had taken his thirty-five-foot Carver down to Key West for a few weeks of fishing. He'd asked Grant to go with him, but with the funeral to attend, he'd said no. Clayton's empty house in Tavernier now seemed like an ideal spot to hide from the Russians.

When he pulled into the canal, he slowed to idle. Once he tied up to the pier, he and Wrench climbed up the steps to the small beach house. Sitting down on his buddy's back deck, he took out his phone.

"Yullo," Macabee answered after the third ring.

"Hey, it's Grant."

"The hell you want now?"

"Tony, some Russian dudes just crashed my house trying to kill me."

"Shit, you calling me?" Macabee asked. "Dial 9-1-1!"

"I'm already gone," he assured his friend. "I figure they're long gone, too."

"What are you into, Grant?"

"Would you believe me if I told you, it was my family?" he asked.

"Is this the supposed sister?" Macabee replied.

"Yeah," Grant explained. "Turns out I have a dad too."

"Everyone's got a dad," Macabee quipped.

"Well, mine might be running around trying not to be killed by Russians."

"I assume we're talking about the same Russians who just stormed your *casa*?" Macabee was half Irish and half Italian, but it didn't stop him from dropping a little Spanish in conversation. He thought it made him seem more Floridian.

"Yeah."

"Shit!" Macabee swore. The word came out like "Sheeyut!"

"Can you run a couple of names for me?" Grant asked.

"Yeah, give 'em to me."

"Daniel Edwards and Diana Turner. Edwards is English."

"Who are they?"

"Tony, those are my parents."

"That's not your mother's name," Macabee noted. "I thought it was Wynona or something."

"Fiona."

"Yeah, that's it," Macabee agreed, as if Grant did not know what his own mother's name was.

As it turned out, he didn't.

"Tony, they changed their names in the nineties. We're guessing they went into hiding."

"Whose we?"

"That'll be the sister part."

"Gotcha," he whistled.

"See what you can find about them. I know they got married. Angie's trying to pull their marriage certificate to see if there's any more information."

"What are we looking for?"

"A reason for the Russian mob to want them dead."

"Your mom, too?" he asked.

Grant swallowed. Each time he thought of it, his throat tightened. "Yeah, I think they killed her."

"I thought some idiot knocked her off her bike."

"Yeah, me too. Now we think it may not have been by accident."

"Oh, man, I'm so sorry."

Grant didn't respond. There was little he could say. Everything felt like it was on edge. His skin prickled as if he was about to burst into flames.

Finally, after what seemed an eternity, Grant said, "I appreciate it, man."

"You got it."

Macabee hung up.

Grant scratched Wrench's ears. The dog panted in the sun.

"We need to get you some water," he realized, standing up and walking to Clayton's water hose.

When the water started bubbling out of the hose, Grant tested it.

"Not yet," he warned the dog. "It's too hot."

After about twenty seconds, the water cooled, and Grant stuck the hose out for Wrench to lap at the stream. He paused and took a drink himself before letting Wrench have it again. Once the dog had his fill, he wanted to play in the stream. Grant shook his head with a smile before turning the water off.

His cell phone rang in his pocket, and Grant answered the call.

"Grant, I got a copy," Angie told him before she even said "Hello."

"Is there an electronic record?" Grant asked, somewhat nervously. "Next of kin?"

"Yes, and no for next of kin. It does have the clergyman's and witness's names though."

"What are they?"

"The clergyman was Reverend Frank Tilly."

"The witness?" Grant asked.

"Timothy Glaser."

"Uncle Tim?"

"Who?" Angie asked.

"I only knew him as Uncle Tim, but I'm sure that's his full name. We used to see him every so often. I think he lived in

Marathon or somewhere south of here. I don't remember, I was a kid. He used to take me out fishing."

"Was he your mom's brother?"

"Not that I remember. More like a family friend," Grant said. "I was just a kid. After I turned ten, he didn't come around much."

"I can meet you back at the house," she said.

"No!" Grant almost shouted into the phone. "Don't go back to the house. In fact, don't go home either."

It suddenly occurred to him that if they were looking for Grant and Charlie, then Angie's place might be the next best bet.

"What's going on?" she asked.

"It's a long story," Grant admitted. "Can you come pick me and Wrench up?"

16

After watching the Grady White disappear, Charlie had stomped through the Blue Fin Marina boat yard, catching a glare from the guy she presumed was the owner, and a wolf whistle from one of the workers. The latter she acknowledged by flipping two fingers which he looked confused about. Upon reflection she recalled in America they used the middle finger for such responses, but it was too late to correct the error as she'd already reached Overseas Highway.

Bringing up a map on her phone, she spotted a place called Ballyhoo's to the north. Their online menu was mouthwatering. She checked her pocket where she found a couple of dollar bills and a quarter she'd grabbed from Grant at some point, plus the credit card which had no chance of working. Across the two northbound lanes in the center section was a Denny's. A quick check of their menu told her that the vast fortune in her possession would extend a lot further at Denny's.

Sitting in a vinyl-covered bench seat in a booth by the window, Charlie watched the cars roll by in both directions, and simmered over Grant. The evidence was accumulating to suggest they were siblings, but in her mind, they couldn't be more different. Why he'd be popping pain pills was beyond her comprehension. As a detective in London, she'd seen so many sob stories of drug-addicted losers and the scum who profited from peddling narcotics of every variety.

The waitress came by the table and Charlie thrust her coffee cup over for a refill, splashing a little over the table in her embittered haste.

"Are you ordering something, hon?" the waitress asked.

Charlie picked up the dog-eared laminated menu. "Still having a look."

The waitress made a sound somewhere between a grunt and a sigh, topped off the coffee, and left. Charlie had already discovered her choices were a couple of pancakes or coffee, and she'd committed to caffeine, but the waitress didn't need to know she was destitute. Her thoughts wandered back to the man she was now thinking of as her brother and her body tensed once more. *How dare he accuse her of being unable to control her anger?*

The fact that he was right wound her up even more. The realization that she had no more control over her issue than he likely did over his, made her swear out loud and thump the table. Heads turned, and she held up an apologetic hand, despite the fact she really wanted to tell them all to piss off and mind their own business. *See,* she told herself, *I can control my anger.* Sometimes.

Charlie melted into the seat, slumping against the windowsill until she felt something sticky on her elbow and sat up straight again. What appeared to be remnants of a marmalade incident was now evenly distributed between her skin and the faded wood of the windowsill. She quickly scrubbed her elbow with a paper napkin, instantly feeling like she needed a shower. As she mopped the mess off the wood, her mind drifted to her father. He liked marmalade on his toast in the mornings. But he wouldn't have launched a dollop on the windowsill.

On one hand, it was hard to believe her dad could be here in the Florida Keys, but on the other, she'd flown to Miami as that was the only trace he'd left behind. She'd followed the thin evidence available and maybe seen him at Grant's mother's funeral.

Her own mother's funeral?

Charlie tried to picture the figure in the distance once more, but her mind wouldn't hold the scene in focus. *Was it her father?* It could have been someone with a similar build and her brain was piecing together a truth she wanted to see. Eyewitnesses were notoriously inaccurate in their recollections of events and details.

If it had been her father, surely, he'd seen her, so why hadn't he called? He would have been as surprised to see her in Florida as she'd been to stumble across him. Which leaned her toward the fact that it probably wasn't Keith Greene.

Or was it Daniel Edwards, and everything she knew about her dad was a lie?

If Charlie was the crying sort, the enormity of the life-altering events happening all around her would certainly turn the waterworks on. But she wasn't.

She looked at the time on her dad's Rolex which hung loosely around her wrist. It was just after 4:00 p.m. Which meant 9:00 p.m. in the UK. Late, but not middle-of-the-night late. She found her contact and called his cell phone number, listening to it ring. John Francis, who everyone called Froggy, worked in one of the numerous data analysis groups within Scotland Yard. He'd been in Charlie's year in secondary school, and while they hadn't been close friends, the police force connection had kept them in touch. She was preparing herself for the voicemail message she was about to leave when a voice answered the phone in a hushed tone.

"Charlie?"

"Hey Froggy, how's things?" she greeted him, trying to sound breezy.

"Buried. Threat level in London is about to go up," he said, continuing to whisper into the phone. "Not that I told you that. Fuck. I shouldn't have said anything. Forget I said that, okay?"

Charlie shook her head. "Stop freaking out. I'm not even in London right now. Are you still at work?"

"Yeah. It's bloody mayhem here. Where are you?"

"Florida. Key Largo. Like in the old Humphrey Bogart movie," she replied.

Her dad used to love watching the old black and white movies with her. That one had been his favorite. He'd watched them as a kid and thought it was some kind of bonding thing. Charlie protested every time, but truth be told, she liked most of them. Now, she wondered if his love for that movie had deeper meaning.

"Humphrey who? What movie? You're in a movie?"

"No, you silly bugger… oh forget it. I'm in Florida, okay?"

"Sure. Got it. Why are you in Florida, Charlie? I thought you were job hunting?"

She felt a pang of guilt as she'd told several of her friends she was looking for a new job, when in fact, she'd been moping around the house arguing with the cat for too many weeks.

"Long story, but the short version is, I need your help."

"Ummm… I don't know, Charlie. I mean, this is really bad timing. JTAC are in knots and have us jumping through hoops. Plus, you're not even on the force anymore. Can we take a look in a week or two when things settle down?"

Charlie stayed quiet, knowing how her friend's mind worked. He'd had a crush on her since school and while she didn't like to take advantage of a friend, her situation was getting desperate.

"Charlie? Are you still there?"

"Yeah, I'm here. Just trying to think who else might be able to help me. I have crazy Russians trying to kidnap or kill me, I'm not sure which, so I don't have much time."

"What? You didn't say anything about people trying to kill you! Bloody hell, Charlie. Have you gone to the police?"

"Of course, but they're way out of their depth," she replied, and left it at that.

Froggy was a great guy, but now wasn't the time to explain about her father. Or the fact that she apparently had a brother. Well, she thought, she'd had a brother for a long time, but now she actually knew about him.

"What do you need?" Froggy asked in an even quieter voice.

"I need a name search for Daniel Edwards, and while you're looking, check Diana Turner."

Froggy read the names back to her and she verified he had the correct spelling.

"Are these the people after you? I thought you said they were Russians," he quizzed.

"This isn't the Russians. We think this may be the people who..." Charlie trailed off, wondering who exactly they thought these people were. Aliases for their parents seemed to be the logical explanation. "They're involved," she finished, and hoped that would be enough to satisfy his curiosity.

"Dates of birth?" he asked.

"Fifth of January 1970. For Edwards," she said, giving him her father's birthdate, then she tried to recall the date on Fiona Wolfe's program from her funeral, but couldn't remember. "Try April 28, 1971, for Turner."

Charlie gave him her own mother's birthday. Every year, her father would buy a cupcake or similar, light a candle on it, and they'd wish her a happy birthday. Charlie made a mental note to check Fiona Wolfe's date of birth. She was sure it would be the same as her own mother's.

"I don't see anything under those dates and names," Froggy whispered back. "Let me expand the search and let the AI do its thing."

The waitress came past and Charlie had her top up her coffee once more. The woman was getting annoyed that her corner window table was being hogged by a single coffee purchase, but Charlie could see the place was barely a quarter full, so she ignored the irritated glare.

"You're getting dyslexic on me, Charlie," Froggy said, chuckling over the phone. "The days and months are backward."

"Huh?" Charlie responded, wondering how April 28 could become the fourth day of the twenty-eighth month.

"The day and month are for the other name," Froggy explained. "The years were correct."

"Really?" Charlie blurted, double-checking herself. "So, Edwards is April 28, 1970, and Turner is January 5, 1971."

"Correct."

Once again, Charlie was faced with a strange coincidence with zero hard facts. It was maddening.

"What's in their files," she asked, moving on and assuming they'd found the right people.

"Absolutely nothing," Froggy replied.

"Nothing?"

"Nothing."

"There can't be nothing," Charlie said. "Everyone has something in there. Place of birth, National Insurance number, addresses. You're saying there's none of that?"

"I'm saying there's not even a file," Froggy replied. "Never seen anything like this before. There's a folder location against the name and DOB, but no files inside. I've come across sealed files, which require clearance to view, but these two don't even have that. It's as though they were scrubbed from existence, but the system wouldn't let all trace of them be wiped. Who are these people, Charlie?"

"I don't think you'd believe me if I told you," she mumbled in response, lost amongst her thoughts of her parents.

"Try me..." Froggy began, then she heard his hand cover the phone and muffled voices in the background.

Charlie thought she heard, "Come with me," but couldn't be sure.

"Damn it, Charlie," Froggy suddenly hissed in her ear. "What have you done to me?"

The line went dead.

Charlie stared at the phone in disbelief. If she wasn't right in the middle of this madness, she'd never believe any of it could be happening.

17

"They shot up your house?" Angie asked incredulously. "How the hell did that happen?"

"I should have thought about it," Grant admitted. "If those bastards killed my mother, it makes perfect sense that they'd know where she lived."

Angie drove her red 2020 Tesla Model 3 south on Overseas Highway. After half an hour, Wrench curled up on the back seat. He seemed to relish the cold air-conditioning, and he let his eyelids droop halfway down. The dog had a habit of fighting sleep whenever other people were around. Grant figured he didn't want to miss out on a random belly rub or ear scratch.

"What about Charlie?" Angie asked. "Isn't she still in danger?"

Grant shrugged. "Probably." He wanted to complain about how it was her own fault at this point. She bailed on him.

"She just left?" Angie asked pointedly.

"Yeah," he responded, slower than he should have.

Angie's eyes shifted to glance Grant's right hand, tapping and touching his pocket, which appeared void of the familiar pill bottle bulge she was used to seeing.

"The pills?" she asked, nodding toward his hand.

"This running around is killing my leg," he argued.

Angie turned back to the road. "I know," she acknowledged. "But those pills are killing everything else."

"C'mon, Ange. You know I'm still good. And you know what I went through."

"Grant, *we* went through it," she corrected. "You, me, Fiona. Hell, even Wrench."

"I know," Grant agreed.

"No, you don't really," Angie said flatly. "You didn't get the call. I did. Not only that, I had to call Fiona. Do you know what it's like to tell the mother of the man you love that he's been shot?"

Grant didn't respond. This wasn't the first time they'd had this discussion. It was the first time in a long time she used the word "love" though. Thinking about Angie going to his mother's house to tell her he'd been shot left Grant with a wave of nausea. It was only a few days ago a deputy showed up at his door to tell him about his mother's accident.

Not an accident.

"Angie," he started, "I'm trying."

The brunette turned to stare at him as she drove. "Try harder," she demanded. "Right now, I'm the only thing you have left. Maybe you have a father and a sister out there too. But if you don't get your shit together, it will just be you and this dog."

Grant didn't respond, but Wrench lifted his head, curious about what was being said about him.

Damn, he thought. She was completely right. His life was a mess. Honestly, he didn't know what he was going to do—much less how he was going to do it. The tip of his index finger traced the outline of where the bottle would have been. He had more at the house. He could just throw them out. Couldn't he?

Angie slowed down, turning off the highway onto a side street. Grant had stopped paying attention as he'd contemplated the idea of not having access to his crutch.

"This is the address," she alerted him. "Doesn't look like much."

The squat, square house sat on Sixty-eighth Street with a Boston

Whaler Center Console parked in the driveway. In the back of Grant's brain, the house felt like an old lost memory. Of course, it also looked like hundreds of houses in the Keys.

Angie pulled into the small driveway, parking next to the fishing boat.

"You sure this is it?" she asked.

"Maybe," he said. "It's been forever. I'm not even sure what I'm supposed to ask this guy. 'Hey Uncle Tim, remember me? Do you know why my parents are being hunted by Russians?'"

"It's a start," she suggested with the half smirk she gave him when she found his frustration amusing. It was the same look that melted him nearly every time she used it.

In that instance, he flashed back to the first time he'd seen the expression. Seventh grade. The second day of school, Grant went back to his new locker to find he couldn't remember the combination. He worked that lock for fifteen minutes. When the bell rang, this brown-haired girl with the bronze skin that came from an entire summer on the water walked up and asked him why he was trying to unlock her locker. Dumbfounded, Grant realized his locker was one to the right. The girl gave him that wry grin, and his face burned bright red with shame.

"I'll be back," he told her, pulling himself to the present.

As Grant opened the passenger door, Wrench popped up, looking for his next adventure. Grant's palm shot up. "Wrench, stay with Angie."

The dog dropped his muzzle and stared up at him.

"Don't give me those eyes," Grant scolded.

"C'mon, boy," Angie urged the pup who immediately turned to her for attention as Grant slammed the door closed.

He walked up to the white door. A semi-circle window at the top allowed light in, but the frosted glass prevented anyone from looking inside. Grant rapped his knuckles on the metal door.

He listened intently for the sounds of life inside the home. It seemed silent. Grant knocked again. Still nothing.

"You looking for Tim?" a voice startled him.

Grant turned around to see a thin woman in her sixties. The lady wore skintight leggings and a sports bra. She bounced back and forth on her feet as she warmed up before her run.

"Yeah, I am," Grant acknowledged. "Is he around?"

"I haven't seen him in a few days, but he's usually either out fishing or down at the Billy Club over on Sixty-third."

"Thanks, ma'am," he offered.

"Don't ma'am me, cutie," she snarled playfully.

"Well... okay... thank you," he stammered, making his way back to the car.

The woman watched him until he was inside the Tesla.

"Make a new friend?" Angie asked.

"Don't start," Grant grunted.

Angie laughed as the woman started her run down the street.

"We need to find the Billy Club," Grant told her.

"I assume that's a restaurant," Angie said.

"The lady told me it was on Sixty-third Street."

Angie reversed the Model 3 onto the narrow two-lane street. In a minute she was turning left on Overseas Highway. Traffic was thickening along the roadway, but in five minutes, she made a right onto Sixty-third, pulling into a small gravel lot halfway down the street.

The Billy Club was a one-story cinder-block building with what looked like a neon bat that would swing over the door when it was dark. During the day, the effect was lost to the sunlight—one of the downfalls of such gimmicks.

The Tesla looked out of place next to the old Jeep and an older Toyota Corolla. Immediately, Grant recognized it as a joint frequented by locals more than tourists. The vehicles in the parking lot gave that away. There were no new rental cars, just everyday vehicles.

When Angie parked the car, she climbed out. Grant glanced at her.

"Wrench and I need some lunch," she pointed out.

"It's almost dinnertime," Grant said.

"Fine, we need dinner."

She grabbed the dog's leash and clicked her tongue twice. The brown dog sprang out of the back seat and followed her inside.

The Billy Club was little more than a fish shack with a bar inside. The Rolling Stones played through a couple of old speakers behind the bar. The interior was dark, having only one narrow strip of windows at the top of the front wall. It eliminated a lot of natural light, but, in turn, it prevented the Florida sun from converting the small concrete building into a solar oven. The brown, wood-paneled walls completed the dive-bar vibe.

A heavy-set black man leaned against the back counter watching a soccer match on the thirty-two-inch television at the far end of the bar. He glanced over at the trio as the door closed behind them. His eyes flitted down to Wrench, appraising the canine.

Grant scanned the room, seeing two other men besides the bartender. One hunched over a half-empty lager while the other one watched the soccer game.

"We'll grab a table," Angie told Grant, tugging gently on Wrench's leash. The dog followed obediently, and when she sat down, he immediately curled up at her feet.

"Two Coronas," Grant told the bartender. "And three burgers."

"Gotcha," the bartender replied with a worn Bahamian accent.

The man pulled two bottles of Corona from the cooler and cracked the tops. "Limes?" he questioned.

"Please," Grant replied. As the barman squeezed two wedges into the open mouths of the bottle, Grant asked, "I'm looking for one of your regulars. His neighbor said I might find him here. Tim Glaser?"

The bartender's eyes registered recognition, but he didn't respond for a second. Finally, he replied, "I haven't seen him in a week or so. Figured he was out on his boat. How do you know him?"

"He's an old family friend," Grant explained, opting for at least a partial truth. "I wanted to let him know my mother passed."

The man behind the counter let his eyes lift up slowly—almost sadly. "I'm sorry, man. Losing your mama is a tough business."

Grant nodded. "Yeah. Know anyone who might have an idea where's he's at? I haven't seen Tim since I was a kid, but I know he was tight with Mom."

The bartender's head bobbed almost in time with Mick's coda of "Paint it Black".

"Can't say I do," he acknowledged, passing the two beers to Grant.

Bright light gushed in as the door behind him opened. Grant turned around automatically and froze in place. The two men he and Charlie had run across at the Cheeca Lodge stared at him. Despite being clothed, Grant recognized the one who'd been wearing a Speedo, and his battered and swollen lips were another giveaway. The second man had several Band-Aids adhered to his neck from his second encounter with Wrench. His jacket sleeve no doubt covered his wounded arm.

In the corner, a low growl came from Wrench, who apparently recognized them too.

"Mr. Wolfe," the shorter, more rotund man, who had sported the Speedo, greeted him. "Where is Miss Greene?"

Grant stared at the two men, noticing the bigger man holding the Makarov pistol pointed in his direction. In his peripheral vision, he saw Angie tense up. Whatever was about to happen couldn't hurt her.

"She's gone back to England," Grant lied.

"That is untrue," the smaller Russian growled. "Perhaps, we can take your friend here until you bring us Miss Greene."

Grant cursed himself for not grabbing his gun from the house. Instead, he went after a damned bottle of pills.

Glancing right, he caught sight of the bartender hunkering down behind the bar. The man who'd been working on the lager had vanished.

The growl from Wrench grew louder.

"Keep that dog back or I'll shoot him," the man with the Makarov ordered.

"To hell with that," Grant said, hoping Angie understood him.

She released his leash, and Wrench launched toward them. The tattooed man jerked his gun toward the dog, and Grant rushed forward.

He hurled one of the full bottles of Corona at the smaller man as he closed the distance, switching his attention to the gunman. The former deputy slammed into the big Russian, and the Makarov fired, echoing in the small confines of the concrete structure.

Grant and the tattooed man struck the metal door with a clang. Grant had dropped the other beer in the skirmish, and now he grabbed the man's wrist, forcing it against the wall.

He heard Wrench howl in pain, but he couldn't focus on the dog now. The Russian struggled with him to pull his gun hand free, and Grant fought back.

"You fucking dog!" the other Russian shouted.

Angie screamed as Wrench let out another yip of pain.

Grant twisted around, dragging the big Russian with him. He hooked his left leg around the Russian's right calf so that the two men tumbled to the floor with Grant on top. His head came back before slamming into the man's face. The crunch of cartilage seemed to echo to Grant, and the Russian, now dazed, went limp long enough for Grant to knock the Makarov free.

He looked up to see another man dragging the smaller Russian away from Angie. Wrench's jaw was clamped down on the Russian's thigh, and the dog was swinging his head from side to side, trying to rip the flesh from the man's bones.

Raising up, Grant punched the bigger Russian in the face again. The blow sent the back of his opponent's head into the tile floor with a thud. He stopped moving.

Grant scampered after the gun. He came up with the Makarov leveled at the smaller Russian.

"Wrench, come!" he ordered.

The dog released the man's bloodied leg, and the stranger

tossed the Russian to the ground. Surprised, Grant recognized the third man as the one who'd been in the corner when they'd arrived.

Grant gave the man an appreciative nod as he grabbed Speedo by the hair, dragging him away from the stranger.

"On the floor," he ordered, pointing the barrel of the Makarov at the two Russians who didn't seem to be going anywhere. Blood soaked through the pants of Speedo where Wrench had ripped into his leg.

Sunlight suddenly streamed in as the door opened again. Grant turned around to see the man who'd just helped him disappear. He turned back to see the bartender rising up behind the bar. The Bahamian waved a cell phone at Grant, saying, "I called the cops."

18

It had taken Charlie forty minutes to walk the two and a half miles from Denny's to Grant's house. She'd spent another thirty minutes carefully approaching and watching the place for signs of the Russians. Alone, unarmed, and without Wrench, she felt more vulnerable and less cavalier than earlier in the day. The sun was losing intensity as it arced toward the horizon, but she was still sweating from the humidity as she crouched behind a neighbor's shrub, deciding no one appeared to be a threat.

As she began to rise, her cell phone rang in her pocket, and she quickly dropped back down to the dirt. Looking at the screen, she saw it was Grant.

"What?" she hissed.

"Got a picture of your dad you can send me," Grant asked in a hushed tone. "Our dad… I guess," he added.

"What for?" Charlie rebutted.

She'd calmed down at her brother before leaving Denny's, but the hot walk and concern over the thugs at the house had put her on edge again.

Grant sighed. "Charlie, text me a picture."

She didn't respond but searched through the photographs on

her phone until she found one that she'd taken of her dad eating an ice cream cone a few months back when they'd gone for a walk back home. Charlie stared at the shot for a few moments, looking into the blue eyes that sparkled back at her as she warmly remembered the day. A day before her world turned upside down.

How could a man so comforting and familiar to her, now seem like a stranger wrapped up in lies and deceit?

Texting the picture to Grant, she waited for his response.

"That's him!" she heard him say to someone else.

"What's going on?" Charlie demanded. "You saw my dad? Grant?"

"Hey," he said, coming back on the line. "You won't believe this. I'm in Marathon trying to find Uncle Tim, and went to his local bar where we were told he hangs out…"

"We?" Charlie interrupted. "Who's we? And who's Uncle Tim?"

"Angie brought me down here," he explained. "Tim Glaser was the witness at our parents' marriage. I knew him as a kid. Listen, we go to the bar and Tim's not there, but guess who showed up?"

"My dad, apparently."

"Yeah, but not at first," Grant responded, getting a little flustered. "Well, actually, he was there first, but I didn't recognize him. No, the damn Russians came in, wanting to know where you were."

"Did you tell them you'd ditched me in Key Largo?" Charlie retorted.

"I didn't ditch you. You threw a fit and made me drop you off!"

"Stop bickering you two, and get to the point, Grant," Angie said, loud enough for Charlie to hear over the phone.

Charlie bit her tongue and waited for Grant to continue.

"I told them you'd gone home, but they didn't believe me. Wrench took on one of them and I got the other guy, but it was fifty-fifty how it would have ended up, until out of nowhere, this guy helped us out. Before I could thank the dude, he left. But Charlie, I'm telling you, it was your dad… our dad… whatever. It was the guy in the picture you sent."

"And you let him go?" Charlie asked bluntly.

"No! I just told you. He bailed as soon as I got the gun on the two Russians."

"I'm coming down," Charlie announced.

"How? An Uber will cost you a fortune," Grant pointed out. "It's over an hour's drive."

"What will cost me a bloody fortune is replacing the keys to Dad's hire car!"

Charlie heard a groan over the phone.

"Where's the keys to your piece of shit?" she continued.

There were a few moments of silence on the line. "In the house, I guess. I probably left them on the kitchen counter. But you can't go to the house, they could still be watching the place."

"They're not. I'm here now," Charlie informed him. "Text me the address where to meet you. We've got to find Dad."

"I suppose…" Grant began, but Charlie ended the call and was already jogging for the stairs leading up to the house.

She slowed at the bottom step, looking up at the front door still slightly ajar. They could be inside, waiting, but she hadn't seen any suspicious cars nearby and it sounded like the Russians had moved on to Marathon. Charlie ran up the stairs and charged through the broken door, hoping surprise might buy her enough time to turn tail and bolt if it was a trap.

The house was silent beyond the air in the ducting trying to cool Florida through the open front door and slider to the deck. She walked over and closed the glass door, then looked for the car keys. They weren't on the counter, but after a short search, she found them on the floor, presumably knocked aside by a scrambling Russian. She noticed drops of blood on the tile.

Pulling the splintered front door closed behind her, Charlie scampered down the steps and swore as she opened the passenger side of the Honda. She ran around to the left side and slid into the seat which was way too far back for her. Adjusting the position, her left foot hunted for the clutch pedal in the footwell. Remembering the car was an automatic, she started the engine, found reverse, and backed out onto the road.

Coolish air belted from the vents as she pulled away, slowly reducing the sauna-like temperature inside the car. At the stop sign for Caribbean Drive, she checked both ways before crossing over to where Atlantic Boulevard became a divided road. Something didn't feel right to Charlie, as she swept by the palm trees in the center divide, but sitting on the wrong side of the car was making everything seem out of whack. When she'd driven down from Miami, every road she'd been on had been divided and she'd gone along with traffic, but now, alone on the street, everything felt awkward. Especially the car coming straight toward her.

"Bloody idiot!" Charlie screamed, knowing her surprise and annoyance was directed at herself.

Turning hard right, she drove the Honda over the curb with a hard thud, aimed between two of the trees, and bounced down onto the correct lane with another crashing sound from beneath the car. The honking horn of the other car faded into the distance as Charlie straightened the Del Sol out, before continuing in the right-hand lane.

Over her own heavy breathing, she noticed the exhaust note had gotten a little louder and prayed the whole system wouldn't fall off the ancient car. At the traffic light, she followed a van in front of her as it turned south on Overseas Highway, relieved she was done with intersection choices for a while.

Charlie let out a long sigh, enjoying the air-conditioning drying the perspiration beading on her face, until it shut itself off at cruising speed.

"Bugger!" she cursed, and wound the windows down, stretching across the passenger side to move the handle in quarter-turn shoves with her fingertips.

Traffic was busy, but most was heading north, and she was able to make decent time. Gaining confidence in her lane of travel, she passed a few slow-moving tourists until the road returned to single lane each direction in Islamorada. From there, a lifted full-size pickup truck with fancy LED lights and huge wheels and tires which made such a racket on the roadway she could hear them inside the Honda, followed a few feet off her bumper. At first, she was worried it was the Russians picking up her tail again, but in the rearview she caught a glimpse of the driver who was wearing a white tank top and sporting a long beard and a shabby-looking ball cap. The confederate flag stitched on the front of the cap confirmed she was either dealing with the best disguised Russian of all time, or a local.

Shutting the tailgating idiot out of her mind, Charlie's thoughts went back to her father. There was no denying he was involved with the Russians in some way, but *how* remained a complete mystery. Grant had mentioned the thugs had asked after her, so it appeared she'd been their target all along, ever since they showed up at the funeral home. *But why?* And why was her dad sneaking around and hiding from her? None of it made sense.

Her phone dinged and she checked the message. It was Grant, sending an address in Marathon. Charlie plugged it into her maps app and saw she still had thirty-one miles to go. The sun was beginning to set over the horizon ahead with the sky turning rich shades of orange and yellow. She fiddled with the stalk on the steering column, hunting for the headlights. The windshield wipers came on instead, smearing the squished bugs and road grime across the glass, making it impossible to see anything until two red lights burned brightly in front.

Charlie slammed on the brakes and stopped just short of the car she'd been following. She fumbled for the washer spray switch to clean the mess off the window, and fortunately, she still had her foot on the brake. The car in front had just pulled away, when the Honda lurched forward with a mighty crunch from behind. Charlie's head was violently jarred, her body caught by the seatbelt, and once she could look up, the rearview was full of the custom grille of the pickup truck. The chrome badge of a naked woman holding an AK-47 in her hands hung limply from the wrinkled black grille, and as Charlie eased off the brake and rolled forward, pieces of LED light bar rained down on the road in shards.

The Del Sol seemed to have escaped with nothing more than cosmetic damage which she'd worry about later, so while the driver stepped from his truck, screaming at the departing Honda, Charlie flipped him the bird out of the driver's window and kept going. She was proud she'd remembered to use the single digit, and that she'd found the washer switch to clean the window. Checking in the mirror, in the dimming light she even saw a red glow when she tapped the brake pedal, indicating the Del Sol's rear lights had survived the incident.

Forty minutes later, Charlie pulled into the parking lot of the Wooden Spoon restaurant, whose sign advertised they served breakfast and lunch. A sleek-looking red car was the only vehicle in the lot, so she parked alongside and saw Grant and Angie inside. They all stepped out, and Grant walked to the back of the Del Sol.

"What have you done to my car? The trunk's all dented!"

Wrench nearly bowled Charlie over in his excitement and she bent down to scratch his ears.

"What have you done to the dog? He's limping!" Charlie fired back.

Grant crouched down and looked underneath the car. "You've damn near knocked the muffler off as well!"

"Hi, Charlie," Angie, said pleasantly. "Wrench came off better than the guy's thigh he had hold of. I don't think anything's broken."

Charlie nodded. "You okay, you crazy mutt?" she asked the dog, who furiously wagged his tail in return. "Okay. Let's find my dad," she said, standing up straight and looking at Grant who picked himself up from the ground.

"We don't know where he went," Grant pointed out. "The police showed up before we could question the Russians, then they hauled them away. We watched from across the road, but all we heard was one of them telling the cops to call someone named Dragon. The guy kept saying it over and over."

"Did he give them a number to call?" Charlie asked.

Grant shook his head. "Not that we could hear. I think he was trying to get them to call from his phone."

"Bollocks," Charlie muttered. "So, what now?"

"I think we should go back to Tim's place and have a look around," Grant replied. "He wasn't home, and it seems like no one has seen him in a few weeks. His neighbor and the bartender said he's usually out fishing, but his boat's in his front yard."

"He must be a part of this if we tracked him down, the Russians were looking for him, and my dad was there too," Charlie thought aloud.

"The Russians could have been following us," Grant responded. "But your dad... our dad... was certainly already there, so he was either expecting us or hoping to find old Uncle Tim."

"Okay, let's go then," Charlie said, ready to get back in the car.

"We'll go on foot," Grant said. "Leave the cars here. It's only two streets over and we can approach from his backyard."

Charlie wound the windows up on the Del Sol and locked the doors before tossing the keys to Grant. "Lead the way."

Grant caught the keys and paused a moment. "Angie, why don't you stay here in your car? You're already more involved than I wanted you to be. Who knows who'll we'll run into next?"

"Wouldn't I be safer with you than sitting here alone?"

"Wrench can stay with you," Charlie offered. "He still has a little limp, and he doesn't really understand a stealthy approach."

"Perfect," Grant agreed, and before Angie could argue, he opened the back door of the Tesla and let the dog jump in.

Angie shook her head. "Fine. But be careful. Both of you."

Grant led them down Sixty-ninth Street toward the ocean. After passing a water storage tank on their right, the street was lined with a mixture of older single-level homes and modest places raised on concrete stilts as required for newer builds. Most had tidy front yards with hardy grass and fences marking the lot lines. A few had boats on trailers in the driveways. They all looked like full-time resident homes instead of rentals or snowbirds' winter escapes.

At the end of the cul-de-sac, thick shrubs and low trees separated them from the water and they moved to their right across the edge of someone's property. Porch lights had guided their way down the street, but now they moved carefully in the dark across a mixture of crushed coral and rough, dusty limestone, trying not to trip over scattered branches and rocks. On the corner of Sixty-eighth Street, a waist-high chain-link fence marked the boundary to an empty lot, and Grant led them along the back of the fence line.

"Tim's is the next one," he whispered.

When the fence ended and an overgrown backyard began, Charlie assumed they'd arrived. "I can't see bugger all," she whispered.

Grant unlocked his cell phone and used the meager light from the home screen to pick their way through the tall weeds and occasional pieces of unidentified junk. As they reached the small single-story building, Charlie noticed the back door was closed but the wood around the lock was broken and splintered.

"Grant," she hissed, and pointed to the mess.

While he moved to a window on their right, Charlie assumed there was no one in the house and tried the door. It easily swung open with an ominous creak. Taking her own cell phone from her pocket, she turned on the flashlight function, shone it inside and scanned the dated kitchen cabinetry and appliances. Ignoring Grant's hushed calls from behind her, she continued inside the little house and swung the beam to her right, where a small, round dining table had three chairs set in place around it. The fourth was turned to face the living room.

Bound to the chair was the blood-soaked figure of a man, his chin slumped to his chest.

"Uncle Tim," she heard Grant groan behind her.

19

"Dammit!" Grant cursed.

"Bugger!" Charlie seemed to agree. "Did those Russians beat us to Tim?"

Grant shook his head, sniffing through his nose. "Yes, but no. You can tell by the smell. He's been dead awhile. This didn't happen today."

Charlie curled her mouth in disgust.

"Haven't you dealt with dead bodies before?" Grant asked. "I thought you were a cop."

"First, we don't go around murdering everyone. Homicides aren't nearly as common as in the States."

"Really." Grant questioned. "Based on every BBC show I've seen they murder people in every small town on the island."

"That's television, you dolt." She turned around in the small kitchen. "We need to get out of here."

Grant shook his head. "We can't," he confessed. "The neighbor met me. When the police do find Tim, the first thing she'll do is give out a description of me."

"You want to report it?"

"I think I have to," he said. "But let's take a look around first."

Charlie walked toward the den.

"Watch out for fingerprints," Grant warned.

"You don't think I know that?" Charlie retorted.

"Just reminding you."

"I'm not an idiot," she mumbled in return.

Grant knelt down in front of the body. Tim Glaser's shirt was ripped open. His bare feet turned outward, and the skin around the ankles and feet were a mix of purple and blue. *Livor mortis*, the pooling of blood in the lower extremities of the body after death, had set in. A coroner would pinpoint the time of death more closely, but Grant knew it was at least twelve hours ago. More likely a few days, given the state of the body.

Draped across the floor was an orange, heavy-duty extension cord. The end was cut, and the red and black rubber coatings had been stripped back about three inches. A metal saucepan lay overturned on the floor. Grant leaned in closer, holding his breath to avoid the stench of decay. Small, narrow burns covered the dead man's chest. He stood up, grateful to be away from the rotting smell.

"Find anything?" Grant asked.

"Uncle Tim seemed to be a confirmed bachelor. He's got nothing here." She nudged a stack of fishing magazines on a table. Most barely looked read.

"What did you know about him?" Charlie asked.

"Nothing," Grant replied. "I haven't seen him in almost twenty years."

"This place is sterile," she added.

Grant pulled the refrigerator open, using his shirt so he didn't leave prints. Three cans of Sprite and one short of a six-pack container of Michelob Ultra. There were some old take-out containers and a pack of hot dogs.

"He wasn't much of a gourmand, either."

"You mentioned a dragon," Charlie said. "What do you think that's all about?

"I'm not sure. They were spitting out words in English and

Russian. Whatever it was, they were intent on getting hold of Dragon. Whoever that is."

"Are you sure it's a someone, not a something?" Charlie asked.

"That's the impression I got," Grant replied without confidence.

"Could be like a code name," Charlie remarked, then switched subjects. "I called my mate, Froggy, and he did a search on the names Diana Turner and Daniel Edwards. He said it looked like they'd been erased. No files at all anymore, just some sort of ghost trace where he could see there had once been documentation. Right after he looked it up, it sounded like the powers-that-be swooped in on him and took him away. I think I may have got him in big trouble."

"Shit. A lot of people are getting hurt around this… whatever this is we're in the middle of," Grant said, staring at the corpse in the chair. "Come look at this," he added, calling her over.

Charlie moved next to him, following his index finger pointed to the array of burn marks on Tim's torso.

"Whoever did this to him took their time," Grant suggested. "And they were good at what they were doing. It's tricky to rig up an electric wire like this. Give it too much juice, and the heart can give out. Not enough, and it's nothing more than an annoyance."

"You know a lot about torture," Charlie commented.

"I've seen some scary things on the force," he admitted quietly.

Charlie examined the burn marks. "Did they stick his feet in the pot of water?" she asked, pointing over at the upturned pan.

"Probably," Grant acknowledged.

Charlie raised up straight. Her tone softened somewhat. "I'm sorry about your uncle," she offered.

"I didn't know him," he assured her. "Now, I'm guessing he was involved with our parents."

"Maybe their handler," she suggested.

Grant shook his head. His mother wasn't a spy. The possibility of that being true was zero. She was a hairdresser who liked to fish and ride her bike. Not once did she ever do anything overly adventuresome. As best as Grant recalled, the most dangerous thing she'd ever done was kayak out through John Pennekamp State Park with her life vest unbuckled. She didn't take chances. She certainly didn't spy on people.

"I know what you're thinking," Charlie told him.

He lifted his eyes to her. The pain in his leg ached slightly, and he thought about the pills floating in the ocean. And the ones he could get from the pharmacy to replace them.

No, Angie was right, he thought. They were holding him too tightly. He needed to stop using them. Stop relying on them to get through the day.

Charlie continued, "It's the same thing I'm thinking. How is my dad a spy?"

Grant nodded. "We don't have much time," he said, pulling them back into the present. "Let's check the rest of the house before I call the cops."

The two moved toward the other bedrooms. Tim Glaser's house was a small two-bedroom bungalow. Each took a separate room.

"Looks like he used this one as an office," Charlie called from her room. "I think he had a computer in here."

"Had?" Grant questioned.

"There's a printer, speakers, and wireless mouse. But no computer."

"Maybe whoever killed him took it," Grant suggested.

"No shit," Charlie quipped.

Grant's phone rang, erupting like an alarm in the still house. He saw Angie's name on the screen.

"You got cops coming," she warned before he could answer.

"Crap!" he mumbled. Then, in a loud voice, he called to Charlie, "Police are coming."

"You called them?" she asked, incredulously.

"Not yet, but maybe a neighbor did," he said. "Come on."

As he made his way to the front room, Grant called the non-emergency number of the Monroe County Sheriff's Department.

"Monroe Sheriff," a female voice answered.

"I'd like to report a murder," Grant replied into the phone.

The voice on the other end seemed to come to attention as Grant gave her the address.

"Why are you doing that now?" Charlie asked.

The back door that the two had come through swung open as two deputies stepped through the door.

"Hands up!" one of them shouted.

Grant lifted his arms still holding the phone. "You guys are fast," he informed the officer. "I just called about this."

Ignoring him, the deputy demanded, "Turn around."

The two complied.

"Son of a bitch," the second deputy cursed.

"We just found him," Grant said. "I used to be a deputy. My name's Grant Wolfe."

"Get on your knees," the first officer ordered.

"Do what he says," Grant told his sister as he crouched down. "I'm on the phone with your department."

A hand grabbed the phone from him.

"Hello," the deputy said. "Who am I talking to?"

A pause.

"Deputy Mason Cruz," the man replied.

Another pause.

"Yes, ma'am. Thank you."

He'd obviously hung up. The second deputy called the dispatcher to report the murder.

"I'm going to cuff you," Cruz explained.

"Are you arresting us?" Charlie demanded.

"I need to assess the situation," he explained.

"It's okay, Deputy," Grant acknowledged. "Cuff us."

"We didn't do anything wrong," Charlie argued.

"Ma'am—"

"Don't 'Ma'am' me!"

"Charlie, calm down," Grant said. "They need to be certain we aren't a threat."

She grunted something as the metal cuffs snapped around Grant's wrists.

"Whoever killed your Uncle Tim is getting away," Charlie snapped.

"Is this your uncle?" Cruz asked Grant.

"He was an old family friend," Grant explained. "I hadn't seen him in years."

"What are you doing in his house?" he asked.

The click of metal indicated the deputy had restrained Charlie too.

"We came down to tell him about my mother's death."

"Mason, this guy's been dead awhile," the second deputy remarked.

"Smells like it," Cruz agreed.

"Tell me who you are again?" Cruz asked.

"I'm Grant Wolfe. This is my—my sister."

Charlie added, "Charlotte Greene."

Cruz stared at the two. "You don't sound related."

"We grew up in different places," Grant explained.

"I think they figured out that much," Charlie quipped.

"Deputy Cruz, the man in the chair is Tim Glaser. He was a close friend of my mother's, and when he didn't show up at the funeral the other day, I wondered if anyone had informed him. It didn't occur to me, of course. I wasn't even thinking of him."

Cruz nodded, glancing between Charlie and Grant.

Charlie said, "We found the door open and Uncle Tim right there."

"We got a call that people were prowling around the house."

"The neighbor I met earlier today, I expect," Grant remarked. "When there was no answer at the front, we came around back and found it open."

In the distance, Grant heard sirens growing closer. Even when he was in the department, he never understood the need to blast the sirens once it was ruled there was no emergency. Tim had no chance of revival, and the situation on scene remained contained. Still, there was a perceived importance in running lights and sirens.

"He used to be up north in Key Largo," the second deputy announced to Cruz. "Got a guy named Hernandez on the line."

"Isn't that the wanker?" Charlie asked under her breath.

"Shit," Grant whispered.

"He said to watch them. Apparently, they shot up a cemetery a couple of days ago."

"Is that true, Wolfe?" Cruz asked.

"No, it isn't. Hernandez is a dick."

Cruz turned to Charlie. "What about you?" he asked.

"I barely met the man, but I think Hernandez is probably a knob, yeah."

"Funny," Cruz said dryly.

"Deputy Cruz, it's obvious we didn't kill him. He's been dead for days." Grant turned to stare up at the officer.

"How is that obvious?" Cruz asked. "You might have been returning to the scene of the crime."

"Bloody hell," Charlie cursed. "I was still in London."

"Mason, just take them back to the station. The detectives can deal with them," the partner said.

"You can't arrest us," Charlie insisted.

"We can hold you for questioning," Cruz replied.

"Can they?" Charlie asked Grant.

"Technically, yes."

"Bloody hell."

Two more officers entered the back door. Grant listened to the exchange between the four deputies as they ensured the scene was secure. After about five minutes, Cruz addressed the pair.

"We're going to take you to the station as we process the scene," he informed them.

"Can't we get a solicitor?" Charlie asked.

"A what?" Cruz asked.

Grant glanced over and scowled at her.

"A solicitor," she repeated, scowling back at her brother. "You know, legal defense."

"A lawyer?" Cruz suggested.

"Yeah," Charlie confirmed.

The officer chuckled. "Listening to you is like watching Harry Potter with the kids."

"Glad I can entertain you," Charlie retorted.

Grant shook his head and sighed. She'd said the magic word, and he'd hoped to hold off on that until they gleaned some information from the deputies. Now, the cops would be wary of stepping over the rights of the two.

"Come on," Cruz ordered, escorting them back outside into the peaceful darkness shattered by flashing red and blue lights. Every house seemed to have people gathered outside, watching the show on their sleepy little street. He put them in the back of the second Monroe County Sheriff's car.

After the door closed, the two were alone for the first time since the cops had burst in.

"They can't hold us long," Grant informed her. "But they might have some information we need."

"How do you plan to get it?" she asked.

"I'll ask. It won't take them long to tie the murder to the two guys in the bar."

A minute later, the two deputies who arrived second came out, then drove north toward the station.

"Is Harper still running the desk in Marathon?" Grant asked.

The deputy in the passenger seat glanced back. "Yeah."

Grant nodded back a "thank you."

"You know him?" Charlie asked under her breath.

"Even better," Grant replied. "He owes me."

The police cruiser pulled into the lot of the Monroe County Sheriff's Substation. The long single-story yellow building housed the deputies and administration for the Marathon area. Since the sheriff's department covered all the Florida Keys, they had a few substations set up throughout. They didn't hold suspects or prisoners here for more than a few hours. If the small holding cell didn't accommodate a suspect, they would be transferred to a detention facility nearby.

The two deputies marched the pair in toward the holding cell.

"Wolfe?" a voice demanded curiously.

"Harper!" Grant called out to an older African American plain-clothes officer behind a desk. The man sported a closely trimmed gray beard that matched what little hair he still had on his head as well as his bushy eyebrows. "I heard they were pulling you in here."

"It's a bad case of being there first."

"Watkins," Harper ordered one of the deputies. "Put them over in interrogation one."

The deputy who'd been driving pointed Grant and Charlie into a side room.

Harper Sexton followed them in. "I just got the call. I'm heading over to the crime scene in a minute. My partner is already there."

"Who do they have you with?" Grant asked.

"Guy named Collins. He moved down from up near Atlanta. Wanted to be a Conch. But he's a smart kid."

"I didn't do this, Harper," Grant told the man.

"Wouldn't assume you did," Harper acknowledged. "Just gotta go by the book, you know?"

Grant nodded.

"Who is this?" Harper asked, nodding toward Charlie.

"She's my sister," Grant told him.

"I didn't know you had a sister," Harper stated.

"Neither did he," Charlie interjected.

"And you're British," Harper observed. "Let's get you guys uncuffed at least. Tell me what's going on, Wolfe."

Grant repeated the story about reaching out to Tim to tell him about Fiona's death.

"Oh, I'm sorry about your mom," Harper offered.

"I think you might have arrested two men earlier who probably know about Tim's death."

"Who's that?" Harper asked.

"Couple of Russians at a place called The Billy Club."

"That was you too?" Harper questioned. "What in the hell are you into, boy?"

Grant glanced at Charlie, wondering what they were willing to share just yet.

"Harper, we don't know."

"Well one of those Ruskies is in the hospital with a bad dog bite. Tore up his thigh. Damn near bled to death. Ain't neither one of them talking though. Except to say call the Russian Embassy."

"The embassy?" Charlie asked.

"The call we got from the State Department said let them go. Some Russian diplomat called Washington demanding they be released."

"What the hell?" Grant spouted.

"What's the diplomat's name?" Charlie asked.

"Shit," Harper cursed. "Hell, if I can remember. Dragon. Or Drag-ann something or other. Russian."

"Dragon?" Grant questioned.

"Yeah, does that mean something to you?" Harper asked.

Grant shook his head slowly. "Did you release them?"

"Like I said, one's not walking anywhere yet. The other will go free when we do the paperwork."

Harper cracked a broad grin. "That might take until morning. You know, we just got another murder."

20

Charlie rubbed her wrists where the handcuffs had chafed her skin. It had been a quiet night so far, so she and Grant had been placed in the same holding cell on their own. Harper hadn't taken Grant up on his offer to share the same cell with the Russian they were still holding. He'd been friendly and accommodating, within reason, but he wasn't foolish enough to put them all together.

She looked over at Grant sitting on the opposite bench. He had a hand on his bad leg, kneading the muscle.

"Does it hurt all the time?" she asked.

He looked up, and quickly moved his hand as though he'd been caught doing something he shouldn't. He shrugged his shoulders.

"Aches, mostly. Sometimes I get a shooting nerve pain down my leg, but usually it's just a constant, nagging sort of thing."

"They can't fix it?" she asked. "Relieve the pressure on the nerve or whatever it is?"

Grant relaxed and went back to massaging his thigh. "Bullet made a pretty good mess in there, so I don't think they know which part is causing which problem. Besides, insurance starts arguing over whether it's necessary, or whether it's elective, meaning they decide I don't need it."

"Wait a second," Charlie blurted. "Some twat behind a desk at an insurance company gets to decide whether you're allowed to have a surgery to stop the pain in your leg? Shouldn't your doctor decide that?"

"You'd think so, huh?" Grant scoffed.

"I'd go stick something through Mr. Insurance Man's leg and then see what he has to say about elective procedures."

Grant laughed. "I believe that's exactly what you'd probably do."

Charlie started to scowl, but realized he was just pulling her leg, however close to the truth it might be. His left cheek had that cute dimple again. She chuckled too. "You know what I've been thinking?"

"What have you been thinking?" he replied, leaning back against the wall.

"I've been thinking we're being way too reactive."

He looked thoughtful for a moment before responding. "We haven't had much to go on except reacting to what's happened to us."

"Perhaps, but I think it's time we took more control over our own fate."

Grant nodded slowly, then looked around the cell with a smirk. "You're right, we're in the perfect position of power to take the bull by the horns."

Charlie rolled her eyes. "You said we'd be out of here tonight, right?"

"I believe so."

"So, let's inventory what we know, and decide what our next steps should be," she declared firmly. "We're both trained in law enforcement. We're supposed to be able to take the facts and evidence then turn them into logical paths of investigation."

"Fair enough," Grant replied. "Now we need a whiteboard to write everything out like in the TV shows."

He followed his words with a grin, so she knew he was kidding.

"The people we now believe to be both our parents were once

married under different names," Charlie began. "We suspect your mother's... I mean our mother's accident was, in fact, murder. Dad flew over from the UK to attend her funeral, or at least to witness it, and we've spotted him at the funeral home and down here in Marathon."

"There's evidence to suggest they worked for or with a government agency at some point in time," Grant said, "and Tim Glaser knew them before they changed their names. Maybe he kept in contact with both of them after that."

"Russians, who appear to be protected by their own government, are pursuing me," Charlie continued. "To what end we don't know yet."

"There's a connection to something, or someone, code-named Dragon or a similar sounding word, who the heavies we've encountered seem to work for," Grant added. "We suspect these men tortured poor Tim for information, but we have no way of knowing whether he gave them anything or not."

They both sat quietly for a few moments.

"Our inventory doesn't take up much room, does it?" Charlie said.

"We wouldn't need a very large whiteboard, that's for sure."

"It does seem like Dad's only a step or two ahead of us, doesn't it?" Charlie suggested. "I mean, we don't know whether he'd already found your Uncle Tim's body or not, but he was waiting at the bar for somebody."

"I presumed it was Tim, but you're right," Grant agreed. "Maybe he was waiting for the Russians to show up."

"Or you."

"He couldn't know I was going to be there," Grant retorted.

"Unless he figured we'd find the connection to Uncle Tim?" Charlie thought aloud. "He may have been expecting me to be with you."

"I feel like he's had plenty of opportunity to contact us since the funeral," Grant replied. "And why did he take off after helping me at the bar? No, he's trying to stay under the radar for whatever reason."

"Trying to protect us?" Charlie said.

In truth, she hoped that was the case. It was devastating to think her dad was running around the Florida Keys deliberately avoiding his daughter who was being chased by Russians hell-bent on kidnapping her.

"That would go on the board as a theory rather than fact, but it fits in my mind," Grant replied. "He may be trying to take care of all this, but I wish he'd clue us in."

"No shit." Charlie took a deep breath to keep her mind in logical, police mode. "With our rather thin list of things we know, what do we do next?"

"We're lacking motive, and we still don't know who's behind all this," Grant replied. "So, I suggest we try to answer those two questions."

"On our theory list, I'd throw out the possibility that the Russians are ultimately after our dad," Charlie said. "If our parents were agents of some sort and the Russians killed Mum, it fits that they're after Dad as well."

"Which is why they want you?"

Charlie nodded. "Yeah. Use me to get to Dad."

"Okay," Grant said, standing up and pacing around the cell. "That gives us a possible motive, so what we need next, is either to find him, whether he wants to be found or not, and ask him what's going on. Or interrogate one of these Russian sons-of-bitches and find out who they're working for and what their orders are."

"We know where Tattoo and Speedo are," Charlie replied.

"Maksim Prutsev. Wasn't that the name Rat came up with for Tattoo?"

"I think so. And he's next door somewhere."

"Not getting out until morning," Grant added.

"I like the idea of our target being already incapacitated," Charlie said with a grin.

Grant nodded. "If they let us out tonight, we go to the hospital. If they keep us overnight, we'll see if we can follow Prutsev."

Charlie liked that plan. It finally felt like they weren't scurrying for their lives like rats in a barn with a pack of terriers set loose. She also liked the way the two of them had worked through the process together.

"We can't split up again," she said, looking up at her brother who now leaned a shoulder against the wall. "But no more pills."

Grant sighed. "You threw them away, remember?"

"Then no getting any more," she replied flatly. "I need you clearheaded and to know you're watching out for me, not a bottle of pills."

He looked away and she waited. Finally, his gaze came back her way. "I get it. No more pills. But I need something from you, too."

Charlie's brow creased, and as quickly as she wondered what he was going to say, she knew the answer.

"I'll try my very best not to get overly wound up," she said.

"Then we have a deal, and we have a plan," Grant confirmed, and gave her another dimpled smile.

They didn't have too long to wait. A little after 10:00 p.m., a deputy unlocked the holding cell and led them to the reception area where their possessions were returned.

"Harper sends his regards and asked you stay outta trouble for a while," the officer behind the desk told them. "Have a nice night."

Walking outside, Charlie brought up a map on her phone and checked the distance to the Wooden Spoon where she'd parked Grant's Honda. It was two miles away. Grant was listening to a voicemail on his phone. Once he was done, he powered his down.

"Shut that off," he said.

"You think we're being tracked?" Charlie asked.

The thought hadn't crossed her mind before, but it made sense.

The Russians had a habit of showing up after they arrived places. She took another look at the map, searching for the hospital.

"Bloody hell. The hospital's right there," she said, pointing to a building less than a block away.

"Angie found a hotel room; she's given me the address. Let's see if Speedo wants to chat with us, then we'll go get the car. Maybe we can still get a few hours' sleep before this night's over with."

Charlie powered down her phone as they walked along the sidewalk toward the hospital. The mention of hotel room and sleep made her realize she was completely worn out.

"A coffee wouldn't go amiss," she mumbled to herself as Grant walked to the left side of the buildings instead of entering through the front doors.

The hospital wasn't big. A single level, with the emergency room entrance to the left of the main building. They continued around the side and looked up to see two nurses standing fifty feet away, outside a door, smoking. Grant stepped behind several palm trees at the edge of the property and Charlie followed. They stood in the shadows where they could see the nurses chatting.

"You'd think they'd know better," Charlie whispered.

"Yeah, but lucky for us," Grant replied, carefully picking his way closer along the fence line, staying behind the cover of tall shrubs.

When the two women were finished, they stubbed out their cigarette butts and dropped them in a tall, metal receptacle next to the entrance. One of them swiped her ID card and pulled the hefty door open, the second woman holding it as they went inside. Grant leapt through the shrubs and lunged for the door, shoving a toe in the jamb, stopping it from closing. He eased it open a few more inches and checked inside. As soon as he opened it wider, Charlie slipped through into a short hallway with storage rooms to each side. The door ahead of them leading deeper into the building clicked closed behind the nurses as they headed back to work.

"Where do you think they've got him?" Charlie asked quietly.

"I'll show you if you'll stop barging ahead," Grant retorted and stepped past her to the inner door.

"You've been here before?"

"Unfortunately, I have," Grant whispered, cracking the door open. "You check rooms on the left, I'll check right."

She followed into a brightly lit hallway and quickly trotted to the first room on the left. The bed was empty. Beeping monitors, muffled chatter, and laughter on a TV show accompanied them as they both moved from one room to the next.

"Here," Grant hissed, and ushered Charlie into a room where Speedo lay asleep, hooked up to an IV and a heart rate monitor.

A tall curtain was drawn back revealing a second bed in the semi-private room, which Charlie was glad to see was unoccupied. She pulled the door closed behind her and they moved to the bed, Grant taking the far side by the IV bag hanging from a stand. The Russian's right wrist was handcuffed to the bed frame.

"Hold his arm down," Charlie hissed, as she placed one hand over the man's mouth and dug her fingers into his wounded thigh with the other.

Speedo jolted awake and tried to scream, but Charlie had the sound muted enough that it was little more than an agonized groan. Grant caught the man's left hand as the terrified patient attempted to shove Charlie away.

"I told you to hold him," she growled as Grant managed to pin him down.

"Go easy, Charlie," he urged. "You promised you wouldn't go postal again."

"Go what? Just hold him still," she said and turned her attention back to the Russian. "I'm going to take my hand away. You yell or scream, and I'll choke the shit out of you. Understand?"

The man's eyes were wide and flitted from Charlie to Grant and back again. He nodded the little he could with Charlie pushing against his face. She slid her hand from his mouth to his neck, ready to squeeze at any time. Her other hand hovered over his wounded thigh.

"Who do you work for?"

"Better you don't know," the Russian said in heavily accented English.

"Give me his name or I'll rip your leg apart far worse than the dog did."

Her hand dropped to his thigh, and he immediately flinched.

"Dragan!" he gushed. "Dragan Lazović."

"And who the hell's that when he's at home?" Charlie asked.

The Russian frowned. "I don't understand."

"Why is this Dragan bloke after me?" she growled.

"I can't," the Russian replied through gritted teeth. "He kill me."

Charlie gripped the man's throat then clenched his thigh with her other hand. He wheezed out a long-anguished moan, and his body thrashed in the bed.

"Charlie!" Grant seethed, trying his best to hold the man down.

She let go of his leg and waited a moment until the Russian's eyes met hers before releasing his throat.

He gasped and spluttered. "Not you. Your father."

"Why, damn it?" Charlie spat. "Why does he want my dad?"

The Russian shook his head. "Not for me to know. I do as he say, this is all. I swear this is truth."

Charlie looked up at Grant. "He knows more."

"I don't think he does, Charlie. What are you going to do? Torture him until he either tells you something or dies?"

"Like he did to your Uncle Tim?" Charlie retorted, her blood boiling as she recalled the sight of the poor man strapped to the chair.

"I not know Uncle Tim!" the Russian insisted. "Not me. I not torture anyone. I swear."

"You lying piece of shit," Charlie snarled. "Where do we find this Dragan bloke?"

The squeal of a cart wheeling along the tiled floor of the hallway caught their attention. Grant grabbed Charlie's arm.

"Quick, we need to hide."

Charlie stood firm as Grant tried to pull her away. She stuck a finger into the Russian's chest.

"Say a word about us, and I'll hurt you something awful before I kill you!"

The man's eyes widened again before Charlie allowed Grant to hustle her away behind the curtain which he drew across the room. The door opened and she heard the cart roll into the room. The patient immediately began babbling in Russian. A second voice responded. Also, in Russian. Grant grabbed Charlie's arm once more and they quickly eased out the second door to the hallway and dived inside the next room. An older man was sitting up in bed watching a television hung on the opposite wall.

"Who the hell..." he began, but Charlie put a finger to her lips.

"Keep it down, mate," she urged. "We got caught visiting after hours. You never saw us, all right?"

The man shrugged his shoulders. "Whatever."

Grant slid past the curtain to the other side and Charlie swiftly followed. A kid lay asleep in the second bed, his arm in a cast. Charlie peeked around the edge of the curtain as she heard the door they'd come through open. It was a nurse in uniform, but she didn't say a word, just looked around the room.

"Can I help you?" the old man asked.

"No," the nurse said in a strong accent, and backed out of the doorway.

A loud beep sounded from down the hallway and the sounds of urgent activity grew, footsteps clattering on the tiled floor. Charlie moved to the door on their side and cracked it open. Staff were running into the Russian's room. At first, she thought they'd been reported, and the nurses were looking for them. Then she realized what the drama was about.

"Crash cart! Now!" one of the nurses Charlie recognized from the smoke break yelled, before she dove back into Speedo's room.

"Bugger," Charlie hissed. "We need to leave!"

Waiting until the hallway was clear, they bolted across to the storage rooms door, then ran down the short hall and burst outside into the humid Florida night.

"What the fuck happened?" Grant gasped.

"I think the Russians just took care of a loose end!" Charlie replied, hopping through the shrubs to remain out of sight.

From the police station, not far down the road, sirens wailed.

21

"Get up!" Charlie seemed to shout as she prodded Grant.

"We just got in bed," he moaned.

"Three hours ago," she corrected. "Wrench, come on!"

The dog bounded off the floor onto Grant's bed. All fifty pounds of him sprawled on the man.

Angie sat on the edge of the bed laughing.

"This is a conspiracy," Grant grunted as he sat up.

"I got you some coffee," Angie told him, pointing to three cups with a local coffee roaster's logo on them.

Grant sat up, taking in the hotel room the four of them had shared for the night. Well, part of the night.

"We need to get to the sheriff's office before they release Prutsev," Charlie explained.

"I'm moving," he assured her, rolling to his feet as he pushed the dog off him.

He popped the top off the closest coffee. "Does it matter?" he asked aloud.

Angie shook her head seconds before he took a big swallow of the coffee.

"Ange, can you take Wrench back with you?" Grant asked after chugging half the cup.

She stared at him for a second. "You don't need me?" she asked.

"Yeah, I do, but not here. These bastards are dangerous. I need you to take care of Wrench."

She let out a sigh that could have been relief. "Be careful," she warned.

"I'm always careful," Grant promised.

The resulting glare earned a response from Charlie. "I'll watch his back."

"You better," Angie replied. She stepped up and kissed Grant. "If you don't come home, I'm dressing the dog up in holiday sweaters."

"Angie, it's Florida."

She shrugged with a grin. "C'mon, boy," she ordered Wrench who jumped off the bed. He paused in front of Charlie and nudged her hand.

"Oh, I'll miss you too," she relented, scratching behind his ear. "But don't tell Stanley."

"Who's Stanley?" Grant and Angie asked simultaneously.

"My cat," Charlie replied, grinning at the deflated look on both their faces.

When Angie and the dog were gone, Charlie said, "You got three minutes to do your business before we leave."

With that she marched out the door. Grant took a minute and a half before he found her leaning against the Honda.

By the time they reached the substation, it was almost seven in the morning. After years as a deputy, Grant knew the schedule. Harper could drag his feet releasing Prutsev, but only until shift change. It was a craft trick, and both shifts did it to the other. Once the shift supervisor clocked in, they'd finish processing Prutsev's paperwork. As if on a timer, Prutsev stepped out of the glass door and into the sunlight at twenty-two minutes after seven.

"Look," Charlie announced, pointing to the black Suburban Prutsev got into. "Do you see who's driving?"

"Is that the nurse from the hospital?" Grant guessed having not actually seen the woman himself.

"If she's a nurse, I'm Adele," Charlie pointed out.

"There's a security guard up north that still thinks you are," Grant chuckled while he waited until the SUV pulled out onto Overseas Highway, heading south. "They're not going back to Key Largo."

"Not yet, at least," Charlie agreed.

Grant pulled out four cars behind the SUV and settled into the busy traffic moving slowly out of Marathon. A few cars cut into the line between the Honda and the Suburban as the miles rolled by, but a couple turned off, keeping them a safe distance behind Prutsev and the nurse. After over an hour, they entered Key West, and Grant straightened up in his seat.

"What is it?" Charlie asked, stirring from the doldrums of riding along Highway 1.

"They turned off," Grant told her.

"About bloody time," Charlie complained. "I could do with a hover."

Grant turned right on the Palm Avenue Causeway and frowned at his sister. "What?"

"A hover," Charlie repeated. "You know, you don't actually sit on a petrol station loo, you hover over the seat to pee."

Grant opened his mouth to respond but couldn't decide what to say about English women's bathroom etiquette and closed his mouth. He checked the Suburban instead. There was only one car between them now.

"Don't let them see you," Charlie urged.

"This isn't my first tail," he told her.

The road bisected the Garrison Bight with piers filled with smaller fishing boats lining either side of the jetty. On the right, they passed the entrance to the Trumbo Point entrance for the naval base.

Charlie stared out the window, watching Key West pass by her. "Where are they going?" she questioned.

Grant shook his head. Three minutes and two turns later, the Suburban pulled into a parking lot.

"They'll see you if you pull in," she warned.

"I know," he groaned.

"Stop!" Charlie ordered.

Grant hit the brakes, and Charlie jumped out of the car. "I got them," she said, slamming the door.

"Dammit, Charlie," Grant mumbled. With no other choice, he went down to the end of the block and turned.

The Russians pulled into the Key West Bight Public Parking Lot, a busy area surrounded by a plethora of businesses near the marina. Grant realized Charlie had made the right call. If she hadn't gone after them, finding them again would have been like the proverbial needle in a haystack.

He turned right at William Street, where he pulled into the lot from the west end. Luckily finding a spot right away, he got out and scanned across the lot to see Charlie's head bobbing along above the car roofs. He sprinted across the parking lot.

His leg throbbed, and he slowed down. She was still fifty yards ahead of him. Grant couldn't see the Russians, but he assumed she had her eyes on them. The sidewalks were busy, but in Key West it seemed there were always pedestrians out. Especially here at the Key West Seaport. Now the Conch Harbor Marina occupied a large portion of the bight, but restaurants and shops lined the port with wooden walkways and sidewalks connecting the various vendors.

Charlie was skirting around the Waterfront Brewery. Ahead of her, Prutsev's head came into view. Grant picked up the pace despite his aching leg. *It's all in your head*, he told himself. It was a lie, but he needed to believe it. Right now he didn't have any oxy to lean on. As he rounded the corner, he almost slammed into the back of Charlie who was leaning against the wall.

"Bloody hell, mate."

"Geez, Charlie," Grant said. "Where are they?"

"They headed down that dock," she said, pointing toward a walkway leading off the shore.

They watched as the female seemed to usher Tattoo toward a superyacht moored to the pier.

"That thing's huge," Grant muttered.

"Bigger than my flat," Charlie agreed. "Who the hell is on it?"

From where they stood, Charlie and Grant watched a few people moving about on the upper deck. One man scrubbed the forward gunwales. Grant judged that the vessel was well over a hundred feet long. Its white hull stretched almost the entire length of the dock. The top two decks shone black, and the bridge, which occupied the uppermost level, was wrapped in glass, offering a 360-degree view of the harbor.

"Do you know what kind of boat that is?" Charlie asked.

Grant shook his head. "Expensive," he whispered as he stepped closer to the wall to let a couple pass along the walkway.

He pulled his phone out and snapped three pictures of the yacht.

"I wish I could see the name," he complained.

The older man in the couple paused. "It's a beaut, ain't it?"

Grant nodded. "Yeah, I wonder what that costs."

"More than I'll ever see," the old guy replied. "I guess it's some foreigner."

"What do you mean by that?" Charlie questioned.

The man balked when he heard her English accent. "Oh, miss, I didn't mean nothing by that. Just that the name isn't in English."

"What is it?" Grant asked.

"Is it Spanish, dear?" he asked his companion, a slightly younger lady. Probably his wife.

"No, it's Italian."

"Right," the man beamed. "She'd know too. She speaks three different languages. I just butcher the one." It was a joke he'd obviously told a hundred times. The woman offered a conciliatory half smile for his efforts.

"*La Tana del Drago*," the linguistic lady remarked. "It means the Dragon's Den."

Grant and Charlie exchanged a quick look.

"Thank you, guys, so much," Grant said, hoping to move them along.

"We have a Hatteras over there," the man stated.

"Come on, David," his wife urged, aware that the strangers didn't care to continue the conversation. "I'm hungry."

"Take care," David said as he was almost forcibly dragged away.

"David likes to natter, yeah?" Charlie noted.

Grant didn't respond, instead staring at *La Tana del Drago*.

"The Dragon's Den?" he remarked.

"I want a closer look," Charlie suggested.

"That might not be wise," Grant pointed out. "They've been trying to grab you for days. I don't know that walking into their den is our best move."

Grant watched the tattooed Prutsev appear on the foredeck. He crossed his arms and stared over the shopping area. At a distance, the Band-Aids made his skin look mottled around his neck. The woman appeared, along with a thick, dark-haired man in a white linen suit. Prutsev towered over him by more than a few inches. The new man's face sported a thick black beard.

"I wonder who that is?" Grant mused.

When Charlie didn't respond, he turned to look at her. His sister's gaze stretched out across the water. Floating on the other side of the marina was a blue and white Polaris Virage personal watercraft. A lean, older man straddled the three-seater vessel and watched the superyacht.

Wait, Grant realized. He was taking pictures of the boat. Even from this distance, he recognized the man who'd stepped in to help him at The Billy Club.

Their father.

"Is that—?" he asked.

"Dad," Charlie finished.

Prutsev locked eyes with Grant, spotting the pair. His hand pointed toward them as he alerted his companions. The newcomer with the beard turned to follow Charlie's line of sight.

"Dammit!" Grant cursed. "They know we're here."

Across the marina, he could hear the guttural orders in Russian.

"We need to warn your father," Grant said, grabbing Charlie's arm.

"I think we're too late," Charlie groaned.

Brother and sister ran north on the wooden walkway as three men came off the yacht's gangplank. Grant glanced across the water to the Polaris where Keith Greene floated. The man noticed the sudden movement, and his head tracked to the line of shops where his son and daughter now dashed along the waterfront.

A screech of a high-powered motor echoed in the harbor, and Grant turned to see a black Sea-Doo GTX rip away from *La Tana del Drago*. Two men rode the Sea-Doo as it coursed across the water toward Keith Greene.

"Dad!" Charlie shouted.

"He can't hear you," Grant advised as he pushed her forward.

They had a significant head start on the three men, and Charlie shoved her way through a crowd heading toward Turtle Kraals for an early lunch.

"What the hell?" a man shouted as she elbowed him aside.

"Sorry," Grant apologized as he tried to catch up to his sister.

A few seconds later, the three Russians collided with the same crowd. Relieved they'd been slowed even more, Grant's head twisted to see Keith Greene racing away from them as the Sea-Doo pursued him. Charlie hit the end of the wooden sidewalk, cutting left to run down the pier.

"Don't go that way!" Grant shouted as his sister ran down the dock past two men cleaning fish at one of the stations along the pier.

Grant stopped as he reached the men and grabbed a gallon jug of bleach the men intended to use to clean the white HDPE plastic bench. Spinning around, Grant swung the jug like a club at the first Russian. The hefty vessel slammed into the surprised Russian's face, throwing the man to the side as Grant rammed him with his shoulder, sending his opponent off the edge of the dock with a splash.

The next two men skidded to a stop, preparing to launch an attack at Grant. Grant pulled the top off the bleach as the two came at him. He squeezed the jug and thrust it forward. A burst of bleach fired from the mouth of the bottle into the face of the next attacker. The immediate burn of the chemical sent the man doubling over in fear of permanent damage.

Grant dropped the bottle when the third man punched him in the face. He'd still been in motion when the strike landed, and it knocked him to the side. Grant caught his footing, turning to defend from another attack.

"Don't you do it!" one of the fishermen shouted, holding a .38 snub nose revolver in the Russian's face.

Grant bent at the waist for a second, catching his breath.

"You okay, son?" the older fisherman asked.

"Yeah. Thank you, sir. Call the cops," Grant muttered before turning to chase after his sister.

He saw her at the end of the pier waving her arms as Keith Greene pointed the nose of the Polaris toward her. Grant realized he was slowing down, and the Sea-Doo was about to close the gap between them. Grant picked up speed, grabbing a ten-foot gaff, hooked on the stern of a Contender center console. Charlie jumped off the end of the pier, landing astride the Polaris as Grant ran after them. Greene squeezed the throttle, and the watercraft leapt away from the dock.

As the Sea-Doo charged toward the Greenes, Grant swung the gaff, the hook catching the driver in the chest, digging into the foam of the man's life preserver. Before he could plant his legs, Grant snapped forward, still holding the gaff in his hands. He hit the water, releasing his grip on the pole as he plunged underwater. When his head surfaced, he saw the Sea-Doo floating powerless without its pilot. The passenger stood on the rear looking back for the driver whose fall activated the kill-switch on the PWC's controls.

Grant scanned the water and spotted the man who floated, either unconscious or dead, thirty feet away. Suddenly, with a roar from the Polaris's engine, the Sea-Doo violently rocked to one side as Greene's outstretched foot slammed the passenger into the water.

"Grant!" Charlie shouted from the back of the Polaris. He swam toward the blue and white craft.

"Get on!" the older Greene ordered, and Grant reached up to grab the handles. Before he'd pulled himself out of the water, Keith started moving.

Charlie caught Grant by the arm and heaved him aboard where Grant slid against her on the seat with half his ass hanging off the back of the bench.

Without a word, Keith Greene leaned forward, putting his mass over the handlebars, and raced out of the marina.

22

"You've got a lot of explaining to do, Dad!" Charlie said once they'd cleared the naval station jetties and approached the bridge through Fleming Key Cut.

Keith nodded and half turned, having slowed to a sensible pace once he was sure they weren't being chased anymore.

"I do indeed," he responded in what Grant would call a British BBC accent. "Much has happened, and unfortunately come unreeled. I certainly never intended for either of you to be involved."

"I'm Grant, by the way," Grant said, trying his best to hang on the back of the Polaris which appeared to be designed for two and a half butts. "There's a rumor going around that you might be my father."

Keith let out a long breath. "We have much to discuss, but let's get off the water to somewhere safe, and I'll explain everything."

Charlie hung on to her father as he accelerated once more, preventing further conversation. Grant bounced around like a sack of potatoes, gamely holding on to the grab handles and Charlie's now-sodden shirt.

Five minutes later, Keith steered the vessel down a mangrove-lined inlet to a rental location just before the North Roosevelt Boulevard bridge. He gunned the engine to ride the machine up the floating plastic dock where a tanned young man with dreadlocks and tattoos down his arms greeted them.

"You still have another half an hour, dude," he said, looking at the other two in confusion. "You're supposed to have life vests on, man."

"Unplanned pick up, old chap," Keith replied, handing the youth the vest he'd been wearing. "Ran like a champ though, thank you."

The man nodded and silently watched the three dripping wet people walk away under the bridge toward the parking lot.

Charlie looked at her father walking briskly along, wearing dark gray swim shorts, a navy-blue rash guard, and water shoes. His trim and fit figure clearly outlined under the skintight shirt. His chin showed several days of unshaven salt and pepper growth and the crow's feet around his eyes appeared deeper than she recalled. He paused by a motorcycle in a line of cars parked in the small lot.

"This won't do anymore, will it?" Keith said, unstrapping a small bag of clothes from the rear of the Ducati Monster.

"You were riding that?" Charlie asked in astonishment. "I didn't know you rode motorbikes."

He turned and his expression softened from deep thought to something she perceived as sympathy. Or regret?

"As you've discovered, there's another side to my life that you've not been privy too. For very good reason."

Charlie had always considered her father to be a classy, debonair man, but if she wasn't currently so confused and upset, she'd admit to how impressed she was. Every kid's dream would be to have an international secret agent for a parent... unless they'd lied to you about it your whole life.

"I see you found my watch and ring," Keith commented, looking at his daughter.

Charlie held up her hand where the Rolex dangled loosely around her thin wrist. "Why did you leave them behind?"

Her father smiled. "Standard protocol, my dear. But that will become clearer when I explain everything."

He turned his attention to Grant who stood dripping salt water onto the asphalt staring back at the man. "You've no idea how good it is to meet you, son. I'm just so sorry it's happening this way. Your mother was a wonderful woman. The love of my life."

Grant swallowed hard and wiped at the water running down his face. "Fuck," he mumbled.

Keith spun around and pointed to a large strip mall next door. "We don't have time for sappy reunions," he said boldly. "We need dry clothes for you both and new wheels."

He strode away, leaving Charlie and Grant both wondering what on earth was happening. They jogged to catch up.

"Charlotte, would you mind borrowing us a vehicle?" Keith said as they reached him. "Something nondescript. Preferably an employee's car from behind the shops so it won't be reported for a while."

"What makes you think I know how to nick a car?" she responded.

"You do, don't you?" he replied.

"Yeah, but you shouldn't know that."

Keith grinned. "Well, I do. Now get us transportation while I procure you and your brother dry clothes."

"You're going to pinch us some clothes?" she asked.

Keith stopped so Charlie and Grant did too. "I'm going to buy you clothes, and as I know your size, I can get yours for you. I'm less familiar with Grant's needs, so it makes sense for him to come with me. Is that satisfactory, Miss Nosy Detective?" The edges of his mouth rose ever so slightly into the suggestion of a grin.

Charlie couldn't stop a smile creeping across her face despite her frustration with her father. "Fine. I'll meet you by your fancy motorbike."

She backtracked to slip behind the row of buildings running parallel to the canal inlet where they'd arrived. Cars were parked along the tree line which divided the lane from the water. Charlie kept moving until she found an older gray minivan with faded paintwork and a small dent in the driver's door. She guessed it may once have been silver before the Florida sun turned the color matte.

She looked through the window to check for any sign of a security system and saw none. She tried the handle, but it was locked. Moving around the front, she checked the passenger door and then the sliding door behind it, which were all locked as well. Checking the rear, Charlie tugged on the tailgate handle, and to her surprise, it swung up. She watched the emblem stating the vehicle was a "Town & Country" rise past her face, satisfied step one had been easier than expected.

Pulling the tailgate closed behind her, she looked to her right, then left. On the left side, a panel covered a storage space, and she undid the two swivel latches holding it in place, letting it fall to the carpeted floor. Inside were two black bags, and Charlie retrieved the smaller one, untying the cord and shaking the tools out before her. She took a pair of diagonal cutters, scrambled over the seats, and slid upside down beneath the dash in the footwell, her feet draped over the center console. Reaching up, she took hold of the plastic shroud beneath the steering column and wrenched it, scattering small shards of broken pieces all over herself. Three more good tugs and the panel came completely free, and she tossed it across to the passenger side footwell.

Finding the wiring bundle to the ignition, she wriggled it free of the cheap plastic tab securing it to the steering column assembly and began locating the wires she was looking for. Using the cutters, she snipped two thicker red wires, then stripped the insulation away from the ends and twisted them together. She was rewarded with a buzz of the fuel pump priming and a ding from the dashboard. Next, she found two brown wires and pulled them away from the bundle, carefully holding the rubber coated handles of the cutters as she snipped them. She stripped the ends, then holding the two wires by their insulation, she touched them together and the starter spun the engine which caught after a few nervous seconds.

"Haha!" she exclaimed, a little louder than intended as she pulled herself from the footwell and sat up, staring straight at a large, middle-aged lady taking a cigarette break outside one of doors to the long building.

The woman took a long inhale on the cigarette, held the smoke in her lungs for what felt forever, then released it in a thick stream which momentarily obscured her face. Charlie dropped across the passenger seat.

"Bugger," she whispered to herself, weighing her options.

She opened the glove box and reached in, finding a baseball cap, and something else she recognized by feel.

"It is the wild bloody west around here," she muttered, leaving the handgun where it was and retrieving the cap.

Sitting up, she pantomimed finding the cap on the floor and slipping it on her head, pulling it down tight above her eyes for the bill to conceal as much of her face as possible. She sneaked a sideways glance at the doorway, but all that was left was a waft of smoke rising from the ground where the woman had tossed her cigarette butt. Charlie hoped she'd not cut her break short to go warn the minivan owner someone was stealing her vehicle, dropped the Town & Country in drive, and turned it around in the narrow lane.

Parked near the motorcycle, she drummed her fingers on the steering wheel while she waited for her father and brother to return. The concept of having a brother was still so foreign it outweighed her shock over her father's story. She wondered what the two were talking about while they strolled the aisles of Ross Dress For Less and picked out the perfect outfits for hunting down Russian thugs.

In the rearview mirror, she spotted the two men approaching. Keith was now wearing a pair of beige linen trousers and a slightly willowy white, collared shirt, with the last two buttons undone. Grant didn't look quite as dashing in long, dark blue board shorts and a gray golf shirt, but handsome nonetheless. Whatever they'd discussed appeared to have been amicable, as they were deep in conversation as Charlie stepped from the minivan and waved them over.

Keith took the front seat while Charlie relinquished the driver's seat to Grant, then hopped in the back.

"I occasionally forget they drive on the wrong side here," she said in way of explanation.

"Did you just admit to not doing something perfectly?" Grant teased, grinning at her in the rearview as he adjusted it.

"I believe she did while still insulting your country for its driving regulations," Keith pointed out, and the two men grinned at each other.

Perfect, Charlie thought. They've been together for ten minutes and they've already formed some macho bonding bullshit.

Her father handed her a shopping bag and she took out a pair of black capri leggings and a dark maroon-colored T-shirt.

"Eyes front," she said, and peeled off her smelly damp shirt she'd lived in for the past few days, glad her bra below was relatively dry. "What now?" she asked as she continued changing.

"If you find your way to North Roosevelt Boulevard, Grant," Keith said. "There's a Marriott up the road on the left. We'll find a seat in their bar, order a drink like civilized people, and I'll tell you all I'm allowed to under the Official Secrets Act."

Grant made a right until he found a road between several chain restaurants on the left leading to the highway, where he turned right again. As Keith had explained, a Courtyard by Marriott appeared on the left-hand side, and Grant found a parking spot shielded from the road by a palm tree and well away from the front entrance. From there they walked around the building and found a covered patio overlooking the hotel's small beach which had been recently formed via truckloads of sand brought in and sprinkled over an area cleared of mangroves. They found a table away from other patrons, a waitress took their drink order, and Charlie and Grant both looked at Keith.

"Your mother, Dee, and I," he began, his eyes locked on his daughter, "worked for a covert group under a combined British and US government division." Keith turned to Grant. "Before you were born in London, we completed what was intended to be our last operation. It was successful, but let's just say it was rather high profile, and we became the targets of very unsavory characters. Diana, or Dee, or Fiona," he said, before pausing for a moment. "Your mother, is probably the easiest name to use. Anyway, she wasn't heartless enough to kill a teenage girl who witnessed the key event in the operation, and we believe by choice, or by persuasion, the young woman gave enough of a description for them to figure out who had been involved."

"Is that where this wanker with his fancy boat comes into it?" Charlie asked.

"Yes, but patience, my dear, I'll get to that in a moment."

The waitress arrived, setting their drinks on the table, and asking if she could get them anything else.

"We're perfect for now, thank you," Keith replied with a warm smile. Once the woman was out of earshot, he continued. "The situation became remarkably intense in the UK, so the branch we worked for suggested the new identities they supplied us with should be completely detached. We would spend some time apart, then join back together when things cooled off."

"You became Keith Greene?" Charlie asked, rocking in her seat impatiently. "Instead of Daniel Edwards."

Keith raised an eyebrow. "That is correct."

"And Mom switched from Diana Turner to Fiona Wolfe," Grant added, and Keith nodded.

"But your new identities used elements of each other's birth dates," Charlie pointed out.

Keith smiled. "You two are quite resourceful." His expression darkened once more as he continued. "Unfortunately, in the same way you were able to discover these details, so was Lazović."

"He's the Dragon guy with the bloody great big boat," Charlie said.

"Dra-gan," Keith corrected. "And yes, he's the son of the man your mother and I..." he paused to consider his words.

"Iced?" Grant offered.

"Whacked?" Charlie added.

"We had an altercation with," Keith replied, wincing. "I'm not sure exactly how, but he found Dee and knew I'd show up looking for him."

"So, my mother was murdered," Grant said between gritted teeth.

Keith swallowed and took a deep breath. "I'm afraid so. Staged as an accident of course. They were watching at the funeral, waiting for me, while I was watching them, hoping they'd lead me to Lazović, when to everyone's surprise, you showed up," he said, looking at Charlie. "You look so much like your mother," he added softly, reaching across the table and taking her hand.

Charlie fought back the tears for a woman she'd never known, but always loved. After a gentle squeeze, he released her hand.

"Since then, it's been an unpredictable galivant all over the Keys."

"You should have told me," Charlie said, her voice more frustration than anger now.

"You're right. I should have. After their attempt to grab you at the funeral, I should have come to you both and explained everything. I stupidly thought I could keep them away from you both while I figured out where Lazović was and took care of the problem, but I couldn't, and Tim paid the price."

"You knew Tim, then?" Grant asked.

Keith nodded. "A wonderful friend I hadn't set eyes on in years. He has been the go-between for Dee and me all this time."

"Why did you never get back together?" Charlie asked. "You said the plan was temporary. How come you stayed apart all these years?"

Keith's shoulders dropped. "It took several years for the threat to die down. About the time it appeared Aleksandar Lazović's wife, who took over his interests after… his unfortunate demise, lost her passion for finding us, I was persuaded to take on one more assignment. And then another. And so it went on. It was only a few years ago, after I was officially retired, that we'd begun discussing the feasibility of getting back together. I don't know how, as we communicated covertly as always, but in hindsight that may have triggered a renewed interest from their son, Dragan. His mother passed around that time as well, so it's possible he took up the torch when he inherited the business. Who knows?"

"Can't you involve whatever department it is you worked for?" Grant asked. "Surely they could help after all you've done."

Keith sighed. "Alas, the combined operation Dee and I worked for was dissolved years ago, and the British branch I continued to be a part of was also disbanded when our beloved Queen passed away, so…"

"You were working for the bloody Queen?" Charlie blurted.

Keith frowned. "Please don't use profanity alongside our monarch's name, my dear," he chided. "And, all of the British government officially works for the crown, but yes, my branch was more closely connected than most."

"Blimey," Charlie muttered, looking suitably contrite yet stunned inside.

The three sat back, took a sip of their untouched drinks, and tried to make sense of their worlds which had all been spun in circles. Charlie couldn't set aside the notion that she'd been kept away from her mother because of some Russian mobster who was now running around Florida like he owned the place.

"Okay, so what's the plan now?" she said abruptly, slapping the table with the palm of her hand. "This Lazović bastard needs to pay, Dad."

She stared at her father and felt Grant ease forward in his seat next to her.

Keith took a beat before replying. "I have a plan, and with your help, I believe it can work. And pay he will, my love. Pay he will."

23

"What do you have in mind?" Grant asked.

Charlie nodded in agreement with her brother. "This Dragan bloke has a lot of resources. Can't we nick him for Grant's mother's —I mean, our mother's murder? Or Tim's?"

"Dragan Lazović is smarter than that," Keith assured her. "He might be more dangerous than his father was. It seems he's garnered some diplomatic immunity here in the States. As I understand American law, the best we could hope for is deportation. That would be of little recompense, in my opinion."

"No shit," Grant replied. "The bastard killed my mother. I'll be damned if he gets to just up and leave."

"Good," Keith agreed with a grin. "I'm glad we agree. Lazović heads one of the vilest organizations. He's taken what his father did and exponentially made it worse. He cannot survive."

"Are you saying we kill him?" Charlie asked, dumbfounded by the suggestion from her father.

"Not we," he corrected. "*I* am going to kill him."

Grant leaned forward suddenly. "No, you aren't," he stated in a low, gruff voice.

"Son, I understand your position, but this man has hurt too many people. He is untouchable by the law."

"First," Grant interrupted his father, "we're not at the 'son' stage yet. Second, I don't care about the law. If Lazović killed my mother —or had her killed—then, you don't get to bench me."

Keith leaned back in the chair. He stared at his son, letting out a long sigh. "It's too dangerous," he slowly replied.

"I'm going," Grant stated flatly.

"Me too," Charlie said.

Grant glanced at his sister, glad to have the support. Keith crossed his arms, and Grant wondered if he wanted to issue some paternal ultimatum. The older gentleman returned his children's glare for several seconds.

"Fine," Keith relented. "It'll be a lot more efficient with three of us anyhow."

Grant's features softened once the former spy agreed to let him join the mission. He felt like a six-year-old, ecstatic to be included with the older boys in whatever game they were playing at the time.

"What's the plan?" Charlie questioned.

"After the scene at the marina, I imagine *La Tana del Drago* will depart the area, but they won't go far. Lazović wants me dead, and failure to get what he wants isn't something he's used to."

"Where would he go?" Charlie asked.

"I'll find him," her father assured her. "I still have some favors I can call in. But we'll need equipment."

"What do you have in mind?" Grant asked.

"Lazović's people will see an assault over the water. Growing up near the water, I assume you can scuba dive, Grant?"

"Yeah, I've been diving since I was eight. Certified when I was ten. While I was with the department, I worked with the rescue divers."

"Perfect," Keith said with what might have been a proud smile. "Charlie, how long since your last dive?"

"Last year when we went to Malta," she told him.

"Good, we'll make our approach underwater. We'll need guns. These guys probably have enough hardware to invade Key West."

"I doubt it," Grant countered. "The Navy might have something to say about that. They'd come running if an army of Russians marched down Duval. That's where all the girls are."

Keith chuckled, "Fair enough. Maybe enough to invade Marathon then. At least until the Navy comes north."

"Are you two bloody serious?" Charlie snapped. "You want the three of us to sneak on board and fight an armed crew."

"Ideally, we don't have to fight," Keith explained. "Our best approach is stealth. We sneak aboard and find Lazović. Once we dispatch him, we slip away. In fact, it would be best if we had suppressors for our weapons. Helps maintain the element of surprise."

"I'll take care of that," Grant assured him.

Charlie stared at the two men. "This is insane," she muttered.

"Charlie, you can sit this one out," Keith told her. "Both of you can."

"To hell with that," Grant blurted out. "He killed my mother."

His face softened a bit, and he turned to his sister. "But Charlie, he's right. You don't have to do this. It's not your fight."

Her eyes narrowed. "Seriously? Just because I never met her doesn't mean I don't care."

"I never said you didn't," Grant interjected.

"I just said it was a stupid way to die," she continued. "Not once did I say I wasn't going along."

Keith smiled. "That's my girl. You can probably find us scuba gear. We'll need a boat too."

"Give me a few hours," Grant said. "I can handle the hardware. There's a guy I know—well, I arrested. But he can get us whatever we need."

Keith nodded before glancing at Charlie.

"Right, dive boat and gear," she acknowledged.

"What are you going to do?" Grant asked Keith.

"If I act fast, I'll track where *La Tana del Drago* goes. That way we know where to hit. And I'll take care of a special item we'll need."

"C'mon, Charlie," Grant urged. "I'll drop you. I need the minivan."

"How come you get the minivan? I'm the one who nicked it." she complained.

"Borrowed," Keith interjected.

"You're getting a boat for us, right?" Grant asked.

Charlie frowned at him, sensing a trap.

"Can't drive the car while you're piloting the boat, can you?"

"I'm getting the short end, but fine," she huffed.

"Is she always this argumentative?" Grant asked Keith.

"Her first word was 'no,'" Keith noted.

"Not surprised," Grant admitted as he headed for the door. "If you want a lift, keep up," he directed at Charlie, then glanced back at Keith. "We'll meet you back here in a few hours."

Keith nodded as Grant walked off the hotel's patio toward the lobby.

Charlie didn't immediately follow. "When this is over, we're having a talk about everything."

Before Keith could respond, she hurried out of the restaurant after Grant.

"Where am I going to find all this gear?" she asked when they slid into the front of the Chrysler minivan.

"Dive shops and charters are a dime a dozen around here," Grant informed her. "Buy or rent the gear you need, and rent a boat."

She curled her nose up at him. "I don't know much about boats," she confessed.

"What?" Grant exclaimed. "There's something you don't know about?"

"Shut up," she snapped. "Just tell me what to get."

"Anything with a shallow draft. Which shouldn't be hard. Everything around here will be one-to-two-foot drafts. You could even get a pontoon boat. As long as it has enough room for all the gear."

Grant drove north, going over the bridge to Stock Island, then turning off the main highway onto Cross Street. Another right turn took him through a residential area until the road ended at a commercial building on the cut between Stock Island and Key West itself.

"Go in there," he advised as he pulled up in front of Chuck's Key West Boat Rentals. "There's a dive shop across the water. I think you can pull right up with the boat and load everything."

"Why don't I come with you first?" she questioned.

"The guy I'm going to see doesn't like people, and I don't need him getting a twitchy trigger finger."

"Seems everyone in this country has that."

"Yeah, yeah," Grant moaned. "Guns bad. You don't have them across the pond."

She huffed with annoyance before getting out of the van. "By the way, there's one in the glove box."

"Good to know," he said, stifling a laugh. "Hey, make sure you get a boat with a chartplotter. Or at least a GPS. I don't want to have to come find you out there on the water."

Charlie's head cocked sideways, and judging from the look on her face, Grant expected her to extend her middle finger. Instead, she held up two, like a victory sign backward, slammed the door and stomped away. He vaguely remembered seeing that gesture in a British movie once.

When he reached Overseas Highway, Grant pulled into a convenience store where he purchased a cheap pre-paid phone. He knew the man's number by heart, and he hoped that the goodwill he'd garnered in the past hadn't been forgotten.

Thomas Johnson was more often called Tommy J. He and Grant attended the same high school. Tommy J would be seen by some as a gun enthusiast. Most law enforcement, though, saw him as a small arms dealer. Or they would if he'd ever been caught.

When Grant ran into him again a few years ago, he busted him for possession with intent to sell. Tommy J had been a much better arms dealer than a drug dealer, and Grant finagled him into a lighter charge when he offered Grant a bigger fish—a high-level dealer in Marathon.

The bust wasn't monumental for Grant's career, especially considering two months later he took a bullet that would end it. However, he expected that a guy like Tommy J might prove more useful in the future.

Now it was time to test that theory.

"Yo!" Tommy J answered.

"Tommy, it's Grant Wolfe."

"Sup, Grant! I ain't done nothing wrong."

"Hey, don't sweat it, Tommy. I'm not a cop anymore," Grant assured him.

"Hallelujah, you've seen the light!"

"Amen, brother," Grant replied, playing along. "I'm private now, and I need a favor."

"Man, for you, anything." His gracious tone seemed genuine to Grant, but the man was a criminal. Even if he only ended up with a couple of months in jail instead of years, it was still Grant who put him there.

"It's been getting dangerous out there," Grant said. "I'm looking to add to my collection."

"You sure you're not law enforcement?"

"No, they kicked me off the team."

"Why's that?" Tommy asked warily.

"Got shot," Grant explained. "Then I started relying too much on oxy."

"Oxy's a bitch to shake," Tommy J agreed. "I'm staying dry since you and I last saw each other."

It was a blatant lie, but Grant didn't care anymore. Right now, all he wanted was enough firepower to take down the crew of Lasović's yacht.

"When you need it?" he asked.

"I'm looking for now. You still down island?"

Tommy J gave him an address. "It's on Sugarloaf Key," he told Grant.

"Be there in forty-five to an hour," Grant told him before hanging up.

Sugarloaf Key was about fifteen miles north, but Grant also knew what traffic could do along Highway One. A small fender bender could back it up for hours. If he got there early enough, he could reconnoiter the place.

For once, traffic seemed to work in his favor, and the drive only took twenty-eight minutes. He cruised past the address, a self-storage place that appeared to house mostly boats for weekenders and snowbirds.

Parking across the street, he sat and waited. He didn't think he'd need it, but just in case, he checked the handgun in the glove box was loaded. Six minutes later, a black Lexus coupe pulled into the lot. Grant watched as a ponytailed blond man keyed in a code. As the Lexus proceeded forward, Grant slid in behind him.

By the time Tommy J stopped the black car, Grant assured himself that the other man was alone.

"Driving a mom-mobile?" Tommy J asked when Grant got out of the vehicle.

"It gets me around," Grant admitted.

Tommy J came close, wrapping Grant in a hug. He assumed the criminal was checking for a wire more than expressing affection, but Tommy J had always been the drunk that shouted, "I love you, man," after three beers.

"What are you looking for?" he asked Grant when he released the embrace.

"I need three automatic rifles."

"You mean semi, right?" Tommy J asked cautiously.

"No, I'm looking to fully invoke my constitutional rights."

Tommy J's head bobbed. "Right on, man. I have some here."

He led Grant to an overhead door. As they walked, Grant scanned the area for security cameras. He saw three, but all of them pointed in a different direction. Tommy J picked the perfect unit. It was situated in the blind spots of all three cameras. His former schoolmate was smarter than he let on.

When the roll-up door rattled open, Grant stared at stacks of wooden crates.

"So, you're private?" Tommy J asked again.

"Yeah."

"What have you got in mind for these?"

Grant stared at the man. "Might be best if you don't know."

Tommy J opened a crate and waved his hands over the contents like a model on *The Price is Right*. Inside, Grant stared at twenty or so black metal rifles. He reached in and picked up the top one, examining it carefully.

The weapon was a Smith & Wesson M&P 15 with a red dot optic sight. He popped the magazine out and inspected it. Twenty-five rounds fit into the magazine, although it was currently empty. With the magazine removed, he pulled back the action, ensuring the weapon was completely unloaded. Grant lifted the stock to his shoulder and peered down the barrel. His thumb activated the laser, and a small red dot appeared on the back of the storage unit.

"You got three of these?" he asked as he dry-fired, listening to the click as the trigger engaged.

"Just one," he sighed. "But look, I have a couple of Colts."

Grant set the Smith & Wesson down and removed two identical Colt AR15-M4s. He thoroughly inspected each of them before stacking them with the other rifle.

"Perfect, I need ammo and extra mags."

"Let's talk money first," Tommy J interjected.

"Yeah, I'm going to need these more as a favor," Grant stated.

"A favor," Tommy J blurted out. "I'm not in the business of favors."

"Today you are," Grant said. "I'll owe you. Or, I can have my friend who is sitting across the street watching call in a friend of mine at the sheriff's department."

"You fucker."

"Calm down, Tommy," Grant soothed. "We're going to work

something out. It's a favor for an old bud. Remember, just like I did for you."

"Man, I still got sixty days."

"Dude, you were facing five to ten *years*," Grant pointed out. "I saved your ass as best I could."

"This is almost three grand worth of goods though."

"Hell, Tommy, if I saved you three years out of the state pen, then that only comes to a hundred bucks or so a month. Seems like the legal fees would have cost you that much."

"Damn it," he sputtered.

"I promise, I'll make it up to you," Grant swore.

Tommy waved his hand at him.

"Ammo?"

"Seriously?" Tommy asked.

Grant shrugged.

"Ugh," the man groaned pointing toward another crate. "Take what you need."

Grant carried the weapons and several boxes of .223 caliber bullets to the minivan.

"Hey, Tommy, one more thing."

"What now?"

"I need suppressors," Grant explained.

"Oh, you've got to be kidding me."

24

Charlie watched Grant drive away in the minivan and realized with a jolt that she ought to be running after him with arms waving. She had no way of paying for anything. How could she rent boats and scuba gear? Instead, she groaned and turned around, looking at the building with its large sign advertising "Chuck's Key West Boat and Jet Ski Rental."

On the left were the Jet Skis with a young man instructing a couple on how to use them. An arrow pointing right told her the front office was around the opposite side. A box truck hid most of the front of the building, and Charlie stepped forward until she could see behind the truck. Halfway along, several large plastic tubes came out of the ground leading to a utility box mounted on the wall. An idea began forming in her mind.

Slipping between the truck and the building, Charlie moved to the gray box and discovered the latch had a combination padlock.

"Bollocks," she muttered and tipped the lock to see the numbers. It read 2-2-3.

She dare not hope it could be that easy and rolled all three numbers to 1. The lock opened and she laughed to herself. Opening the cabinet door, she studied the myriad of wires, lines, and connections, finding a coaxial cable which she traced to a junction block marked 'Xfinity'.

Charlie had never heard of the company, but she couldn't see any fiber optic lines, so she assumed it was cable and internet. Yanking on the coaxial cable, she tried pulling it free of the block, but it wouldn't give. She growled and wrenched harder. The block pulled from the back of the box, but both ends of the cable were still connected to the block itself.

"Bugger."

Quietly moving along the side of the building, she poked her head around the corner. The renters were bobbing in the water aboard their Jet Skis as the young worker shouted more instructions to them. On the wall behind the young man, Charlie saw a bench with tools scattered about. She spied a pair of cutters and nipped over, grabbed them, and scurried back around the corner. Back at the utility box, she quickly severed the coaxial cable and waited a moment. From inside the building, she heard a man's voice yelling something and figured she'd cut the right line.

Closing the cabinet door, she paused with the lock in her hands. Someone would be coming outside soon, so she didn't have much time, but she tried to remember how to re-code a combination lock. She'd had to do it often in school as some of the idiot guys liked to watch the girls when they unlocked their lockers, then break in later and leave them little gifts. Usually something dead and smelly.

Rotating the shackle ninety degrees, she pressed it down against its spring, then set the three numbers to 3-8-2 and released the shackle.

From closer by, the same man's voice echoed around the building. "Maggie! The fuckin' internet's down. The Marlins were winning for once! Where the fuck are you?"

"Stop yellin', you old goat, I'm right here," a woman replied, with the gravelly voice of a career smoker.

Charlie snapped the lock closed on the latch and spun the numbers, then ran around to the back of the truck, just in time. She heard heavy footsteps on the stony ground and the rattle of the lock she'd just set. She moved carefully away from the truck, then walked boldly toward the office as though she'd just arrived.

"Maggie! Did you change the damn combination!" Charlie heard from behind the truck.

She passed a gaunt, leather-skinned woman in her sixties heading the opposite way with a scowl on her face and a cigarette hanging from her lips.

"Why would I do that, Chuck?" she growled.

Charlie continued to the dock where an array of small boats were tied up. They varied in size and shape, but Charlie had no clue which one would be best for a covert diving operation in the Florida Keys. *Shallow draft*, he'd said.

"Help you?" came a male voice from behind her.

She spun around to see a guy before her who looked remarkably similar to the Jet Ski helper, except he was wearing jeans and a T-shirt, both of which were stained with dirt and oil.

"I need to rent a boat for a day," she replied. "Shallow draft."

Charlie hoped the young man wouldn't look at her like she had two heads, but if he did she'd slap Grant silly when she saw him next.

"Sure, I can help you. I'm Jason," he said. "Pretty much everything we have is shallow, but the flats skiff is the best for bone fishing if you're thinking of getting near the sandbars."

Charlie now looked at the guy as though *he* had two heads. She hadn't understood any of the important words he'd said.

"We're going diving," she blurted.

The young man laughed, rubbing his hands on a filthy rag. "Then you definitely don't want a flats skiff. Only thing we have with a decent ladder and enough space for gear is that pontoon over there," he said, pointing to a vessel that looked to Charlie like a covered patio attached to a pair of elongated barrels.

192 | NICHOLAS HARVEY & DOUGLAS PRATT

She recalled Grant also mentioning something about pontoons, but couldn't remember if he'd said they were good or bad. She guessed good.

"Okay. I'll take that thing. I need it now for twenty-four hours."

The young man grimaced. "Don't know if we can do that. Our internet just went down."

"That's a shame," she responded, tilting her head, and pushing her chest out a little. She felt like the Barbie doll she liked to twist into ridiculous poses when she was a kid. Right before she made her action figure soldier kung-fu kick Barbie in the face. "Can you direct me to a boat rental that has internet so I can rent a boat from them?"

Her half-ass flirting must have worked, as the young man's face creeped into a grin. "I guess we can figure something out to make it work."

Oh shit, she thought, now he thinks he's getting a quickie behind the building. "I'm sure you have one of those old-fashioned credit card swipes, right?"

Jason looked slightly deflated, but quickly recovered. "We have dive gear you can rent as well if you don't have your own."

"You do?" Charlie responded, having seen nothing about dive equipment on the signs, or the obligatory red and white dive flag. "I need three sets of everything."

"Sure. It'll be my personal kit, plus my brother and sister's. But I'll run you a good deal."

"Got tanks?" she asked.

"Yeah, but only the three, so you'll have to bring them back between dives to get filled," he said, grinning at the thought of seeing her again. "Fifty bucks a set-up, but that's the cash price."

Charlie shook her head. "All gotta go on my card. I don't carry cash around when I'm on the water," she said, quickly coming up with a lame reason.

Chuck and Maggie reappeared from around the building, bickering and swearing at each other.

"Hey, Dad!" the young man called out. "This lady wants the pontoon. Can we do a credit card swipe or something?"

"Come back in an hour when we have the stupid internet running again. Your mother's screwed something up and it ain't workin'."

Maggie smacked her husband across the arm with an impressive strike for someone her size. "I ain't fucked anything up! Come inside, hon. I'll see if I can get this working over a cell connection."

A surge of panic rippled through Charlie. Her credit card was a worthless piece of plastic with a decline message at the end of any actual connection to Visa.

"I'll get the pontoon and the gear ready," Jason said, giving Charlie a wry smile. "She's getting dive gear too," he shouted to his mother. "One fifty."

He winked at Charlie.

"Thanks," she replied, giving him a nice smile before joining Maggie who led her inside the building.

The place reeked of oil and cigarette smoke and looked like no one had cleaned any portion of the store since it had opened forever ago.

"It's seven fifty a day," Maggie told her, stepping behind the counter. "Taking it now and bringing it back tomorrow'll be two days. Fifteen hundred. Plus the dive gear."

"Last I checked there's twenty-four hours in a day," Charlie responded, trying to keep her voice pleasant. "I'll only have it a day."

"That ain't how it works, lady," Maggie snapped back, her cigarette flying up and down like a toggle switch between her lips. "I'll do it for twelve fifty. Take it or leave it."

"Including the dive gear," Charlie replied firmly.

"No fuckin' way!" Maggie said, sounding offended. "Thirteen fifty with the gear."

"Thirteen hundred even, and we have a deal."

Maggie took in a long drag from her cigarette and looked at Charlie through squinted eyes. "Fine."

It didn't really matter if the woman charged her ten dollars or a million dollars, the result from the credit card would be the same, so Charlie had no idea why she'd haggled, but she hadn't been able to help herself. Although, she sensed Maggie had expected a battle, and respected Charlie for negotiating.

"Fill out these waivers and rental forms," Maggie said, sliding a bundle of paperwork across the counter.

While Charlie filled out the reams of paperwork, using a squirmy version of her handwriting to support her future claim that her card had been stolen when this was over with, Maggie fussed and cussed over the credit card machine and her cell phone.

After ten minutes, Charlie slid the completed paperwork back to the woman. "Here. Can we run the card so I can go, please? I'm in a bit of hurry."

Maggie looked up from the credit card machine, staring at Charlie through a haze of smoke from the third cigarette she'd lit.

"Fuck it," the woman mumbled, and reached under the counter.

To Charlie's relief, Maggie had an old-school manual swipe machine which made an imprint of the card on carbon paper. She fished out her impotent credit card and handed it over. As Maggie dragged the slider over the card, the door burst open, and Chuck bowled into the office.

"Some fucker cut the internet cable!" he roared.

"You remembered the combo?" Maggie asked, pausing the credit card process and looking up.

"No, I chopped the lock off," Chuck growled. "Cable was cut inside. Wire cutters were still laying in the fuckin' box."

"Who the hell would do that?" Maggie asked.

"How the fuck should I know?" Chuck barked back, pacing around the store.

"I'll call the police," Maggie said, and picked up her cell phone.

"No, you won't," Chuck snapped, coming to a stop. "That's the last thing we need!"

Charlie saw the man's eyes flick to the back of the shop for a moment before he frowned at his wife. She put the phone back down.

"Right. Suppose not," she grumbled.

"I'm sorry for all your trouble," Charlie said politely. "But I really do need to be on my way with the boat. Everyone is waiting for me."

"You get the cell link fuckin' thing working?" Chuck asked.

Maggie shook her head.

"Well, she can't take a boat without at least a deposit now, can she?" he raged, resuming his pacing. "You got cash?" he asked Charlie.

"I don't, but your wife has my credit card, and we're staying at the Hilton place just down the road," Charlie lied, pointing in the general direction of Key West, recalling a Hilton hotel on the way.

"Hilton Garden Inn?" Maggie asked.

"That's the one," Charlie replied.

"Oi!" Chuck screamed, seeing his Jet Ski son walking by the door. He shot outside and began a tirade of questions and general abuse aimed at the young man and his association with dodgy people. Maggie shook her head and handed Charlie the slip to sign.

Charlie wondered how bad the son's circle of friends must be if his parents were running dope or whatever it was they were up to out of the shop. Certainly, an illegal enterprise worthy of keeping the police away.

She signed the slip and waited impatiently while Maggie sorted the paperwork, then handed Charlie her copies. Maggie looked at her watch and wrote down the time.

"It's three o'clock. Three oh one tomorrow and you pay for another day."

Charlie rolled her eyes. "Should be the time I leave the dock, not the time now."

"Can't rent that pontoon to any else now, can I?" Maggie growled back, a fresh batch of ash raining down from her cigarette as she spoke. "Three oh fuckin' clock."

"Fine," Charlie relented and stomped from the office, keen to get under way before someone found coaxial strippers and a connector to fix the internet.

Jason had the dive gear aboard, which all looked like it had been well used. The BCDs were faded, and the tanks battered and scratched. Beggars couldn't be choosers, she decided, and quickly made sure there were three full sets of equipment.

"I almost forgot," Jason said. "I need to see your cert cards for the tank rentals."

Charlie's certification card was at home in London, and she certainly had no idea about Keith or Grant's.

"You'll have to look them up through PADI," she replied impatiently, keeping her fingers crossed.

"Yeah, we don't really have access to the PADI stuff," he replied hesitantly.

Charlie shrugged her shoulders. "Then I guess you'll have to trust that I'm a qualified diver, and I'll trust that these tanks are current with their inspections and you're legal to rent them out."

She followed that up with a playful smile. At least that's what she'd intended but had no idea how it really looked. She realized her brows had creased as she overthought her expression, and she was now scowling at the young man with her mouth in a weird half smile.

"Bugger," she groaned to herself, looking down and berating herself for being so useless at putting on pretenses.

"Yeah, fair enough," Jason said, then began the boat briefing.

Relieved, Charlie listened carefully, while trying her best to look like it was all information she'd heard before and knew. Which it wasn't. Her prior boat experience had been happily letting someone else do the boat part, while she did the enjoying the sun and diving part.

"Any questions?" he asked when he was done showing her around.

"I don't think so," she replied, looking over to the building where Chuck and Maggie were arguing once more.

"Go try it!" she heard Chuck yell, and noticed Maggie was heading to the office.

Jason had the outboard motor idling, so Charlie hurried to the helm and looked at him.

"You're welcome to come along," she said, and he stared back, seemingly confused.

"I'm leaving now, so you're either coming with me, or getting off the boat," she clarified.

He seemed to consider the offer for a moment, and Charlie held her breath. She hadn't expected him to say yes.

Jason glanced back toward where his father was stomping back and forth in front of the electrical box. "I'd love to, but he'd kill me," he said, much to Charlie's relief. "How about a drink when you bring it back tomorrow?"

"Yeah," she said, dropping the boat into reverse as he'd shown her. "I'd love to. See you then," she said, figuring it was unlikely she'd make it back alive anyway.

Giving it a little throttle, the pontoon boat eased backward out of the slip and Jason flung the bow line over the railing to the deck. Charlie turned the wheel and the boat reacted, with the stern swinging to port as she'd hoped. Once clear of the dock, she pulled the throttle lever back and put the transmission in drive. Easing into the throttle, the boat began turning back into the dock and she realized she hadn't turned the wheel again. Fortunately, the boat moored in the other side of the slip had fenders over the side as she heard one squeaking and groaning as the port pontoon banged against the little center console.

"Watch out!" Jason yelped from the dock.

"Bollocks," Charlie muttered and selected reverse again. "See, you got me all flustered thinking about tomorrow," she said, and Jason's face almost made it from grimace to grin. But not quite.

"It's working!" Maggie shouted from the doorway to the building.

"Oh shit," Charlie groaned and slammed the pontoon boat in drive.

This time, she swung the wheel starboard before giving it more throttle, cleared the other boat, then the end of the neighboring slip. She shoved the throttle forward, and hung on, waiting for the boat to jump up to speed. But it barely rocked her as it sluggishly accelerated away.

"Fan-bloody-tastic," she moaned. "I've rented the slowest boat in Florida. Grant will never let me live this down."

25

The banging on the door snapped Grant out of his slumber. He hadn't remembered falling asleep, but obviously he had. He blinked a few times, trying to focus. Some annoying cartoon played on the hotel's television.

"Grant!" Charlie called through the door.

"Hang on!" he shouted as he rolled his feet to the floor.

The digital clock beside the bed read 10:32. He'd only been asleep an hour. When he'd made it back to the hotel with the guns from Tommy J, neither Charlie nor Keith were there.

Keith, he mouthed the name. He hadn't gotten his brain around the idea of calling him "Dad" yet.

Grant opened the door, and Charlie pushed into the room.

"Have you seen Dad?" she asked.

"Not since earlier."

"What are you doing in here?" Charlie demanded, her voice raising to a level Grant envisioned as the red line on a gauge.

"Charlie, calm down."

As soon as he said it, he regretted it. He immediately recalled a domestic call he made several years back with Jacob Wilson, an older deputy in the department. The wife was angry and excited, both with her husband who'd given her a black eye, and with the two deputies trying to disarm her of the cast iron skillet she'd just used to bludgeon her husband. Grant's mistake was asking the wife to calm down only to barely dodge the flying skillet.

Later, Wilson pointed out to Grant that "Never in the history of the world has telling a woman to calm down resulted in her actually calming down."

Now, he'd just made the same mistake, and Charlie greeted those words with a low growl. "Don't tell me to calm down."

"I'm sorry, Charlie," he tried to tell her.

"What were you doing?" she demanded, looking down at the rumpled bed. "Did you take more pills?"

"No, I just fell asleep."

"How nice for you," she remarked. "I can't find Dad anywhere, and you're napping."

"What do you mean?" Grant asked. "Is he not back?"

She shook her head. "No, and he hasn't been back to his room."

Grant was awake now. "After I left you earlier, I came up to Keith's room to take a shower, and figured I'd rest while I was waiting. What have you been doing for the past…" He looked at the clock again and did the math. "Five hours?"

Charlie gritted her teeth. "I may have fallen asleep on the boat for a bit."

Grant stifled a laugh. "Okay, I get it," he responded. "You're upset, but don't take it out on me. Let's find him."

"I don't need to find him," she snapped. "I know exactly where he went."

Grant understood. "Damn him," he muttered.

"Exactly."

"Fine, we need to find the yacht," Grant said.

"How do you expect to do that?"

"I need a computer," he told her.

"Come on," she urged, leading him to the door.

"Wait, I need some shoes," he said, pulling out of her grip.

"Hurry up."

Once he was no longer barefooted, he followed her to the lobby. She marched past the front desk to a small, windowed room labeled "Business Center" on the door. Grant slid behind a computer which appeared to be at least three or four years old. The letters on the keyboard were faded, but years of typing up reports gave him adequate skills to work around that.

"What are you looking for?" she asked him.

"A yacht that size is going to have AIS—Automated Identification System. It sends out a signal telling other vessels the name or at least an identifier. It works like a GPS using satellites so they can be tracked."

"You can find any boat out there?" she questioned.

"In theory," Grant explained. "There are a few websites now that show the signals wherever they are in the world. Geeks like to track some of the cooler yachts, and families keep an eye on loved ones. That sort of thing."

"Blimey, there's no end to how we're being watched these days," Charlie muttered.

"Well, this is a safety system for ships to avoid collisions in poor visibility and what-have-you, but now it's become like train spotting."

He pulled up a website. A black background appeared that looked like an old weather map. Using the mouse, he zoomed in closer until he centered Key West on the screen. The outline of the island was now visible.

In a search bar, he typed *"La Tana del Drago"* and hit return.

No results.

"The Den of the Dragon."

No results.

"Dragon's Den."

A dot appeared.

"Is that it?" Charlie asked.

Grant zoomed in closer on the screen. The identifier noted the yacht was flagged in Belarus.

"Where is Belarus?" Grant asked.

"Don't Americans learn any geography outside of the States?"

"I know where England is," Grant remarked.

"Belarus borders Russia."

"Seems like a big coincidence if it's not them," Grant pointed out.

"I never liked those," Charlie commented.

Grant opened another window and typed in a web address. Another map opened up, and again, he narrowed the view until he could see Key West. Icons popped up over the map. Each had its own symbol: anchors, fish, dive flags, and boats. He traced his finger across the screen to the location the other website indicated for *La Tana del Drago*.

"They're at the USS *Vandenberg*," Grant realized aloud.

"Where's that?"

"It's an old Navy vessel about seven miles offshore. It was sunk —I don't know, maybe fifteen years ago to create an artificial reef."

"You think this Dragan guy is diving it?" she asked.

"Could be," Grant said. "But I doubt it. He's probably just laying low out there overnight. The wreck has bigger mooring lines that can handle a boat that size. The shallower sites don't. But, he can't stay there long. The marine police will chase him off if they don't ticket him, although it's not likely they'll come by at night."

"We need to go," Charlie demanded.

Grant considered protesting but realized he wanted to go just as much as she did.

"Okay," he agreed, pushing away from the computer. "Where'd you tie up the boat?"

It took them twenty minutes to carry the duffle bag of guns from the stolen minivan to the pontoon boat tied to the hotel's seawall.

"Dang, girl. How'd you get it in here?" Grant questioned. "This water is virtually nonexistent."

Under the hotel's decorative lights, Grant could see the sea grass jutting out the surface. He hadn't checked the tides, but the last week or so had seen high tide around three to four in the morning.

Charlie followed his gaze to the water. "It looked really shallow," she replied. "But I figured they wouldn't put a place to tie up boats if the boats couldn't get there."

Her brother let out a chuckle. "Sometimes the best way to do something is to not know you can't."

"Will we get out?" she worried.

"Tide's coming in so if you got in earlier, we should be fine going out," he assured her, adding, "Assuming we don't add too much weight."

"It would only be you," she told him as he untied the bow line.

"You want to drive?" he asked.

She shook her head. "You know the waters better than I do."

He nodded, not telling her that he'd only spent a couple of days down here. No point in admitting that. As long as he didn't mess up.

The motor rumbled to life, and Grant eased the throttle forward. The front of the pontoon lifted slightly as the boat got underway. He didn't think the pontoons would run aground unless he hit some shoaling he wasn't expecting. However, the propeller on the outboard dipped lower in the water, and it could easily drag through the bottom long before the pontoons did.

At the helm, he watched ahead for the lights of other boats out on the water. When he saw the red or green glow of another vessel's running lights, he steered away from them.

"Good job getting one with a chartplotter," Grant said.

"A what?"

Grant laughed. Whether she'd recalled his instructions or not, the pontoon had a chartplotter, so he keyed in their destination and a line appeared, offering him a suggested route. As long as they were close to shore he'd have to keep the pontoon slow as most of the area was considered a no wake zone.

A glow of lights off the starboard side attracted his attention.

After a moment, he realized it was a spotlight, and it swept across them. Marine police patrolling the waters.

"Are those coppers?" Charlie asked.

Grant nodded.

"Can we get away from them?" she asked nervously.

He lifted an eyebrow. "No chance. You didn't exactly rent a speed demon," he said, noting she seemed nervous. "What's wrong?" he questioned.

"Uh, it might be that the credit card I used was bad," she explained. "The rental place probably reported the boat as stolen by now."

Grant shook his head with a half smile. "We have several illegally obtained firearms and enough ammo to storm a small frigate. I don't think I'd worry too much about the boat being reported stolen."

"Actually, I doubt they called the law," she said after pondering Chuck's earlier reluctance in dealing with the authorities.

He shrugged. "If we do get pulled, the last thing we need to worry about is the boat being rented on a bad card."

"I thought everyone carried guns here," she remarked.

"Not fully automatic ones. Those are frowned upon."

"I'll never understand," she sighed.

The route they were taking suggested they would arrive in a little less than two hours, putting them there close to one in the morning.

Over the next couple of hours, he wondered how they would get close to *La Tana del Drago* without being noticed. The upside to the superyacht's location was the fact that they'd moored to an active dive site. While the daylight hours were the busiest, it wasn't unheard of for several boats to head out for night dives on the deepwater wreck. But not usually at one in the morning.

Grant had never dived this particular ship, but he'd always been interested. The ocean floor where the vessel rested was over 140 feet deep. He wasn't sure the depth of the main deck, but he guessed it was close to a hundred feet down.

He watched Charlie who sat on the bench staring ahead into the darkness. They'd rounded the point forty-five minutes ago, and now Grant had the throttle down. The fifty-horsepower outboard took its time getting up to speed, but finally pushed the pontoons through the small waves at nearly nineteen knots. Faster than he'd predicted.

When they were within a mile, Grant could clearly see the lights on the superyacht. This far out there were almost no other boats ahead. In the distance, a couple of freighters chugged along, but *La Tana del Drago* stood out like a beacon.

He backed the throttle off before turning back to survey the waters behind him. The closest vessel running was at least a mile away, and it seemed to be taking a northern heading.

Satisfied no one was coming up behind him, he flipped the switches, turning off the navigation lights. It didn't do anything for his vision as the lights were only there to alert other boaters of their presence. Right now, the last thing he wanted to do was warn the crew of Dragan's yacht they were approaching.

As they drew closer, Grant began to make out the outline of the vessel. He steered the pontoon south of the yacht. If he came in from the east, the lights of Key West might illuminate their boat. Instead, Grant wanted to swing around and approach from the west where the black night would be at their back.

"That's it?" Charlie asked.

Grant only nodded. Her fist clenched the railing as she stared at the vessel where she suspected her father might be.

"How do we moor if they're on it already?" Charlie asked.

"There's a bunch of buoys here," Grant replied. "Five I think."

"How big's this shipwreck?"

"Over five hundred feet."

"Bloody hell. So that's not creepy then," she groaned. "We're planning on diving over the top of a bloody enormous shipwreck at night, and we'll not be able to use dive lights, right?"

"Did you rent some?" he asked.

"Would you turn one on if I had?" she countered.

Grant chuckled and already knew his sister well enough to picture the look she was undoubtedly giving him.

It took another fifteen minutes at about ten knots to get in position. As they approached, Grant saw a shape in the water. He slowed as they came closer. A center-console fishing boat floated at the second mooring from the bow—if Grant was recalling correctly that the wreck lay with the bow facing east. They'd made a wide arc around the yacht on the stern tie.

"That might be Keith's boat," Grant pointed out. He stared at the two three-hundred-horsepower motors on the back. With that kind of power, their father might have gotten here in less than half an hour.

"Can we tie up next to him?" Charlie asked.

Grant turned back and caught sight of another buoy about a hundred feet to the west. Reflective tape on the float signaled its location.

"Let's move closer," Grant suggested. "There's another buoy ahead."

The boat idled toward the next mooring, and Grant pointed toward the boat hook attached to the railing. "Use that to snag the line as we get closer," he said in a hushed tone.

"Why are you whispering?" she asked, imitating his volume.

"Sound is funny on the water," he explained. "It can carry a lot farther. It's bad enough we have the outboard going."

She nodded as she took the hook and extended her arms over the railing. Grant pulled the boat's throttle to neutral, and the pontoons glided through the water next to the orange float.

"Got it," Charlie announced.

As she looped the line to the forward cleat, Grant turned off the engine. He took another look at the fishing boat, convinced now it was definitely Keith's. Maritime laws required anchor lights at night, but that vessel didn't have one illuminated.

"Let's move," Grant stated. "He's had a big head start on us."

Immediately, he stripped off his clothes, leaving only a pair of board shorts.

"You didn't get wetsuits?" he asked.

Charlie shook her head. "I didn't think we'd want to be wearing them once we boarded Dragan's boat."

"Makes sense," Grant agreed. "But I don't want you complaining about getting chilly."

"It's always chilly in England," she boasted. "Just man up."

Grant let a smile cross his face at her barb. He knelt down and strapped the BCD to the air cylinder, diverting his eyes as Charlie turned around, took off her shirt, removed her bra, then slipped back into the shirt. Leggings and a tank top would have to be her dive outfit.

"There's current," Grant muttered, and Charlie stared into the darkness around them.

"How the hell can you tell?"

"See how all the boats have swung around and are tugging against the buoys in the same direction?"

Charlie looked over at *La Tana del Drago,* with its salon lights glowing in yellowish-white stripes above the bow facing them more than a hundred yards away.

"Bugger. Guess we'll have a nice drift over there, but coming back will be a workout."

"Let's hope we get to come back," Grant muttered.

A minute later, he had the regulator attached and tested the air. Satisfied, he grabbed his fins and a mask before dragging the BCD and tank to the bench next to a gap in the stern railing, beside the outboard. He flipped the folding ladder into the water, ready for their return, hoping they'd still be alive to use it.

"I'll drop in, and you can pass me the guns," Grant suggested as he slipped his toes into the fins.

"Will they still work if they get wet?" she asked.

"Wars don't stop for rain," he replied.

Charlie nodded as she watched him slide his arms into the BCD and latch the waist buckle. She was still connecting her regulator when Grant stepped off the stern with a splash and sank below the surface.

Grant realized he'd forgotten to put any air in his BCD, so he was already sinking and fumbled for the inflator button. Before he could find it on the unfamiliar gear, a low droning noise came his way. It sounded like it was in stereo. Unable to determine which direction the sounds were coming from, Grant spun around in the inky blackness, finally spotting two faint red lights above him. He was still sinking, so he finned hard and finally found the inflator button. He was about to squeeze when he realized what he was seeing and hearing.

The stars in the sky and the lights from *La Tana del Drago*, were just enough to silhouette two figures, stretched out behind underwater scooters… arriving at the stern of the pontoon boat.

26

Charlie leaned on the railing with the hefty tank hanging in the BCD strapped to her back, wondering whether she should put her fins on yet, or not. The pontoon rocked gently in the mild ocean swells, the distant lights from the superyacht allowing her to make out silhouettes and shapes. She searched the water below for her brother, who hadn't reappeared to take the guns from her. Squinting, she finally saw a form breaking the surface.

"Where have you been, you bloody plonker. I thought you'd buggered off without me," she whispered in the still night.

She reached for the gun lying on the deck.

"I would not do that," came a heavily accented female voice, and Charlie froze.

"Step back and raise arms."

Unable to see the woman clearly, Charlie instinctively knew it was the Russian nurse from earlier... or, more accurately, the assassin posing as a nurse. There was a loud clatter as an underwater scooter appeared through the opening in the railing, landing on the deck. A figure clad in a black wetsuit followed, climbing the ladder with a gun clutched in one hand.

"More back," the woman ordered, and Charlie did so.

"That probably won't work now it's been in the water," Charlie said, nodding to the gun, figuring it was worth a try.

"Happy to make test and see," the Russian replied in amusement, keeping the firearm trained on Charlie.

She heard another splash from behind the pontoon and a male voice spoke in Russian. The female barked an order in return, and the man disappeared. The woman shoved the M&P 15s aside with her foot, unclipped a small light from her BCD, and turned it on and off several times, aimed toward the superyacht. She then shone the light directly into Charlie's eyes, blinding her and throwing off the night vision she'd built up. As Charlie blinked and tried to recover her sight, she realized the woman was now checking out the rest of the pontoon, before raising her light across the water, and illuminating the center console.

"Who is this boat?"

"Are you trying to ask me whose boat that is?" Charlie responded, knowing she shouldn't provoke the Russian, but unable to help herself.

"Yes. Who is?"

"How the fuck should I know?" Charlie spat back. "A diver I suppose."

"In middle of night?" the woman retorted. "I do not think you tell truth."

"You should go over there and harass them, then. I'll toddle off back to shore and get out of your way."

The light beam swung toward Charlie, and she quickly looked down and closed her eyes before it blinded her again. She swayed with the movement of the boat and wondered if she had any chance of overpowering the Russian woman. In the distance, she heard the sound of a boat engine approaching.

"So, what now?" Charlie asked, opening her eyes again as she sensed the light moving away from her.

"Now we go," the Russian replied. "Take off diving things and catch rope from him."

Charlie turned around as a rigid inflatable boat glided toward them, its spotlight trained on the water in its path. As she slipped from her BCD, letting the tank drop to the bench seat, she wished their rental gear had come with dive knives, but none of them had. Her only hope now, was that Grant had gotten away... and the second Russian hadn't found him.

Grant had no idea how deep he'd dropped. The low-toned drone of the underwater scooter continued, and he watched the headlight the diver had now turned on, making circular search patterns above him. There had been two and now he could only see one, so he presumed the other attacker had boarded the boat. He prayed his sister was okay.

Moments earlier, he'd heard another vessel pass overhead. Their hastily assembled half-assed plan had fallen apart almost immediately. What was it Mike Tyson had said? "Everyone has a plan until they get punched in the mouth." Grant felt like he was currently lying on the canvas seeing stars and tweeting birds circling his head.

Except, looking up, he was seeing a light, and that light was getting farther away. His pursuer had chosen the wrong direction, but Grant's brief moment of relief was short lived. His fin hit something solid, and he instinctively pulled his foot away, confused. His jerky movement spun him around and he gulped in air through his regulator, which then made him rise in the pitch-black water column.

"Calm down, you idiot," he muttered into his reg, and began rotating himself back around to keep an eye on the light.

Before he made it, he gulped again as something hit him across his thigh. *It had to be sharks!* He'd dived with sharks around the Keys many times, and never feared them... except for the bull sharks. He personally didn't know of anyone who'd ever had a problem with one, but the beasts commanded respect, and he'd always been wary of them. For a second, he was sure he was being rammed by a bull shark.

But whatever it was, didn't move, and his shoulder hit the same thing. Grant swung an arm out and his wrist smacked against a line. He grabbed hold. Now gasping deeply from his regulator in near panic, he turned the rest of the way around and found the headlight continuing its search pattern in the blackness.

The current! Feeling like a fool, he realized he'd been drifting in the current and had hit the top of the wreck, then the next mooring line. The diver with the scooter hadn't moved away, it was Grant who had drifted. That put him halfway between the pontoon boat and *La Tana del Drago*. And at least sixty feet deep if he'd touched the top of the wreck.

Charlie's words about the creepy sunken ship in the dark suddenly made him shiver as he contemplated over five hundred feet of ghostly steel shipwreck, just below him.

Trying his best to settle himself down and shake off the eerie feeling, he pulled himself up the mooring line to get clear of the USS *Vandenberg*, and ascend to a shallower depth. After he'd moved what he hoped had been thirty feet, he risked a quick look at the glow-in-the-dark dials of his gauge console. He was now at thirty-five feet and had already used too much of his air. He quickly turned the console around once more, so the dials were hidden against his body.

He was now at about the same depth as the searchlight, where he clung to the line with the current tugging at his body. The light was also getting closer. Each new oval-shaped pattern brought the beam nearer to Grant, and he noticed a second light was now penetrating the darkness, swooping pathways of illumination like long swords in the night. The diver was using a handheld dive light to help him hunt... and Grant certainly felt like the prey.

Charlie reluctantly climbed over to the RIB, where the pilot pointed to the bow seat. She sat as directed, and in the bright spotlights mounted to the T-top, she searched around her for anything she could use as a weapon. But her captors weren't that stupid. The woman stepped aboard, bringing the line with her and barked an order. The pilot moved away from the pontoon and headed for the center console Charlie presumed was her father's.

The Russians both raised their handguns as they approached the strange boat, lowering them again as the spotlights revealed no one on board. The woman leaned over as the rubber sides of the RIB bumped against the center console. The name "Olga" sprang to Charlie's mind, picturing the determined expression of a stereotypical communist-era Russian gymnast.

Charlie peeked as best she could from her seated position. The shirt her father had been wearing earlier was draped over the back of the helm chair. Her heart skipped a few beats. Confirmation that her dad was indeed somewhere near filled her with a mixture of fear and comfort. Scared he could be in the same danger she'd landed herself in, yet hopeful he might still save her. Which of course, she determined, was why she was being held captive instead of shot and tossed overboard.

Olga barked another order in Russian, and the man spun the RIB around and made for the superyacht, one hundred yards away. The nimble boat skimmed across the calm water, making short work of the distance. They traveled the entire length of the impressive yacht, which was pulled down current and tugging hard on the stern mooring ball of the USS *Vandenberg*.

Charlie gazed into the dark ocean rushing past, and wondered where her father and brother both were. The woman had seemingly abandoned her cohort with the other scooter, but maybe he'd taken care of Grant and headed home. The thought made her catch her breath.

Arriving at the stern, a man she recognized with a gun holstered to his chest caught the line thrown by Olga. It was Prutsev. Now wearing a black T-shirt, Charlie saw the bandaged arm and Band-

Aids on his neck. She couldn't stop from grinning and thinking warmly of Wrench.

Once they were nestled against the low, teak-floored rear deck, which extended fifteen feet to a salon, Olga pointed to the yacht. In the glow of the lights of the rear deck, Charlie finally had a clear look at the woman. She was tall, lean, with dark hair pulled back into a tight ponytail, and a stern face which exuded confidence. She was older than Charlie had first thought, perhaps forty. By the way the men jumped when she barked orders, the woman was obviously in charge.

"Go," Olga ordered.

Charlie stood and looked at Prutsev who'd already tied the line to a cleat and now stared at her with cold, dark eyes. She placed her foot on the side of the RIB and hesitated. The man extended a hand to help her, and Charlie pushed against the rubber side, yanking him off the back of the yacht. She stepped back as he bounced against the RIB, and hit the water with a loud splash. Charlie immediately felt the muzzle of a gun against her temple.

"Bad idea," Olga said, sounding unfazed. "Mister Lazović understand if I kill you. I prefer it too."

Charlie slowly raised her hands, then nimbly used the side of the RIB to step unassisted across to the deck of the yacht. Glancing back, she hoped the salt water would cause Prutsev's wounds to become infected, but then she realized something. He hadn't surfaced.

Grant waited until the diver searching for him came close enough that his light almost reached where he clung to the line, weighing his options. Which were limited. Up, down, or let go and drift to *La Tana del Drago*. None felt very appealing. If he went shallower, he risked being chased to the surface where he'd be trapped. Down, meant using more precious air. Letting go sent him on his way to the superyacht… without Charlie. Or a weapon.

A few moments earlier, Grant had listened to what he presumed was the boat he'd heard before, return in the direction it had come. Convinced Charlie was likely aboard, he made his decision. His best choice was to go up. Maybe he would be able to see the pontoon and confirm she'd been taken, then he'd drop under, let go of the line, and drift to the yacht. What would happen next, he had no idea, but he couldn't abandon his newly discovered sister to the Russians.

Hand over hand, he ascended the heavy rope until he made out the silhouette of the large mooring buoy above him. The diver continued his search below, his light lingering on the line where Grant had been moments before. The low drone of the scooter's electric motor slowed, and the handheld beam hunted the waters all around, above and below. The diver steered downward, spiraling around the mooring line like a corkscrew heading down to the top of the wreck which Grant caught flashes of in the diver's light.

If the man returned up the line, Grant knew he'd be a sitting duck. He wanted to steal a quick look at the pontoon but glancing back down he saw the lights now angling upward, coming his way. The diver couldn't ascend too quickly, or he'd risk giving himself the bends, but Grant still didn't have enough time to surface, duck back under, and drift clear. He had no choice, he had to go.

Releasing the line, the current immediately pulled him away, just as one of the light beams swept across his fins. Grant held his breath, praying the diver hadn't spotted him. The beam traced the mooring line to the surface, illuminating the base of the buoy, then dropped down, before swinging away in the direction of the superyacht. Grant was drifting about thirty feet above the diver who appeared to accelerate his scooter away. *He had to be low on air, or had simply given up!*

Grant sighed loudly into his regulator, relief flooding through his body. His thoughts quickly shifted from escape to forming a plan for when he reached *La Tana del Drago*. He pictured the yacht in his mind from the short time he'd seen it at the dock in Key West.

He recalled the low, open rear deck which appeared to be the only option to board the boat when at sea. He'd have to drift past the last mooring line which the yacht was tied to, and continue underneath the hull to the stern, where he'd have to find something to grab... or he'd be lost to the open ocean.

As he contemplated the treacherous task of getting aboard the Russian's boat, he detected a change in the note of the drone he'd become accustomed to hearing. Something was different. The lights had disappeared completely, but he could hear the sound getting louder—*or were there two sounds?*

Blinded as the diver suddenly switched the powerful headlight back on, Grant lifted his finned feet just in time for the scooter to smash into him. The impact shoved him backward, and his fin deflected the slashing blade of a knife, as the diver tried to reach his prey.

Flailing his arms to right himself and form some kind of defense against his attacker, he felt a hand grab his BCD. The light swung wildly around, and Grant saw the blade plunging toward his chest. With no time to react, he knew he was helpless, and braced for the inevitable, searing pain. Memories of being shot raced through his mind, followed by a vision of pills, scattered across a table.

That would be his final thought? The damned oxy he'd allowed himself to become addicted to. It was a crystal-clear message which hit him like a sledgehammer...

Except, his chest felt like he'd *actually* been hit by a sledgehammer.

Gasping, with his regulator knocked from his mouth and mask askew, quickly flooding with seawater, Grant swung his arms trying to locate the other diver before the blade came his way again.

Desperately needing to breathe, and not finding his attacker, he windmilled his right arm until he recovered his reg and shoved it in his mouth. Forgetting to purge the regulator, all he got was a mouthful of salty water, causing him to cough before the air finally made its way to his lungs. The water churned all around him, and something banged against his legs before riding up his side.

Confused, Grant heaved in deep breaths with his heart rate hammering.

Kicking at his attacker, he grabbed for the man's BCD but found his assailant's arms in front of his chest. Grant held on tightly, keeping his enemy away so he couldn't wield the knife. The diver bucked and wriggled in his grasp, as a light came on and Grant reeled backward, yelling into his regulator.

The man he held was clutching his own throat where blood pumped into the water all around them, the man's eyes wide in terror, his mask gone.

The light flicked away, and Keith illuminated himself so Grant could see who it was. Shoving free of the dying Russian, Grant and Keith rose to the surface where Grant spat out his reg and gulped in the balmy Florida air.

He reached over and took a firm hold of Keith's BCD. "Thank you," he gasped. "Thank you."

"Sorry to bash into you with the scooter. But you're welcome, son," Keith said calmly.

This time, Grant didn't correct him.

27

"Where's Charlie?" Keith asked, grabbing the buoy line as the two drifted to the last mooring.

Grant craned his head to the pontoon boat. From a few hundred feet away, it appeared deserted, but it was little more than an outline in the blackness.

"I think someone took her," he told his father. "A couple of sea scooters showed up as I went in. You just took care of the one who chased me."

Keith twisted his head back to the superyacht. Despair crossed his face.

"What?" Grant questioned.

"They would have taken her to *La Tana del Drago*," Keith replied.

"Yeah, we need to go get her," Grant responded. "They probably have our guns too. I suppose we could go back to the boat and call in the Coast Guard."

Keith shook his head, still appearing sullen. "Not enough time," Keith told him.

"Why? Are they leaving?"

"No, but I set an explosive in the engine room. The timer was set for an hour, but that was at least fifteen minutes ago."

"Shit!" Grant jerked around to the superyacht looming in the darkness. "Charlie's on there. What were you thinking?"

"That I'd have enough time to make it back to my boat and be halfway to shore before it blew," Keith answered. "You two were supposed to be at the hotel."

"We have to stop it," Grant said, letting go of his father's BCD and adjusting the mask over his eyes.

Keith caught him by the leg before he could go farther. "Wait," he ordered.

Grant righted himself in the water, catching the front of Keith's BCD again.

"We need a plan," Keith informed him. "It's a big boat. I'll need to reset the explosives."

"What about Charlie?" Grant questioned.

Keith lifted a pistol out of the water, handing it to him. Grant recognized it as a SIG Sauer P228. On the end of the barrel, extended an almost six-inch suppressor.

"Damn, Dad," Grant quipped. "You mean business."

Keith grinned. "That was your mother's gun," he told Grant. "She used it to kill Aleksandar Lazović. Dragan's father."

"You kept it?" Grant questioned.

"She loved that gun," he explained. "Although we should save this discussion for later."

Grant nodded.

"You don't have a problem using it?" Keith asked warily.

His son released the grip on his BCD, saying, "Hell, I'll kill everyone on that boat if I have to."

Keith dipped his head in acknowledgement as he pulled the mask over his eyes. "Hang on," he told Grant. "The scooter will make it a lot easier."

Charlie stumbled into the salon where a thirty-something-year-old man sat in the corner of a white settee. He held a flute of champagne. The man had a dour face that seemed punctuated by large dark-brown eyes and Slavic cheekbones.

"Miss Greene," he greeted with a thick Russian accent.

"You must be the Lazović bloke," she noted.

"You can call me Dragan," he replied.

"Think I'll skip the chitchat," she responded. "Seeing as you've kidnapped me."

"Sit down," he ordered. "Have some champagne."

"Champagne?" she snapped. "I thought you Ivans all drank vodka."

"Vodka is for everyday. Champagne is for celebration."

Charlie crossed her arms. "What are you celebrating?"

Dragan Lazović grinned, showing a gap-toothed smile. "The end of a long road."

She shook her head. "What's that supposed to mean?"

"What do you know about your parents?" Lazović asked.

"Less than I thought," she admitted.

He continued to hold his Cheshire-cat grin. "So, I have learned. Please, sit."

Charlie didn't move. "I'll stand, thanks."

The mirth vanished from his face for a second. "I won't ask again."

Olga's hand shoved Charlie's shoulders down, and she was forced to relent, sitting in a chair across from the Russian.

"Twenty-four years ago, your parents visited my father's home in Kosovo. But they weren't there on a romantic excursion. Instead, they came to kill my father, a Russian patriot."

"Patriot?" Charlie questioned with a tone slathered in scorn.

"Yes, Aleksander Lazović was nothing more than a businessman whose status in the new Russian state would have made him a forerunner in the government under Vladimir Putin's regime. Instead, your mother killed him."

"My mother?" Charlie repeated.

"Diana Turner. Code name Gray Fox. She shot him dead in his bedroom, in cold blood as you say in English."

"Gray Fox?" Charlie muttered to herself, almost ignoring the man as she absorbed another piece of the puzzle.

"CIA," Lazović explained. "Of course, her counterpart in MI5 was Daniel Edwards. The British and US governments conspired to murder a Russian civilian."

"Because he deserved it."

Lazović gripped his champagne flute and scowled. "But your mother made a mistake. She left my father's lover alive."

Charlie cocked her head. "I thought your mother took over after your father's death. She must have frowned upon his lover being around."

"You will not speak of my mother," the Russian demanded.

"So, you waited twenty-four years to come back for revenge?"

Lazović shook his head. "No one knew exactly who pulled the trigger. Marta, here, gave an accurate description, but both the Brits and Americans have security measures in place to protect their agents. But like many things, time wears away the varnish. That information becomes less important, and it only took finding the right person to get what I needed."

Charlie turned to look at Olga, or rather Marta, who while not smiling, sported a smug countenance.

"You know this won't work, right?" Charlie suggested, turning back to the Russian.

"I think your father will be more than happy to sacrifice himself to save you," Lazović stated. "If not, he'll endure the loss of a loved one."

"The Americans might have something to say about you waging a small war in Florida," Charlie pointed out.

"Unlikely they would even notice," Lazović responded. "But no matter."

He turned to Marta and ordered, "Tell the captain to get under-way." To Charlie, he said, "It doesn't matter where we go, I do think Windsor will come for his precious daughter."

Grant's head lifted slowly out of the water. The aft platform of *La Tana del Drago* floated only ten feet away. Keith popped up on the other side of the deck just behind a RIB.

A man in black stood, staring out into the black night. The light cast from a spotlight on the aft deck fell short of Grant by a foot, leaving him invisible to the man on deck.

Raising the P228, he squeezed the trigger.

Pfft, the SIG whispered before the man pitched into the water with a splash.

Keith moved in quickly, grabbing the body and pulling it under the surface. Grant waited for several seconds but no one came to investigate.

Keith's head emerged from the water again. He signaled for Grant to board the boat. Kicking his fins, the younger man propelled himself to the back of the yacht.

His father lifted a Smith & Wesson forty-five-caliber pistol.

"Take that off him?" Grant asked. When Keith nodded, Grant whispered, "Do you want to swap back?"

"No, son. Hang on to that one. Your mum might like to know you had it."

Without a word, Grant unfastened the BCD and slipped out of the vest.

"I'll pin it under the deck," Keith told him. "Hopefully it will stay there until we get back."

"Roger," Grant acknowledged.

"Don't let the bodies under there startle you," his father warned.

Grant stared at him, and the former agent replied, "I didn't want anyone to see them."

"How many are down there?" Grant asked. "I only shot one."

"One guy dove in as I was leaving. I thought he was coming after me, and I pulled him under."

Grant almost made a joke about how their first father-son excursion left three people dead so far, but he held his tongue and pushed up onto the swim platform. Keith submerged once more, popping back up a moment later without his BCD. Father and son shed their fins and masks, leaving them on the swim platform.

The hull of the boat began to vibrate.

"The engines," Grant stated.

"Dragan is leaving," Keith hissed urgently. "Grant, go. We don't have much time."

The superyacht was huge, and as Grant stared all the way up to the conning tower almost fifty feet up, he wondered how he'd find Charlie. He now had less than half an hour to do that.

Once they climbed to the aft deck, Keith started forward. He pulled a six-inch knife from a sheath and slipped the Smith & Wesson under his waistband. He'd be going below deck to the engine room.

Charlie felt the engines more than heard them. The noise must have been well muffled, but the rumbling still shook through the deck to her feet. She watched Marta in the reflection. The woman seemed agitated. The Russian appeared highly trained to Charlie, perhaps former military or government agent. She had to know even if Grant had been eliminated, Keith was unaccounted for, and they were luring him into attacking. With Charlie as bait.

Dragan seemed nervous too. Was he thinking the same thing? It's possible his life's goal was so close he didn't know how to respond.

They were on the middle level, whatever deck that was called. Charlie calculated how fast she could run for the open sliding glass door. Once the ship was underway, she could run for the rail and dive over the side. In the dark, it would be nearly impossible for them to find her.

On the other hand, she'd be stranded in the middle of the ocean. Not a prospect she relished, but maybe it would stop her father coming after her. If he had a way of knowing what she'd done. Which, she realized, he wouldn't.

———

A guard came down the spiral staircase ahead of him, and Grant ducked behind the small bar meant to service anyone lounging in the area. He peered around the side as the burly man moved rigidly aft.

Grant wondered which of these men was the one who ran his mother down. Gritting his teeth, he lifted the barrel and pulled the trigger. Even the sound from the small puff of air that the suppressor made was drowned out by the throb of the boat's motor beneath them. The guard jerked as the round hit him in the side of the head. His body collapsed in a heap, and Grant stepped around the bar, not gracing his victim with a second look.

———

The sound of something falling echoed up the staircase, and Marta reacted immediately, pulling her gun from its holster and rushing to the steps.

The yacht was barely moving but this was Charlie's chance. She jumped up in a dash for the doors. In the reflection of the glass, she saw Marta turn and fire. The gunshot boomed in the salon as the glass door shattered, and Charlie threw herself sideways behind a table.

Dragan swore in Russian. "That was unwise," he said to Charlie, recovering his composure.

———

Grant almost fired up toward the staircase when he heard the gunshot. Someone was talking. He couldn't quite understand what was being said, but the voice's owner had a thick Russian accent.

Who on this boat doesn't? Grant thought.

A figure ducked down the stairwell, and Grant whipped the P228 up.

It was a woman, and he froze as some part of his brain tried to decide if it was Charlie. When the woman fired at him, he realized his delay was a big mistake, which almost cost him his life. He threw himself back as he fired in the attacker's direction. Landing hard, he rolled behind the bar, gasping in relief only a second before the woman fired again. Wood splinters flew all around him as bullets chewed at the wood and fiberglass. When her volley ceased, he blindly returned fire, hoping to slow down her reloading. The woman released a guttural yowl and opened fire once more. Grant dropped down and mentally counted how many shots he'd fired. He guessed it was over half full.

"Which is it?" the woman called. "American boy, or father?"

Grant twisted around and peeked through a bullet hole. The woman stepped closer, aiming her gun carefully at the bar. Her eyes flitted around as she tried to predict where he would pop up like a dangerous game of whack-a-mole.

"Come out," she insisted. "We talk about your mother. Or your wife?"

She moved closer.

"She make mistake. Letting me live was soft. But she pay price."

Grant fought to keep his composure as the thought of the Russian woman launching his beautiful mother from her bicycle filled his head. He swallowed back the pain and directed all his anger into focusing his next move. Placing the barrel of the SIG Sauer against the bullet hole, he prayed his sightless aim was on target, and pulled the trigger. Twice.

The woman screamed something in Russian as he heard her drop to the deck. Grant scrambled up, moving quickly around the bar to where she thrashed on the ground, clutching a grisly wound where both bullets had shattered her shin. Her hand came up with a Makarov, and Grant stepped on her arm, pinning the gun to the deck.

"Fuck you," he spat between gritted teeth, and shot the woman between the eyes with the same gun she'd been spared from by a kinder heart.

"Is that Mr. Wolfe?" a deep voice called from upstairs in a Russian accent.

Grant stared up the spiral staircase.

"Come. Your sister is waiting for you."

Slowly, he climbed the steps, holding the SIG at the ready. He came up through the deck to see a dark-eyed man holding a Makarov pistol to Charlie's head.

"You can shoot him, Grant," Charlie shouted.

Lazović pressed the barrel against her scalp until it shoved her forward. "Where is your father?" he asked sternly.

Grant remained steady. "Not here," he lied.

"How did you get away from my people?" the Russian asked.

"Dumb luck," he retorted. "Now, I'm going to ask you nicely to let her go."

"Not until you put that gun down," Lazović remarked.

"Do you know what gun this is?" Grant asked snidely.

Lazović stared at him. Grant continued, "This is the gun that my mother killed your father with. Kinda poignant."

"This doesn't end well for either of you," Lazović growled, his annoyance at Grant escalating with the details of the SIG in his hand.

"In a western, we would call this a 'Mexican standoff,'" Grant explained flatly.

"What is this?" he asked.

"It means you don't win," Grant lied again.

"Your sister will die for certain."

"I'm not really sure I like her," Grant responded.

"Bloody, tosser," Charlie retorted.

"See," Grant replied. "She's a pain in the ass."

"Ugh," Charlie groaned. "I'll show you pain in the arse."

"Silence!" Lazović screamed. He took a breath and turned to the aft door where the crunch of feet on broken glass caught all their attention.

Keith Greene stood at the door with a man in black holding a twelve-gauge shotgun to the middle of their father's back.

Grant sucked in air between his teeth. The Mossberg tactical shotgun would cut his father in half if the man pulled the trigger.

"Dad!" Charlie called.

"It's okay, dear," Keith Greene told her. "Everything is going to be just fine."

Lazović laughed. "Who wins now, Mr. Wolfe? I have all of you. If you shoot me, you'll lose both your sister and your father. I came here for Windsor. Walk away now, and I'll let your sister leave with you."

Grant locked eyes with Charlie. Unable to tell her what to do, he hoped she'd sense his intentions.

"You already took my mother," Grant snarled. "You don't get anyone else."

He spun and pulled the trigger. *Pfft.* The shotgun wielder's head snapped back as the round caught him between the eyes.

Lazović jerked his gun toward Keith as the Brit lunged forward. The moment the barrel pulled away from Charlie's head, she threw her weight into Lazović, the two stumbling back as Grant swung the SIG back around.

Charlie rolled away from Lazović, knocking into Grant's legs. He stepped back, losing his aim for a second. Lazović brought the Makarov toward them as Keith dove at the Russian.

"Go!" Keith shouted as he knocked Dragan's gun hand away, a bullet smashing more glass.

Grant caught Charlie by the upper arm and yanked her to her feet.

Keith pulled back his head and slammed it into Lazović's nose. The blow stunned the Russian, but Keith gave him no time to recover, punching him again and again as blood exploded from the man's shattered face. The dark eyes of the oligarch rolled back, and he groaned in disorientated agony.

Keith turned and shouted. "Grant! Get your sister off the boat! I didn't make it to the engine room."

Grant's eyes widened, and he pulled Charlie toward the aft

doors. Charlie hesitated, turning to see her father push to his feet, about to follow them.

"Where are we going?" she screamed, spinning around to see where Grant was dragging her.

"The ship's going to blow!" Grant shouted as they ran out into the darkness, crossing the sun deck.

"Jump!" he ordered, helping Charlie up onto the railing.

"What the hell!" she shouted. "What about Dad?"

"Go!" Grant called. "He's right behind us." Without a thought, he shoved her forward just as a gunshot exploded behind him. Looking back, he saw Lazović sitting up, blood streaming down his battered face; the Makarov aimed toward the door. Keith dove for cover, but his shoulder was already bleeding. Grant raised the SIG Sauer and fired two shots into Lazović's chest.

The entire yacht shuddered for a split second before Grant was lifted off the sun deck and thrown backward.

Time slowed as he flew over the railing and watched as a ball of fire erupted from below deck. A moment later he hit the water. From beneath the surface, he saw a bright orange flash. The concussive wave stunned him for a second, and when he regained himself, thrashing to the surface. He was still holding the SIG Sauer in his hand, and he almost raised it instinctively toward the fiery hulk lighting up the sky. For an instant he thought he was still seeing the face of his father in that last second. Keith had turned to stare at his son who had just saved his life.

He was alive—his father could be too.

The only way to find him was to get out of the water. He saw the gray RIB floating away from the carnage. Its painter must have burned or come free in the explosion.

Grant tucked the SIG into his waistband and swam for the tender. He caught the line and examined it. Singed rope, but it looked like the boat itself had come away mostly unscathed.

He scrambled aboard, and started the engine, desperately scanning the waters for Charlie. Following the trail of the floating inferno, he spotted her, swimming toward the fire. Racing over, he helped her into the RIB where she fell to the deck, exhausted. "You pushed me," she snarled between gasps.

He didn't respond. Charlie sat herself up and glared at his face.

"Where's Dad?" she forced; her face wrought with fear.

Grant shook his head. "He didn't get off."

"No! Grant! Where is he?"

All Grant could do was shake his head again.

EPILOGUE

The wind blew loudly through the open windows of the Honda Del Sol. The drive to Miami airport across The Stretch had mostly been spent above the air-conditioning's operational speed. Grant and Angie sat up front, with Charlie in the back seat, Wrench's boulder-sized head resting in her lap. Panting, the dog's tongue hung out and drool-soaked Charlie's leggings which she was about to spend the next eight to ten hours wearing. On the freeway beyond Florida City, trucks rattled over the uneven concrete surface, and occasionally motorcycles flew by, zipping between the busy traffic as the sun set over Charlie's left shoulder.

They rode in silence, partly because the rushing wind made conversation difficult, and partly because there wasn't much to say. Both Grant and Charlie had each recently discovered the parent they'd never known, only to lose them again, along with the one who'd raised them. Their only relatives left were now each other, and while Charlie didn't want to face the London flat without her father, her obstinate Bengal cat, Stanley, had worn out his welcome with her neighbor.

The previous two weeks had tumbled by in a chaotic array of police and FBI interviews. Law enforcement had found Grant and

Charlie circling the burning superyacht, still desperately searching for their father. The medical examiner had been challenged with the unenviable task of reassembling the corpses from the pieces they'd found, and dental records had confirmed that one of the heads belonged to Dragan Lazović. Blood found on a piece of debris floating clear of the fire also matched that of Keith Greene.

It was clear that an explosive device had been used, and many of the dead had bullet wounds, so naturally the siblings had been vigorously grilled about the incident. Grant and Charlie stuck with their story that they'd gone out to the USS *Vandenberg* searching for their father, whom they never found. They'd been smart enough to switch back to their rented pontoon boat before the Coast Guard had arrived, adding a smidgeon of credibility to their story, which no one really believed, but couldn't disprove. Finally, the police gave Charlie permission to travel, and she'd booked her flight for the following day.

Grant wound around the airport roads, dodging tourists trying to find their airlines, and pulled to the curb at the central terminal. Wrench sat up and stuck his head out of Charlie's window, standing in her lap to do so.

"Move, you stupid mutt," she fussed, all the while scratching his chest as she nudged him away.

Grant retrieved his sister's duffle bag from the back, and Charlie met Angie on the sidewalk where they embraced.

"I hope you'll come over and visit," Charlie told her.

"Let us know about your father's services, and I'll try to take a few extra days off," Angie replied. "I'd love to see London."

Grant dropped the bag next to Charlie, and she turned to him.

"Thanks again for paying for the ticket stuff," she said. "I'll send money once I figure out Dad's affairs. I'm hoping I can keep the flat, but who knows."

"Let me know if you need help," Grant said, shoving his hands in his jeans pockets. "Once I finish this Robertson case, I might have some free time."

Charlie shrugged her shoulders. "I've no idea what to expect. I have to sort out his business and let all his customers know, but I'm not sure whether he really even had a business or not."

They stood in awkward silence for a few moments.

"I wish you could stay," Grant blurted.

Charlie was taken aback. "And do what?"

"It would be good for you both," Angie chimed in. "Make up for lost time and all that. Besides, Wrench won't know what to do without you."

Charlie reached over and rubbed the dog's head as he hung out of the car window.

"Stanley would hate you," she told Wrench.

"From what you've told us, it doesn't sound like Stanley likes anyone," Grant said.

Charlie managed a laugh. "He's more the tolerating type. If you're lucky."

"I was thinking," Grant began awkwardly. "You know, maybe at some point, we could work together again. Partner sort of thing. If you came back."

Charlie wasn't sure what to say. She gave Wrench a kiss on the top of his head and picked up her bag.

"I don't think it was all bad, is all I'm saying," Grant added.

She realized her brother was quite serious. "But we did just about everything wrong, Grant. Our dad's gone as a result."

Grant shook his head. "We can't look at it that way. Lazović was always going to be coming after our parents. We got caught in the middle of it. Sure, we screwed up a few things, but we also did a lot right."

"Dad went back onto that yacht because of me, Grant," Charlie countered. "It was my fault."

Grant reached for his sister and pulled her to him. She dropped the bag, and let him hold her. After a few moments she allowed herself to relax and embraced him firmly in return.

"We can't know what would have happened if any of us had done anything different, Charlie," he whispered. "So, let's take what good we can from the whole thing. We found each other."

Charlie pushed away and swept a sleeve across her damp eyes. "Listen to you, Mister Philosopher," she teased. "I might prefer you back on the pills if you're going to get all sappy."

Grant grinned. "Ain't happening."

"Not on my watch," Angie added, smiling and putting an arm around him.

"Bloody, right," Charlie said, reaching for her bag again. "Oh, that reminds me," she blurted, straightening up and slipping the Rolex from her wrist. "You should have this."

She handed Grant the watch, which he took, his mouth slightly open.

"I have his wedding ring," Charlie said, holding up her thumb. "Only right that you should have something too."

"I don't know what to say," he murmured. "You should have this, Charlie. You grew up with him."

"And you missed out on having the best dad ever," she replied. "This doesn't make up for all those years, but you'll always have a part of him with you."

Grant grabbed his sister once more and held her tightly. "Thank you."

"That's really cool," Angie said softly.

"I can't breathe," Charlie finally gasped, and Grant let her go, laughing.

"Go get on your plane already," he said. "Dork."

"Tosser," Charlie retorted, as she swooped up her bag and began walking away.

"And try not to get into any more fights," Grant called out.

Several people turned, giving them both a concerned look. One woman pulled her daughter closer.

Charlie kept walking, sticking two fingers in the air behind her.

"What *does* that mean?" Grant asked Angie. "She does it a lot."

"Perhaps it's a British sign of endearment?"

Grant grinned. "Pretty sure it's not that."

Charlie found her seat, dead center in the middle row of five. The overhead was already full as she was boarding with the other discount ticket passengers at the end of the line. She asked a woman with her young son to step out for a moment so she could shuffle into the row. The lady huffed and rolled her eyes before moving into the aisle, dragging the kid with her.

Charlie scooted down the row and shoved her bag under the seat in front. The kid plonked himself down next to her and stared. He had a Mickey Mouse ears hat on and wielded a large foam hand protruding from his own.

"I went on a Disney cruise," the boy informed her.

"Yeah, I guessed that much," Charlie responded reluctantly.

Grant had given her a hundred dollars cash, so her plan for the flight involved a drink or two, maybe an inflight movie, and sleep. The foam hand began swinging back and forth like a metronome, except each sweep brought it closer to Charlie until finally it smacked her in the side of the head. The kid giggled, then did it again.

"Do you like your big foam hand?" she asked him, forcing her lips into a smile.

He nodded vigorously and bonked her on the head again.

"Well if it hits me one more time, I'll rip one of the fingers off and shove it some place you thought was a one-way street. Understand me?"

The kid's face froze in shock, then he quickly handed his mother the lump of foam.

As Charlie slumped back in her seat, she felt her phone buzz in her lap. She unlocked it to see who had emailed her. She groaned once she saw it was her monthly bank statement. At some point, she presumed, she'd get whatever her dad had saved up or invested, but until then, she was heading home to poverty.

For the weeks leading up to her trip to Florida, she'd been buried in a sea of self-pity and despair, and her father had given her the space to work through her demons with his usual encouragement. But he was gone now. Her choices were even deeper despair or pulling her life together and moving on as best she could. There was no one else around to sort out Keith Greene's affairs, so the responsibility was hers. She might as well start now and face up to what awaited.

Staring at the link in the email, she finally clicked, and her phone, remembering her password, logged her in. Charlie looked, then looked again, before double-checking she was in the correct account. It didn't make any sense.

Her balance was £60,132. She'd expected the 132 pounds, but the other sixty grand was a complete surprise.

"Where the bloody hell did that come from?" she muttered to herself, unable to stifle a grin as her mind began imagining the impossible.

The adventure continues for Grant and Charlie in
Missing in Zanzibar.

Listen to Doug and Nick's entertaining podcast;
The Two Authors' Chat Show.

ABOUT THE AUTHOR

Author of the AJ Bailey Adventure series and Nora Sommer
Caribbean Suspense series

A *USA Today* Bestselling author, Nicholas Harvey's life has been anything but ordinary. Race car driver, adventurer, divemaster, and since 2020, a full-time novelist. Raised in England, Nick has dual US and British citizenship and now lives wherever he and his amazing wife, Cheryl, park their motorhome, or an aeroplane takes them. Warm oceans and tall mountains are their favourite places.

For more information visit HarveyBooks.com

ABOUT THE AUTHOR

Author of the Chase Gordon Tropical Thriller, Max Sawyer, and Corsair series.

Douglas Pratt, a best-selling action author hailing from Memphis, Tennessee, captivates readers with his unique blend of charm and intensity, reflecting his Southern roots. His works keep audiences on the edge of their seats, infused with a sense of adventure and exploration. Beyond writing, Pratt's personal interests lead him to sail the seas, exploring vibrant coral reefs and sunken shipwrecks, which fuel his imagination and inspire enthralling adventures in his stories.

For more information visit Douglas-Pratt.com

Printed in Great Britain
by Amazon

48006064R00136